Out There

by

Sarah Jane Wilson

Sarah Jane Wilson was born and brought up in North West London. After a mid-life crisis in which she lost most things, including her sanity, she embarked upon a Creative Writing degree at the London Metropolitan University, commuting for hours with a broken foot from her adopted home in Oxfordshire.

With a background in public relations, marketing and hospitality, Sarah has written about most things including concrete and myxomatosis and had her articles published in everything from trade magazines to the national press. She now specialises in natural health, wellbeing, culture and the arts with a social/community twist.

Sarah lives in rural Oxfordshire with a rescued Staffordshire Bull Terrier called Smurf who, when not playing in the river Thames, can usually be found with Sarah's feet under her battered writing desk.

GW00374842

Lorelei Press
Out There
Copyright © Sarah Jane Wilson
The moral right of the author has been asserted.
*This book is a work of fiction. The characters,
incidents, and dialogue are drawn from the
author's imagination and are not to be construed
as real. Any resemblance to actual events or
persons, living or dead, is entirely coincidental.*
Published in the United Kingdom by Lorelei Press.

ISBN: 978-1986120722

For CaLex

To Eileen
Happy Reading
Sarah Jane Watson
Cholsey 118.

I MET HER IN THE queue for soup. Her head was down, hands thrust deep inside pockets. Drawing level, she looked up, her hair blowing diagonally across her face – a no entry sign.

Clutching my rucksack close to my chest, my eyes followed her; the khaki hood shielding like armour; there was something ethereal in the way she held her body, the blondness of her straggly hair. I believed in her.

The queue was grumpy, murmurings of disease escaping from under anoraks as they reached for the polystyrene cups with begrimed fingers. Minestrone soup was being poured in; tiny rings of pasta in a viscous fluid which smelled like school dinners. I remember the soup, scalding my lips as I drank from my cup, dipping white sliced bread until it stretched with the weight of rehydrated tomatoes and peppers. It sticks in my mind, a detail, the beginning of something.

She was alone on the cold city street blackened by night, her parka so large she could have wrapped it around her twice. Had it ever fitted her or been donated by a larger woman with a big heart? As the wind blew the hood from her head, I noticed a tattooed tendril behind her ear and wondered where it went.

"What are you staring at?" she said.

Blushing, an apology slipped immediately from my lips. I stepped backwards out of the queue. She grabbed my hand, pulling me sideways. "He nearly stood on you," she said, nodding at a squat man close by before returning to her soup.

"Thanks," I said sticking a bony hand in her direction. She took it with an equally small one, dropped it and wiped her own on the grubby parka.

"First hot meal of the day?" I said, floundering.

"No," she said. "I had a full English this morning and a carvery at lunch. Just thought I'd pop out of my penthouse apartment and pick up some of this delicious soup."

I laughed but it caught at the back of my throat and my face reddened as the soup threatened to return. She slapped my back and I caught a hint of a smile on her pale face. We stood in silence, watching the queue disperse and the Crisis people clean down the van.

A large man in a black wool hat saw us and shouted, "You two okay?"

We nodded.

"Come see us after nine tomorrow. Carlton House?"

"We know," said the girl. She glanced at me.

"Shall we go?" I asked.

"Pointless," she said. "Been three times already. They put me in a mixed hostel."

I nodded. This I understood. Another agency. Another mixed hostel.

"What's your name?

"Beano."

"Jay."

We shook hands again, a clumsy grab. This time she didn't wipe me off.

"Haven't seen you before," I said. She shrugged, so I fixed my eyes on a flashing neon sign on the other side of the street, appearing preoccupied.

"No good at small talk," she said after a while. "Never know what to say."

"Nor me," I said and stared at the light until the pattern of it was burned into my retinas and everything I looked at flashed hot pink and blue.

"You can carry on talking," she said, "I just won't reply."

Searching all the available compartments of my brain for a sentence to begin a conversation, while Beano flashed hot pink and blue, took longer than expected. She was turning away when I found my voice.

"Do you want to get off the streets?"

She laughed. "Stupid question."

"Some people don't."

"I'd like a house with a bath and a fridge full of food, so, yes, I guess I'd like to get off the streets."

"Me too. Maybe we can, together I mean. I have a plan."

"I don't know you," she said. "Don't presume."

Every sinew of my body wanted to turn and stare into her eyes, to read the stories written in the lines in the transparent skin which surrounded them. None of us is here by choice and generally not by chance either. Most of us have a litany of disasters which follows us. Sometimes we carry it in bags or push it in abandoned shopping trolleys near Victorian canal paths, but we all have it. Beano's was obvious from the oversized parka; mine from the ingrained dirt under my finger nails and the crow's feet around my eyes. I rummaged in my rucksack for something familiar and found the nail file, fiddling with it.

"Have you got a weapon in there?" she asked.

"No."

"You can't be too careful," she said, pushing a wayward strand of hair back under her hood.

"Where are you sleeping tonight?"

She shrugged.

"I've got a railway arch I can share with you. It's a walk but it'll be worth it."

She shrugged again and looked over her shoulder at a man with dreadlocks and piercing eyes.

"What are you staring at?"

He tried to speak but thought better of it, shifted his feet and turned away.

"So, would you like to come to my shelter?"

"Why would I come with you? I'll get there and there'll be a group of psychos standing round a fire and you'll have been a decoy and that's not how I'd like to go, thank you very much."

"There's only me," I said, regretting sounding pathetic when she spat and it hit my shoe.

"Hey!"

She laughed and my heart soared. "I'll follow you," she said. "At a distance where I can escape if you start any funny business or piss me off in any way."

"Fair enough," I said. Draining the last of the lumpy soup from my cup, I threw it in the bin, zipping up my anorak until only the top part of my face was visible.

The road to Holloway was dark and wet. I had discovered the railway arches the day before, crouched low behind a crumbling wall to see who came and went. No one had been, not a vagrant, a villain nor a security guard. From one of the arches, buddleia grew stubbornly through the rotting brickwork, an unlucky seed making the best of its surroundings. It would bloom in late spring, thrusting purple flowers up towards the sky, food for the brave butterflies which ventured there. It had hope.

We walked in silence as my mind raced with subjects to talk about but none left my lips. She plodded behind me, her feet slapping in too-big trainers.

In Great Russell Street, I stopped outside the British Museum hoping to see the one friend I already had. Tutankhamun's mummified body hauled itself up to the left-hand window and waved at me. I waved back. Beano darted behind a wall and disappeared.

"I'll see you tomorrow," I called, motioning him back into the shadows and he slunk back into his sarcophagus. Several Greek statues giggled behind marble hands.

A white flash appeared from the wall where Beano was hiding her face, followed by khaki cotton ballooning behind her.

"Who was that?" She screamed, breathless.

"Tutankhamun," I replied. She took three steps back.

"It's all right," I said. "He's not coming with us."

I trudged on, pausing every now and again to check that she was still there, skulking in the shadows behind me.

"Are you mad?" she asked.

"No."

"Tutankhamun has been dead for thousands of years, you know."

"His body died thousands of years ago, but his soul still drifts over the earth."

"You said you weren't mad."

"I'm not," I said, aware of a wave of redness rushing up my cheeks. "There are lots of things that are real that we don't understand." I thrust my hands in my pockets.

"You talk to dead Egyptians," she laughed.

"He has given me some very sound advice over the years." I sniffed, turning away from her.

"Can't be worse than the advice you get from the living," she said.

AS WE NEARED CAMDEN Lock, the clubs were tossing out the drunks and one-night standers. A woman draped herself across a drunken man, dropping her handbag. I watched as they staggered towards a waiting cab, giggling, their legs buckling. As the cab drove away, I picked up the bag, stuffing it under my anorak before checking the contents. There was cash, a chap stick for my dry lips and a pair of nail scissors. I stuffed the booty into my own rucksack before hanging the bag over the club door for someone else to find.

Beano watched from behind a bus shelter.

"How much?" she hissed as I hung the bag up.

"Forty."

"Good haul." She smiled; I was ten feet tall.

"Thanks. Fancy a coffee and a pastry?"

She joined me then, walking at the same pace as me, next to me, matching my footsteps as I sashayed through the emptying streets.

"There's an all-night Italian five minutes from here," I said. "They do pastries and the best coffee."

"Caffeine will keep you up all night."

"I won't sleep. I'll be look-out so you can sleep. Then tomorrow you can do the same for me."

"You're joking, right?"

"No."

Beano went to cross the road then returned. "You'll do it first?"

"That's what I said."

"Then I guess that's fair. Or I might just disappear before bedtime tomorrow and leave you to it."

"Fine." I said. It wasn't fine. I wasn't going to share my home and my money and my food with someone who had no staying power. But I reasoned that a good night's sleep might change her mind and continued up the road toward Holloway.

There was a queue outside the all-night Italian from which drifted the most amazing aromas. Basil, pesto, starchy spaghetti and sweet almond pastries jostled for prominence in the still, damp air. I ordered two pastries, two coffees and eyed up the spaghetti. It was five pounds per carton. An eighth of my haul. Glancing over my shoulder I noticed Beano pocketing a bottle of Balsamic vinegar. The spaghetti was a treat too far. This was my café, my port of call on a lonely night when I'd got lucky with some cash. Paying for the coffee and pastries, I handed her half the delights and listened as her teeth ground the pastry into something she could swallow.

A few steps later, the bottle of Balsamic vinegar tumbled out of her pocket, smashing, splashing sticky, black liquid all over the pavement. Beano shrugged. My shoulders tightened. I hate waste.

The run of arches down by the railway had been businesses before the downturn came. A battered sign swung, squeaking from a rusty nail over the first doorway but the second was unencumbered and, with only a little resistance, the door opened revealing a black space which smelled of old dogs and pigeon droppings.

"Here we are," I said with more enthusiasm than I felt.

"This place is disgusting."

"Yeah, but there's no one else here."

"And damp."

"Yeah, but we could make it something."

"What?"

"Home."

Beano curled her lip and prodded my shoulder with a bony finger. "I followed you all this way for this?"

"It's inside, not a doorway."

"I'm off. I'd rather take my chances in a mixed hostel."

"Go then. I don't need you." A lump formed in my throat.

She swept her parka around her and peered into the darkness outside. The frigid air hung blanket-like around our shoulders, suspending time. Engines revved at traffic lights a million miles away and above, stars twinkled in a light polluted sky.

She turned, filling the doorway. "Not tonight. I'll stay here with you tonight."

"Fair enough," I said placing my rucksack on the floor so she couldn't see the relief on my face. I had a wind-up torch which I switched on, pointing the light into the corners of the cave-like shelter. A stinking mattress was propped up against the wall. Someone had been here before. A pile of fast food wrappers lay next to it, old and decaying.

"Someone died here," said Beano, her face emotionless.

"How do you know?"

"I can smell it," she said.

"I've got a bin bag I can split open and spread over the mattress so we can lie down."

"I'm not lying on that thing."

"Suit yourself." I rummaged for my black plastic bag which I had caught when, whipped by the wind, it had plastered itself around a lamppost. It didn't cover all the mattress but sat in the middle, a black hole amidst the grime. I sat cross legged in the middle, spreading my possessions around me, checking them over and over until I was sure that every item was there. Car lights from the main road sent strange shadows against the back wall. Beano closed the door and crouched behind it, resting her chin on her knees.

"You comfy there?" I asked.

"I'm blocking the doorway."

"If anyone wanted to come in, they'd push you aside in a second."

"Got a better idea?"

I looked around the room, pointing my torch up and down along the walls until I saw a broom handle half-obscured by the mattress I was sitting on. Pulling it out, I slid it across the floor in Beano's direction. She took it in her hands, brandishing it like a light sabre in a dramatic re-enactment of an epic battle.

"Prop it against the door," I said.

Beano concentrated on the handle, forcing it into the place on the door where the lock should have been and into a crack on the floor where a cobble should have been. Satisfied that no one was going to sneak in and murder us in our bed, Beano crossed the uneven floor and sat cross legged next to me.

"This mattress stinks."

"I know but it's softer than the floor. Lay your parka over it. I've got a towel to cover you." I showed her the grey towel which had once been white and which I had found, dropped in the loos by Oxford Street station.

"I've got a plan to get off the streets," I said, "But it needs two of us."

"Mm?"

"Yes, a robbery, but not a nasty one. Make enough for a deposit on a flat and then get a job."

Beano laughed, good and hard.

"It's not a dream," I said. "I've been planning it for months. But it needs two. Are you in?"

"Depends what it is," she said. "And quite frankly I don't want to hear about it in this dark, miserable hole." She turned her nose up, laid the towel on the bin bag, wrapped herself almost completely in the parka and closed her eyes.

I stared at the only patch of pale skin which was visible, a line of knuckles on her right hand. A tattoo curled from under the cuff, reaching out towards her fingers. I pointed the torch to see what it was.

"Sod off with that light," Beano said, piercing the darkness.

"Sorry. I'll tell you about it tomorrow. It's a proper plan, not pie in the sky stuff."

"I'm going to sleep now," she said.

"I'm going to stay awake."

"You said."

"Okay. Go to sleep then."

"I will if you keep the damn light away from me."

She turned, the parka, towel and black bin liner all rotating with her. I got off the mattress and sat on my rucksack facing the door. If the broom handle moved I could grab it and use it to defend us.

WHEN I WOKE UP, the broom handle was lying across my lap. Beano, the towel and twenty-seven pounds left from the windfall had gone. A shard of cold air struck the side of my face, an icy dagger blade. I cried for about five minutes, for the loss of first real friend and the towel. The grey sky looked down on me, disinterested in the pathetic creature huddling for warmth in an old anorak. I, too, looked down on the pathetic creature who was crying over the loss of a towel and a person who, for a moment, had given me hope.

I was still snivelling and wondering what to do next when I heard a whistle and three knocks on the door. Scuttling behind the mattress, I looked up to see Beano smiling in the doorway, holding a tray of Macdonald's breakfast and steaming cups of tea.

"I thought you'd gone," I said, wiping a filthy tear from my face.

"I slept. Wanted to say thanks. But you were asleep as well and anyone could have walked in and done anything to us so I was pissed off and stole the money and the towel and left but then I thought about the sleep and your plan so I bought food and came back instead."

She grinned, revealing even teeth, laying out breakfast on the towel which had been dropped in a puddle. I stopped myself from mentioning it, grabbing a cardboard cup of tea, warming my hands on it, sipping the sweet contents. Beano was still talking:

"I thought you said you were going to stay awake."

"It was light. And I wasn't comfortable. I squatted on my rucksack and saw the sun come up. I must only have had a few minutes' sleep."

The sausage patty sat in my mouth for some time before I could swallow it, grainy and greasy. I swigged tea, washing it down. Beano chomped on hers, clearly relishing the over-processed, instantly gratifying mush. A grin covered her face as she wiped it with a paper napkin.

"That's better," she said and the following burp echoed around the arch.

I looked at her for the first time. A teenager, I guessed, undernourished either from drugs or from the streets or both. Her straggly blonde hair hung in lifeless strands around her tiny face, perfectly heart shaped and as pale as death. Large, round blue eyes peered out, deep with knowing things they shouldn't, framed by golden eyelashes. Her lips were thin and withdrawn around her mouth, her teeth still healthy. The parka covered her body from neck to knees; stick legs held up the unfeasibly large torso and dirty trainers hugged her feet. She was like a million other girls forced to live in railway arches and on unfriendly streets. A KGB spy; someone you wouldn't notice if they were following you.

Her nails were long and broken. I searched my rucksack, pulling out the small, metal treasure inside. Its mother-of-pearl handle shone white in the gloom, a beacon. I handed it over and she took it with an expression of gratitude but no words.

"You can't keep it," I said.

She began to file, the sawing sound filling the surrounding silence.

"Makes you feel more human with nice nails," I said. She nodded and switched fingers, her head bent over the job in hand.

"What's your plan, then?" she said.

"I go pickpocketing around Camden Market. I watch the gangs of foreigners, all organised and very good at what they do. But they're missing a trick."

Her eyes brightened. "How much you get pickpocketing?"

"Enough. But it's hard for one. The gangs get much more. But they always look the same. The cops watch them 'cause they know who they are. They don't get them though 'cause they pass the stuff between them and you never know who's got it."

"And your plan?" She looked up from the nail file.

I felt in my rucksack once more. This time I brought out a comb with several teeth missing, running it through my own hair before placing it in Beano's lap. She threw me the nail file and ran the comb through her hair before cleaning it and dropping her own hair over the side of the mattress.

"So, we rob this guy from Leicester who sells wigs and clothes. I know where his van's parked and he leaves it open when he's unpacking in the morning. Most of them leave stuff there but he's always moving stock around so he's an easy target."

"Then?"

"A month of work, you and me, pickpocketing tourists. Not Londoners; they're too savvy. The tourists with backpacks and phones and

19

wallets in their back pockets. I can make fifty quid a day from them."

"What do you spend it on?"

"Food, booze, drugs sometimes. But I'm not an addict. I can do without."

"Me too." We nodded at each other, a secret code. She was in on my plan now. We could make it work and get a flat with a bath.

"Why wigs?"

"So the cops don't recognise us."

"And the bloke from Leicester?"

"He won't see us. He'll never know it was us. And if he ever asked where I got the wig, I'd say I was mentally sick and how dare he question me."

She laughed again and I liked the sound more than any I had ever heard.

"Tutankhamun gave me the idea. They wore wigs. They didn't all have thick, black hair, you know." She laughed again but the sound was different. "Anyway, two of us can do between a hundred and two hundred a day I reckon. Let's say two. A month's work is six grand. If that doesn't get us a deposit on a flat, I don't know what will."

"Don't you have to have a job?"

"Yes, but I know this girl, works as an estate agent. She gives me food sometimes, talks other times. She said if there's ever anything she can do and I said could you take a phone call or write a reference for a job and she said yes, but only if I've got enough money to put down a deposit. See, I'm not so stupid after all. And Tutankhamun said it wouldn't even be wrong; it'd just be getting a leg up when the world pisses on you from a great height."

"It's a plan, I'll give you that. It needs a lot of work but it's a plan. I need to meet the estate agent first, check her out."

"That's fine."

My face formed a grin which hurt because the muscles hadn't been used for a while. "Shall we go to Camden and get a few quid and celebrate?"

Beano stood up immediately, brushed down her parka and bit her lips to redden them.

"Let's. The two of us could go far," she said.

"It's written in the stars," I said.

An hour later I spotted some Spanish tourists with back packs who hadn't bothered to zip them up. Beano followed her own mark in the street food market. We met up by the statue of Amy Winehouse, Beano posing next to her, not even reaching her shoulder.

"I got twenty," she said.

"Well done. Let's see what I got." I moved to a quiet corner and dumped the empty wallets in a bin, covering them with an old plastic bag. I shuffled the notes like a deck of cards, twenty, forty, sixty, eighty…

Three hundred and forty pounds.

"See," I said, delighted as her eyes widened. She reached a bony hand towards the stash.

"Can I have some?" she asked, her head tilted to one side, puppylike.

Handing her fifty, I asked what she was going to do with it.

"Some gear," she said. "I'd love a high, just one, to celebrate and to set me on the path to my new life."

"Our new life," I reminded her.

"What you going to get?"

"Some pancakes with chocolate spread and a litre of cider. I'll meet you back here."

I leant against the wall, pulling my hood up against the rain which was now falling steadily, eating sweet, sticky pancakes. The crowds ebbed and flowed through the food section, carrying Peruvian chicken and Argentinian beef; Jamaican patties and Belgian waffles. Intoxicating aromas transformed at every turn, spicy, meaty, sweet. An oversized hot dog nearly took my eye out.

It took a while, an hour and a half to be precise, but Beano turned the corner and expected to find me crouching by the bins where she had left me. I saw fear cross her features, moulding them into something I hadn't seen before. She looked over each shoulder, panic etched on the lines which should not have disgraced her young skin. I felt sorry then and rushed towards her, touching her arm.

"I thought you'd left me," she said, teary eyed.

"Let's go somewhere we've never been before," I said. "It's not like we've anything to do today. And I don't know anything about you. We can walk and talk and plan."

She smiled then, her mouth creases reaching up through her face until her eyes were smiling too.

"What do you want to do?" she asked.

"I don't know. A museum, an art gallery, something normal people do. I saw Tutankhamun's possessions once in an exhibition at the British Museum. Everything gold and painted and beautiful, like people cared about him as much in death as in life. I wondered what that would have been like."

Beano stared at me. "You're not like other people, are you?"

"What do you mean?"

"Not like other people on the streets. You're a criminal, a pick pocket but you're not like the others."

I ignored her. "I want to go to Tate Modern. I'd like to remind myself that some people create beautiful things."

"Fair enough," said Beano straightening the collar on her parka. "Let's go."

I WAS GLAD I had eaten the pancakes because it took ages to walk to Embankment where we stared at the London Eye before crossing Westminster Bridge. Beano stopped in the middle, peering over the side at the rushing water below.

In the Tate foyer, a security guard followed us as we read the signs.

"The toilets are for visitors to the gallery," he said as I caught his eye.

"We're visitors," said Beano, dropping a two-pound coin into the donation bin.

It was white, a lot of white walls and large pieces of work which I didn't understand but which transported me to another world.

"I think I'm glad I met you," said Beano, skipping along the corridor.

We travelled every escalator and visited every floor. Self-expression met us at every turn, bold and colourful or small and delicate, each piece said something about the artist and the world they inhabited. Each room had a different feel; each artist a different filter. My pleasure came as much from Beano's as from the art we were experiencing. Her skin shone, her eyes twinkled and her lips seemed to set in a smile. She floated on worn trainers, a face and feet with the enormous parka in between. I suggested she take it off but she grabbed at it, wrapping it around her body tightly. I didn't push it.

When I felt that we had seen and discussed every exhibit, I said that we should get the tube home.

"I can't believe that it's free. All this and it's free and I've never even been. It's a disgrace!" She laughed, and I thought I had never seen her so free or so happy nor loved her so much.

"Libraries, galleries, museums; all the good stuff is free."

"Thank you," said Beano fidgeting with her fingers.

I paid for our tickets and we descended the underground with all the normal people who did it every day. In less than half an hour we were back in Holloway, discussing the take-away restaurants and deciding which we would go for. I opted for a Lebanese flatbread with falafel and chilli sauce. Beano chose a burger and chips but I felt that, in time, she might be up for trying something else. We sat in a small, tree lined square, sheltered from the wind, eating in silence. When the wrappers had been discarded and the soda cans drained, Beano turned to me and took my hand.

"This has been the best day ever," she said. "Really, really, really, the best day ever. And we can round it off with a trip to blow your socks off if you like?"

I shook my head. "Thanks, I appreciate your offer, but I won't join you. I'll keep look out, so no one can hurt you while you're gone."

She touched my arm as I had hers. "The National tomorrow then?"

"Yes," I said, settling onto the bench with a full stomach and a heart whose beat I hadn't heard in months.

We watched the sun disappear over the rooftops. "It's been the best day ever," she said again, slipping off the bench to watch a squirrel bury an old, brown acorn.

A chill settled on the bench, creeping into my bones.

"Time to go," I said, "Or we'll freeze to death and that would be a shame with so many plans." As we turned down the road towards the railway arches, someone had left a donation outside a charity shop in a large black bin liner. We carried it between us, checking to see that the coast was clear before entering our arch.

"We should buy a blow-up mattress with all that money you've got," said Beano.

"We'll get one tomorrow."

"We could start collecting stuff for our real home." She was still skipping.

"We could and we will," I said, unpacking the bag to see what we'd got. Several men's jackets in tweed and wool made a good mattress covering and cut out the smell a bit too. The rest was old vests and shirts which, rolled up and stuffed inside each other, formed comfortable pillows.

"Dead man's clothes." Beano said.

"Kind of him to leave them for us," I said.

"Kind of his wife. Or the house clearance people."

I wound up the torch and closed the door, setting the broom handle against it to keep out intruders.

She settled then, leaning back on her new pillow, fiddling in her pocket for her gear.
"The National Gallery tomorrow," she said.

I heard the foil scrunch and held my rucksack close while she stuck a needle in her arm.

I couldn't drink the cider, couldn't risk losing my mind while Beano was losing hers. My hand dipped inside the cotton canvas, feeling the nail file; the comb with teeth missing. There was the scarf too and the reading glasses which were too strong for me but helped on days when my head hurt and my resolve faltered. I felt my treasures, recalling the story of each find while behind me, Beano travelled further than the stars. Her breathing slowed and my rucksack nestled into my stomach as I lay beside her, back turned, staring blindly at the broom handle which I knew was there but couldn't see. Tired and strangely peaceful, I closed my eyes and allowed sleep to creep up from my toes.

A PALE SHAFT OF light slipped under the door, a runway of possibilities. I opened one eye only, unprepared for the day, happy to be sharing a jacket covered mattress with money in my pocket.

Silence dripped from the walls gathering around me, safe and snuggly. Tucking my knees up, I sighed. Tutankhamun called to me from his death trap in the British Museum. Beano was sure to be delighted with him and if not, there were plenty of other ancient civilisations to whet her appetite. Perhaps she'd prefer Vikings or Romans or even the people of pre-history. I thought I saw a butterfly land on the straggly branch of buddleia which pushed and shoved through a hole in the roof towards the light; a butterfly with radiant, blue/green wings, shimmering and fluttering.

I lost it for a moment and then found it again; it brushed my cheek as if to kiss me and then, as if it knew what to do, it rushed for the gap under the door and disappeared into the morning sky.

I stretched, rubbing my eyes like a six-year-old, rubbing my feet like a seventy-year-old. I hadn't walked so far in weeks. Gathering a thousand thoughts to share with Beano when she woke, I took off my socks and massaged my stinking feet with rough hands, then wiped them on the clean lining of one of the tweed jackets.

Time passed, and I lay next to my friend, visions of the fun we could have together playing out on the inside of my eyelids, filling my heart with something it couldn't name.

The hum of an insect woke me out of my stupor and I wound up my torch to see if Beano was ready to wake.

As I turned over on the mattress, shining the weak, white light on her, I knew immediately. She was slumped, nose pressing into the mattress, crusty vomit stuck to her beautiful mouth. I hadn't heard or smelled it. I hadn't known that, while I slept, she...

Standing up and backing away, my heart pounded and my guts went into spasm sending my own vomit across the arches' floor. Purple marks covered her arm, dead where a tourniquet still tried valiantly to push a vein forwards. But the vein had crashed and stopped pushing blood around her tiny body.

"Beano's dead," I said in the hope that she would answer, "No I'm not." Silence met me.

"Beano's dead," I said again, a ball of iron settling in my throat.

"Beano's dead," I whispered as I sunk to the floor and the emotion took over and I sobbed into the dirt. "Beano's dead; Beano's dead; Beano's dead. I should have stopped her from shooting up." Pain crept into my feet, legs, stomach, higher and higher until it engulfed me.

"It's my fault," I screamed at the walls, "It's all my fault." My knees buckled and the dirt came up to meet my face. "If I hadn't lied to her she'd still be alive. If I hadn't told her I knew an estate agent; if I hadn't said I had a plan." The cruelty of truth crushed my heart between the rocks of my lies. The plan I'd made up on the spot to keep her with me, the friend I'd always dreamed of; the love

I wanted to share. "If I hadn't lied to her, she wouldn't have celebrated," I spluttered into the murk. "If she hadn't celebrated, she wouldn't be dead. I killed her. Oh my God, I killed Beano."

A primal scream filled the arch.

Emerging from it, new hope flooded me. "Perhaps she isn't dead," I said. "Beano, you're not dead, are you?"

I crawled to her side, laying my hands on her body, shaking her. "Please," I whispered. "Beano, please don't be dead."

Beano was dead, her body empty of the girl I had met in the queue for soup. I held her for a moment, kissing the forehead of a child for whom I was the only mourner, easing the parka away from her so that I could feel her for the first and last time.

"I'm so sorry," I said and the words were nothing.

As I pulled the khaki fabric away from her neck, the tendrils of the tattoo I had noticed got larger, stretching all around her neck and down under her clothes. A shirt covered a T-shirt, once proudly announcing a tour of a world-famous band. I wondered if Beano had been to see them at Wembley or Manchester. Did she have an accent? I couldn't remember. No, London. She'd have gone to Wembley and stood near the front, cheering and singing loudly before being crowd surfed over the more ordinary fans. When she was full of life and love and hope.

She wore jeans, pale and too large for her narrow hips, hanging from the bones which stuck out from there, reaching down to trainers and odd socks. And everywhere on her body was the suggestion of a tattoo, something creeping out or scuttling in, a thousand images hiding under cotton and polyester. I prized open the shirt and under the collar I could see strange symbols in black and white, an eye and some Latin letters emblazoned across her chest. I couldn't move her arms, so I tore at the T-shirt and unceremoniously pulled at her jeans until they were round her ankles. I covered her nakedness with a jacket then pulled the jacket away. From neck to toes and down to her wrists, Beano was a picture, a piece of art to be treasured and stared at in the British Museum. Bees buzzed from her bottom, flying in all directions to join the goat heads, pentagrams and eyes which seemed to make up the basis for the work.

I sat next to her, unable to take in what her body was trying to tell me. They say that people can be read like a book. Beano was a book. I knew I had to read Beano. I knew I had to make it up to her. My lies struck my heart, arrow-like. I touched it, checking for blood but the bleeding was internal. The tattoos stared back at me, accusatory and cruel. Eyes glaring into me, pentagrams threatening spells of revenge. Every deed I had done leading me to this moment. And now it was here and I had no idea what to do with it. I remained sitting, staring at her body. The butterfly escaping into the morning light had been Beano saying goodbye. I knew this to be true. Tutankhamun would not have doubted it. "The Book of the Dead" told of these things, spirits rising as animals and birds and Beano was a butterfly. Maybe I could catch it and bring it back to her.

I ran to the door, stepping out into the drizzle, searching the buddleia and the surrounding weeds for a glimpse of the beautiful creature which carried Beano's soul. But I couldn't find it and I couldn't leave her alone in the arch for the rats to discover so I ran back inside, slamming the door on any possibility of saving the woman/child I loved and had killed.

I SAT FOR AN hour, maybe more, next to her body. Sometimes I shone the torch on her skin; sometimes I turned her to see more of the tattoos which snaked under her arms and around her rib cage down to her vagina, inner thighs, knees, calves, toes.

On her back, a goat headed human with large breasts sat cross legged, the moon shining behind its head, a white snake under its feet. At its back were large, feathered wings and on its lap, a phallus. It was surrounded by demonic faces peering back at me with foreboding. It sat on a sphere of earth, wrapped in a black snake which coiled itself around the creature's leg, snapping at the bees which fled from her buttocks.

Filing the images in the back of my head, I held Beano, cradling her in my arms, keeping her warm. She was more than a girl, more than a friend. She was a sign. A canvas for another's art? Or her own?

We rocked together, as I hummed a lullaby for my sleeping beauty; an enigma in an ugly world, the girl who had relied on me to save her from her situation, whom I had lied to and killed. Each realisation hit me like a hammer in my chest, forcing sobs from deep within. The beautiful, trusting girl who had believed my lies and celebrated the only way she knew how. She had flown to the stars and never returned.

Time passed. I told her about my life, the secrets I had never shared, the love I had never given pouring out into her in the hope that her afterlife would at least be something better than she had received from me in life.

Cold crept into my hands; my fingers moved, warming them. They crept into her pockets but I found nothing to tell me more, nothing official like a name and address or date of birth. I found foil containing more of the brown filth which I had bought for her and killed her with and the remainder of the money, a few coins which I slipped into my own pocket. I found an earring with a dolphin on it which, hoping she had treasured it, I forced through the closed hole in my own, left ear.

Knowing I couldn't stay with her any longer and help her, I took internal photographs of her body, the tattoos which covered it and her face, serene in death. Then I wrapped her in the parka, covering the creatures which adorned her, shivering at the vile figures and demonic symbols which I was certain she hadn't chosen for herself.

Doing mode clicked in. Clothes were folded, the broom handle stored away; the rucksack snatched up from by the door. I didn't check the contents. I placed more shirts under her head, softening her position and laid my towel over the lower portion of her legs so that she was a secret once again. With Beano's dolphin in my ear, I pushed open the door of the arch, blinking as the light struck me blind and a vicious wind blew up under my clothes.

COMMUTERS PUSHED AND JOSTLED for pavement space outside the tube station. The ticket office was open and I waited in the queue until my nose pressed against the glass and a burly man with Dickensian sideburns smiled at me with crooked teeth.

"Can I help you?"

"There's a body. I found a body. I was looking for somewhere to rest and there she was, on a mattress in a railway arch. I didn't know what to do so I came here. She's in the railway arch down the road."

The man stared as if checking to see if I were lying.

"She's there. Can you call the police or something? I have no phone."

"You homeless?"

"Yes."

"And you found a body?"

"A girl. Young. Overdose, needles and such. In the railway arch. I've got to go."

I heard him calling, "Don't go," as I slipped behind a man with a big, grey coat and disappeared into the throng of students and commuters arriving for another ordinary day behind desks. As I walked, dipping down side roads and watching from doorways, I heard a siren and knew that the ticket man had made a call. I was pleased. Beano wouldn't be alone any more. I slid my hand in my rucksack; the comb and nail file were still present and correct. My other treasures I had left in the arch, covered in finger prints which they would never match but proclaimed my guilt in her death. The police were on their way. Beano was dead.

THE BRITISH MUSEUM was open by the time I arrived. Tutankhamun had been waiting for me, he said, waiting for news from the outside.

"There's a lot," I said.

"You were with someone when you came by."

I told him about Beano and her tiny body wasted by misery; about the ticket man with Dickensian sideburns; about the tourist who had dropped her bag and about the lucky find of men's clothes which covered the mattress.

I told him about the wonderful day we'd shared and about the lobster telephone and the 'Snail' by Matisse; about Beano dropping a donation in the gallery. Every detail of the time we spent together was etched in my mind. Permanent marker. I told him I had loved her and I had lied to her and that because of me, she was on her way to a marble slab and a feeble investigation to find out who she might have been. The tattoos were next, each description vivid and disgusting to my own ears. The figure who adorned her back, the buzzing bees and eyes and pentagrams and symbols from the occult. I said that maybe the Devil himself had tattooed her tiny body and he nodded.

"The tattoos must mean something," I said.

"Everything means something."

"That's not helpful. I need your vast knowledge."

He wasn't forthcoming. I huffed.

"Patience is a virtue," he said.

"Virtue is a grace, Grace is a little girl who wouldn't wash her face."

"I don't understand."

39

"Something my grandma used to say."

"You have a grandma?"

"I don't know now. Probably not. She said weird things like that and always had a sweetie tin which smelled of chocolate even though there wasn't any inside." My mind wandered backwards away from the pain.

"Concentrate," Tutankhamun said. "Don't fly away, it won't help. It'll all be there when you come back down."

I knew what he meant and hated him for saying it. I told him so.

"As your friend, it is my duty to guide you not fool you."

"I killed her."

"You had responsibility but she chose the manner in which she would celebrate your good news."

"I lied to her."

"You gave her some hope and maybe your plan would have worked, although I don't see how. And now you still have responsibility because you have placed it on your own shoulders. If you want to find out who she was, you must stay focused and work out how to do it."

"Help me."

A group of visitors wandered past the sarcophagus and he dropped down into it to give them the full experience. When they left he emerged again, death mask on, a look of certainty in his made-up eyes.

"The library," he said, "Go to the British library. You can ask the librarians and they will help."

"Did you have libraries when you were alive?"

"I had anything I wanted, including tablets and great writings and knowledgeable people who would tell me what I needed to know. I never had to search. I ordered."

"I would like to have been alive then."

"I don't think you would."

"Beano would like to be alive now."

"She is. In your heart."

I stuttered. "I, I, I can't leave her. I mean, I left her in the arch but I can't leave her unknown. Someone knows why she was covered in those things. I killed her and I was all she had."

"Then do right by her."

He always comes up trumps, does Tutankhamun. I sat for a while, the presence of ancient death a security blanket around my shoulders which shook uncontrollably. My feet did a dance at the end of my legs which threatened to remove the soles of my trainers. Tutankhamun said that it was delayed shock and that I should cry and release some of the pain I held in my heart. But my heart wouldn't release anything it felt so strongly about and I let my body jump to its rhythm.

TIME IS A FUNNY thing. Sometimes it rushes
past and I feel like I'm moving in slow motion
while everyone around me is a blur of over activity.
Other times it stops around me and I'm the one
rushing while everyone around me stops to enjoy
the scenery. A game of musical statues and I am not
part of it. That day, time stood still for me. The
world went about its business while my head
remained in the railway arch with the body of a girl
I loved. Over and over, the tattoos floated in and
out of my eyes, blurring real life. The tiny girl; the
filthy arch.

Overwhelmed by a sudden urge to make
certain she had been found, I ran from
Tutankhamun and his grand home, not saying
goodbye nor thanking him for his infinite wisdom. I
ran while the soles on my shoes flapped and
slapped on the pavement. I ran without seeing,
blinded by panic which swelled my chest and
pounded my heart. Up the Holloway Road I ran,
ignoring the students queueing outside the kebab
shop, running until I turned the corner by the
railway arches. I stopped, peering around the
crumbling wall.

A cordon hung like bunting across the door
of my arch, a police officer standing to one side
while another walked past in conversation with
someone who looked homeless like me. The
buddleia nodded above their heads as if agreeing
with their words.

They'd found her; she was safe then, safe
from the vile smells and rats and creeping damp.
Beano was safe now, in a police issue body bag,

43

clean and dry and safe. I had done my best to look after her and failed. I had killed her with dreams of a better life and a bath and a fridge full of food and a job and an estate agent who didn't exist. Beano had something to live for and she made a mistake. Beano didn't kill herself. I killed her.

My hand dug deep into the rucksack; nail file, comb and some loo roll I had grabbed in the ladies at the British Museum, all present and correct,

Black and yellow tape fluttered in the breeze. Beano was dead. I loved her. She was my everything. I would have given her the world. I have no home now, either, no stinky mattress on which to lay my weary head. Nowhere to sleep to escape the awful reality. Grandma's sweetie tin flashed before me and I pushed it away. Tutankhamun was right. Flying into the past wouldn't help me now. I had to think and focus and concentrate on surviving now. All dreams of something else had flown away.

THE HOLLOWAY ROAD EBBED and flowed and I trudged up and down it until my leg muscles screamed at me to stop. At a bus shelter, I sat next to a woman with a silk scarf who was staring at the screen of her phone.

"My best friend died this morning," I said.

She looked at me but did not reply. "It was awful," I said. "I've been walking all day trying to make sense of it. And she died in my home. The police have cordoned it off."

The woman shifted away from me along the bench.

"I don't know what to do."

A bus pulled up and the woman rushed aboard, pointing at me as she spoke to the driver.

"My best friend died today," I said to a now empty bus shelter, "And I don't know what to do."

Darkness descended on the shelter and large numbers of students and commuters jostled to get their seat. I didn't tell them about Beano. It seemed wrong when they were so busy. My hand felt the nail file, the comb and the tissue. I had money in my pocket and I couldn't face lying in a doorway being kicked or moved on or worse. I owed it to Beano to be my best self. I needed shelter. Walking up side road after side road, I looked for sheds with dodgy locks or bin stores where the occupants hadn't bothered to store them. There were none. Desperation clutched at my chest, forcing blood in and out of my withering heart. Stopping outside a brightly painted B&B, I stared at the sign saying 'vacancies'. My body screamed at me to ring the bell.

A grey-haired woman with a headscarf wound like a turban opened the door and looked me up and down. "You can't stay here," she said.

"I've got money." I showed her a hundred pounds in notes and she grabbed sixty and invited me in. The room was small but clean and there was a small en-suite shower room.

"Come this way," she said. "I'm not going to ask where you got the money from. You're lucky I've got space. Normally full during the week. How long d'you want?"

"Just one night. My best friend died this morning."

"I'm sorry for your loss." She peered at my face but I couldn't read her expression.

"Thank you," I said.

"If you want breakfast it'll be seven pounds fifty." She held out her hand but I couldn't think about bacon and eggs when my heart was broken and I had lost the only person I had ever truly loved so I asked if I could decide in the morning and the turban woman said, "No" so I handed over seven pounds fifty, just in case.

"Sleep it off. You'll find it quiet here. We're just enough removed from the main road. But if you're not staying longer, I'd like you out by ten so I can clean the room for the next one." Her floral scarf stroked my cheek.

"I don't know," I said.

"Let me know at breakfast. No dancing, men, alcohol, drugs, swearing or cooking in this room. Understand?"

I nodded.

She left, creaking the floorboards with her oversized frame. The double bed was covered in peach candlewick which I vaguely remembered from a childhood visit to another grandmother. She was mad, dementia Mother said, shouting obscenities at me when I approached. I had been terrified of her. But the bedspread was soft and, as I peeled off the layers of clothing which protected me from the world, I wrapped it around my nakedness allowing the little cotton fronds to stroke my skin.

The shower spurted at strange angles. I got under the scalding water, dumping my clothes in the shower tray, and emptied the tiny bottle of shower gel into my hands. I rubbed and scrubbed in between my toes, fingers, bum cheeks and arm pits, scraping and scratching at my skin until the grime pooled around my feet and the shower tray filled up. The water tank juddered and creaked and I stayed under the water jet until a loud voice reminded me that hot water had to be paid for. She knocked twice. I turned off the water then turned it on again, lower this time, so that I could wash the clothes which carried months of dirt and moments of despair. As the dirt swirled, seemingly running from the fabric, I watched it curl around the plug hole and disappear into the depths below. I laid as many clothes as I could across the lukewarm radiator, draping the others over the back of a chair which sat in the corner of the room. Wrapping the candlewick bedspread around me once again, I curled up on the bed.

When I woke in this strange, warm place, darkness had enveloped the room, a full moon casting a search-light like stream of light through the nets. For the first time, I noticed a kettle and sachets of tea and coffee and sugar. I made a cup of tea and laced it with three sugars. The liquid warmed me inside but brought me back to the world where Beano no longer lived. I didn't notice the tears pooling in the candlewick until my skin felt damp and clammy. I let myself cry then, like Tutankhamun had said, racked and sobbing until a fraction of the pain in my heart was released with the salty water.

AS THE SUN ROSE over the B&B off the Holloway Road, so did I. Steam escaped from my jeans on the radiator when the heating clunked on at five thirty, curling up towards the window where it patterned, like frost. I turned them several times, checking the waistband for the damp which would set my kidneys into overdrive. They were crisp when I pulled them back over my legs, tight and sweet smelling. Everything else was cleaner but more threadbare and as I shoved an arm through my sweatshirt, it came through the elbow and I had to tuck the frayed edges under so they wouldn't show. My trainers now looked even more filthy; new splits had appeared and the soles bore holes. I would have to search outside charity shops until I found some more.

Cleanliness is definitely next to Godliness. Clean makes your mind work better. I suppose it's because you're not aware of yourself, not scratching or rubbing or trying to remove something and, sitting in a shaft of sunlight which warmed my skin, a plan slipped into my psyche. I would find out who Beano really was and inform her family so that they could mourn her with me. Perhaps I could have a hand in the memorial service, attended by hundreds, filling the church with scented blossoms in scarlet, vermillion, gold and white. They wouldn't know it was me who had killed her. They would thank me for bringing her back into the bosom of her family.

I hadn't had a plan since Tutankhamun suggested pickpocketing to survive. It was exciting. It was daunting. I had to *live* in honour of the girl who couldn't. I had to make sure that her thin, pale life was worth something.

Beano wouldn't have wanted me to fold like dead-man's clothes. She would have hated weakness. She loved art and plans for a better life - and burgers. She loved burgers. I knew this much about her. It was a start. I wiped a stray tear quickly, daring the others which built up behind it to try and escape.

Nail file, comb, tissue, present and correct.

What to do next?

Where to start?

Pen. Pen! I needed paper to draw the symbols I had seen. I needed paper and a couple more pens and a trip to the British library to research the symbols and their meaning.

I would start with a pen from the stationery shop I had passed a thousand times, next to the shop where a toothless, fat man sits in the window threatening to tell your fortune. He was telling my fortune now, twisting and moulding the ideas in front of me, pointing a fat finger downwards in the direction of the kitchen. The fat man wouldn't start the most important phase of his life on an empty stomach, and neither would I.

Glad that I had paid for breakfast, my body sat down in the dining room at a Formica table laid for one, the toothless grin still playing in my head.

The woman appeared from behind a swinging door. She had changed her turban but not her mood.

"How long did you shower for last night? I should charge you extra."

"My best friend died yesterday," I said, avoiding her eyes.

"Well that doesn't mean you can go and waste other people's hot water."

"I'm sorry", I said. "I had to get clean."

"Hmm." She left, returning almost immediately with a pot of tea and two slices of white toast. A square marmalade sachet sat on top.

"Fried or scrambled?"

"Fried please."

The dining room was dingy and definitely 1970s retro without the mid-century glamour. Pine cladding had soaked up years of frying smells and was now leaching them out. Small wooden tables with different coloured Formica tops hugged the walls, which were littered with laminated signage about what you could and couldn't do in the building. No smoking, visitors, loud music, cooking in the rooms, over indulgence with the shower…

Red pleather seats shone; a Spanish dancer clapped her hands above her head as a bull faced her; bland, pastoral scenes fought for space on the walls with the numerous signs. In the corner, a toy parrot sat on a perch surrounded by plastic greenery.

I had barely begun to take it all in when the woman returned holding a plate groaning with food.

"I've given you a bit extra because your friend died," she said, placing it in front of me.

I thanked her and cut into the first of three slices of bacon. The food was as hot as it was delicious and when I had finished every morsel on the plate, I realised I hadn't eaten anything on the day Beano died. I had marked it with fasting. I would be fasting in the future too, every year, to mark the passing of Beano. Perhaps her family would fast with me when we laid gerberas on her grave.

The woman sidled up to the table. "Can I sit down?"

I nodded and she lowered her bulk onto a pleather seat. Her ample bosom rested on the table as she adjusted her rear.

"You can stay another night, free of charge because your friend died," she said suddenly.

"Really?" I said.

"Yes. It's a difficult time and you paid up without trouble and you don't smell too bad today even if it was my water that cleaned you."

"Thank you."

"You're welcome. I won't give you a free breakfast tomorrow though. Food costs me so I have to pass those costs on."

"I understand."

"So, that'll be seven-pounds-fifty for tomorrow's breakfast."

I handed over the money.

"Thank you very much. It's very kind of you."

"Yes, it is." She grinned and the bridge between her teeth slipped and shot from her mouth. She retrieved it from the floor, blew a dust bunny off it and pushed it back in her mouth without so much as a raised eyebrow. I was still staring when she continued,

"Life can be very hard sometimes. One night won't break me, but it might save you." She turned and disappeared before I could ask what she meant.

Draining my cup, I went back to the room which was mine for one more night and looked round it as if for the first time. Another seventies time-warp, swathed in peach candlewick and flowers. I liked it. It was warm and dry and clean. It was real and not frightening. I could be safe for one more night, could take the risk of falling asleep without one ear open. I moved to the window, resting on the sill as I watched the world pass by under my window. Women with pushchairs and men with suits on under warm coats. Maybe they had lost someone they loved too. I stroked my rucksack whispering, "Nail file, comb, and tissue. Nail file, comb and tissue." The night stand drawer was slightly open; I pulled it and a biro slid backwards and forwards across the top of a Gideon bible. Treasure! I picked it up and put it in my rucksack. "Nail file, comb, tissue and pen!"

Back at the window, Beano's face peeped out from behind a wall across the street. I peered. She disappeared. I caught her again running down the path which led to the square and again at number twenty-seven when she knocked on the door with a parcel from Next. She was everywhere, blonde hair trailing behind her in lustrous curls, clean clothes gracing her slender body.

I met turban woman in the hall when, afraid Beano was going to knock on the door of the B&B, I went in search of something to distract me.

"There's nothing for you down here," she said. "We don't have a residents' lounge."

"That's okay. I was just looking for something to look at."

"Go and sit in the garden. Gardens are good for a broken heart." She smiled and the creases in her face smiled too.

Stepping out of the back door into a tiny oasis of green, Spring had arrived overnight. The sounds of London were muffled here, giving way to bees and hover flies and birds who twittered in the trees which edged the small plot. It may have been the garden of Eden.

I lay back on the cool grass, feeling the dampness soak through the cotton of my T-shirt, the smell of it filling my nostrils, thawing my heart. It may have been hours that I watched the sky, allowing the pictures in my mind to float through, the demons on Beano's body, the creatures, the dark archway…

SLEEP TOOK ME, RELEASING only when the clouds spat tiny raindrops on my face. Hauling my stiff body up, I shuffled inside, crawling up the stairs because walking seemed too difficult. On the candlewick bedspread, I sprawled, once again succumbing to the rhythm of sleep breathing as I wrapped myself up, cocoon-like on the bed.

I woke with the dawn chorus, showered for less time than before and waited for the noises of the house to tell me when breakfast was being served.

There were two rashers of bacon on my plate, a sausage, fried egg, tinned tomatoes and baked beans. The woman, whose hair had become purple overnight, explained that as I had the room for free, breakfast was smaller than yesterday. It was still a lot of food to me, a delicious mountain of sustenance after all the sleeping.

And all the while I ate, the purple haired woman hovered in polyester silk, not far from my table, ostensibly straightening the pictures. Eventually she sidled over.

"Can I sit down?" she asked.

I motioned to the chair opposite, my mouth too full of tomato to make sensible sounds.

An orange scarf with yellow flowers partially hid her now purple hair.

"I might have a proposition for you."

The scarf had distracted me from piercing turquoise eyes which now met mine with intensity. Her skin was soft with a bloom of fine hair across it, making her look out of focus. The blouse which strained to detain her breasts, was fuchsia; her trousers tan and the look was pulled together with an orange cardigan. I felt tired looking at her.

"Thing is," she was saying, "Since I had my hip…"

She may have talked for an hour or a minute. My mind went up to the ceiling and the relative safety of Artex. Cobwebs hung from the light fitting; fuzzy bunting. Her voice became music which I drifted on until I heard her say, "So, what do you think?"

Not wanting to appear rude, I muttered about it being a lot to take in before ten in the morning.

She laughed and it was light and tinkly and I liked her for it. "Well, mull it over. It's hard committing when you've been on the street. I should know."

My ears pricked up. "How did you know?" I asked, my sudden enthusiasm shocking her. Leaning on the table to haul up her tremendous torso, she stopped, falling back onto the chair which groaned under her weight.

"It's not rocket science." She laughed. "Look at the state of you, I mean, you're clean now and that's much better but your clothes, your hair, your expression? Surely you've seen yourself in a mirror."

I told her I hadn't looked for a long time, preferring an idea of myself to reality.

"It bothers most people. Why not you?" I asked.

"Three years I was out there," she said, "Three of the worst years of my life and in the end, I knocked on every door in Holloway asking for a job and I got chamber maid, here. Margaret, the owner, had been homeless too, after she had an illegitimate baby. Parents kicked her out. Things were different then, a real scandal having a baby and not giving it up for adoption. She raised that child good, too. I slept in the shed at first, proved myself and worked my way up. When Margaret died, her son had gone to live in Australia with a wife and four children and a very good job, I might add. So, she left me this place. I've been running it twenty-seven years." She stopped, scratching under the headscarf at purple wisps of hair. "Must have been fate that you turned up out of the blue, just like I did all those years ago," she said. "Last thing I was expecting. But that's what they say, isn't it? Things come when you're least expecting them?" She smiled.

I searched the turquoise eyes, trying to make sense of the stream of words.

"I'm not sure I understand," I said.

"About Margaret's son? Nice man. Very grateful to his Mother but couldn't wait to get away. Didn't like the stream of people in and out when he was growing up. Couldn't understand why she had to keep this place on. He wanted her to get married and settle down but she couldn't. Said she'd walked the streets for weeks with him as a babby and now people walked to her and she offered them a nice bed and a good breakfast and sent them on their way, not the other way around. See?"

"Not that," I said.

"Oh, the job! Breakfasts and chamber-maiding, three days a week to start and the shed's yours."

"What?" My head spun. Words filled every available space.

"Karma in a way. What goes around comes around." She scratched under her turban and a wisp of purple hair fell across her ear. "I'm offering you what she offered me. Never thought I would do it for someone else. And don't go thinking about bumping me off 'cause I've put this place in my will for you. I won't do that so there's no point. Rather a cat's home had it than I got killed for it."

"I don't kill people," I lied.

"So, you'll take it?"

I stopped, a lump of bacon stuck in my throat. The hairs on my neck stood up. My body flushed ready to sweat it out.

"Tell me again," I whispered.

"I'm offering you three days a week to cook breakfast, do some cleaning and you can live in the shed where I lived to start with. If you take a room it's less money coming in and we can't have that now, can we?" She smiled and her face softened into something beautiful.

"I don't know what to say," I said. "It's so out of everything I thought was going to happen today."

"I know. But you're ready after your friend."

Was I? Didn't I have her family to find? Surely that wasn't possible when there were breakfasts to cook and rooms to clean. "I've never cooked or cleaned," I said.

"I can teach you. It's not hard."

"And I have to find Beano's family."

"Look… I don't even know your name."

"Jay."

"Jay, it's an offer you won't get anywhere else. It's a shed and some work. Work hard and there's a wage. Work hard and there's time to find Beano's family too. Who's Beano, anyway."

"My friend that died."

"Funny name. Not real, of course, a pseudonym for the streets, no doubt. Beano, Jay, New Boy, Cider Jack; I've heard them all.

The ball of fear moved up from my stomach and sat on my chest. The bacon was above it. I retched, holding a napkin over my face.

"I'm sorry," I said, not wanting to be rude to this woman who was offering me the world, unsure that I was able to take it.

"What's the problem?" she said.

"It's not a problem as such…"

"Not worthy of help I suppose. Or too bad a person for people to help you. Or even that you're just no good and can't trust yourself not to steal from me."

"No! No, not at all. Not worthy, yes, but I'd never steal from someone like you."

"Then take it."

"I'll take it," I said, believing in fate at that moment, with every fibre of my being.

"Let me show you the shed. We'll take it week by week. If you can't hack it, we can talk or you can leave and we won't fall out. Just tell me what you're doing and we won't fall out. Don't walk and leave me to find your dirty towels in the shed. Know what I mean?" I nodded. "At some point, you can move into the house but you've got to pay for that. This is free."

I followed her out of the French windows in the dining room, down the pretty, abundant garden of Eden, and, nestling between rhododendrons, a Hobbit house made of wood with cedar tiles on the roof. There was a little window at the side and as I tried to peer in, turban lady pushed past, unlocking the padlock with podgy fingers.

She opened the door and stood back. I had expected to see a lawn mower but there wasn't one. Instead, a little camp bed hugged one wall with a shelf on the other and several books, mouldy and green, sitting sadly on it. There was a picture on the back wall of a landscape with heather which I assumed to be Scotland and a rag rug on the floor.

"It's perfect," I said.

"Isn't it?" said turban woman.

"What's your name?" I asked.

"Heather," she replied. And I understood the picture and checked the spines of the mouldy books to find Burns, Walter Scott and Robert Louis Stevenson.

"Is this where you lived?" I asked.

"Yes, my bed, my books, my picture. I couldn't take them down. They belonged to this part of my life."

"Wow."

"Wow, indeed. Better than a doorway or an old, smelly railway arch don't you think?"

"I do," I said.

"You can change it, do it right for you."

"Really?" I asked.

"Of course," she said and touched my arm in a gesture so gentle that I knew this was real help in a real world where no one had cared for years. "I reckon you need a bit of time and space to sort things out. And if you do the work how I say and within time, you'll be getting fifty pounds a week after your trial period, and this. But no jacking up in here. No drinking cider 'til you can't feel your face. And definitely no men. You're on a month's trial and I can sack you at any time if you let me down."

"I no longer drink or do drugs and I hate people," I said.

She laughed. "Then you're the perfect person for it. I knew when I saw you and when you tried to wash the world off with all that hot water. Oh, there's a loo and a basin in the scullery off the kitchen. You can use that for now."

"Thank you," I said. She took my hand then, stroking the back of it in contemplation.

"And twice a week you can have a shower in that room you've been in as long as it's not occupied."

"Thank you," I said again although the words seemed inadequate.

"We all need a bit of help now and then. I need some that you can give and I can give you some in return. Winner, winner, chicken dinner."

I laughed and with a pat on my head, she turned and waddled back to the kitchen. I took in the six by six space which was to be my home, imagining a tiny stove and fridge, colourful bunting at the acetate window and a fluffy duvet encased in Egyptian cotton on the bed.

Beano would have loved it. We would have papered the walls with modern art prints and toasted marshmallows on the little stove. Because of her, I had this safe haven in the garden of Eden. It meant I could honour her memory and do the research I needed to do. It meant becoming part of the world again, leaving the side-lines to play a central role. It meant changing everything I knew about my life. My shaking hands told me I was daunted. It meant benefitting from the fact I had killed her.

Carefully placing my rucksack under the bed, I hung my anorak on the hook and sat down. It didn't matter that the space was tiny. It didn't matter that I could see the cobalt blue sky where a tile had slipped. It didn't matter that I was, at the moment, sharing the space with three types of spider. It mattered only that it was mine.

I JOINED HEATHER IN the kitchen. She was standing by the stove juggling fried and scrambled eggs over four plates. She looked me up and down before speaking, all the while dancing around the stove as full English in all its glory appeared from her pans and floated into perfect position on the chipped plates.

"Have you got any money?" she asked.

"A bit."

"Go and buy some new clothes. Those have died."

The heat rose swiftly from my toes, spreading out in a beetroot rash on my face.

"Don't be embarrassed. Fact not criticism. Those clothes have given up because you've been sleeping rough not because you're a dirty bitch." She laughed, high and bright and despite myself, my own cheeks rose in a semblance of a smile. "It was my water you washed them with, after all!" She laughed again.

"I'm sorry," I said.

"It's how you caught my attention. I wouldn't be sorry if I were you." She wiped her hands on a stained tea towel. "I'd recommend a pair of jeans and a blouse of some description for work. Seven Sisters market. Go there. Jeans are a fiver for someone as small as you. Yes, jeans, a shirt, knickers and socks, shoes if you can?"

Feeling the diminishing bundle of twenties in my pocket I replied, "I can," turning away before my shame engulfed both of us.

"Nothing special, just clean and for work. Makes you feel better about things with clean clothes on your back and you won't be transferring germs to customers."

The tinkly laugh followed me down the path to my new home, where the rucksack with the nail-file, comb and tissue were waiting exactly where I had left them. Nothing missing except for the teeth in the comb.

I sat on the corner of the camp bed and breathed, noticing my chest as it rose and fell.

THE SALIVA STIMULATING SMELLS of Seven Sisters market stunned me five whole minutes before I got there. Oriental and Asian spices, knock off perfumes and artisan breads jostled for pole position. I followed them, pocketing a pasty for later, blinkered towards women's wear and the fabrics which would transport me from tramp to working woman. This working woman could go to the British Library and research with a pad and a pen, the tattoos which adorned the body of the girl I had loved. They would push me towards finding out who she was. My shoulders pushed back as I drew myself to my full height. A working woman with a home shouldn't slouch.

I bought jeans and a white shirt, white to show the world that I could wash when I wanted to, a pack of five pairs of cotton briefs, and one of socks with the days of the week woven into the toes. I imagined the joy of slipping a clean foot into new socks and the idea sent a shiver of anticipation down my spine.

A man with a Manchester accent and an unfeasibly large paunch, wanted thirty pounds for a pair of ordinary trainers so I waited 'til his back was turned and put them in my rucksack, remembering Camden as if it were a lifetime earlier, not yesterday. I had disappeared into the barber's shop long before he noticed they were gone, reappearing with a short back and sides and a long fringe, my straggly, mousy hair now shiny and soft. The trainers were already on my feet as I skipped to the flower man and bought the most garish bunch of flowers I could find for Heather, guessing that they would please her more than the

65

subtle, sweet smelling pink roses which drew me in.

With forty pounds remaining of my stolen money, I spent a tenner on a jumper, knowing as I do, the misery of the cold. It was red and fluffy, almost reaching my knees and I wanted it so badly that my heart raced and my breath came in short bursts. The sun had been shining all day and it was too warm to wear it, so I threw it over my shoulders, enjoying the flashes of red as the arms swung when I walked. A bag of broken biscuits and one of all butter fudge also found their way into my bag as the stall holder talked to an ancient woman with a tartan shopping trolley, the crumbly fudge sticking to my teeth as I walked on air-filled soles back to Holloway.

HEATHER TURNED PINK WITH pleasure when I gave her the flowers. She took them straight to her 'parlour', closing the door behind her but not before the aromas of tea and biscuits and disinfectant had leaked out. She returned a moment later with rosy cheeks and wet eyes and admired my clean shirt and dark jeans.

"You don't half scrub up well," she said and I blushed a little. "In the scullery are all the cleaning things you need. Do rooms two and three please, and be good at it. Then you can do the shed and I've left you a pile of linens that I don't need anymore. Have what you like and recycle the rest. I'll see you in the kitchen at six tomorrow morning. Six sharp, mind."

"I have no alarm."

She winked and her face softened. "I've left one in the scullery," she said.

I whistled in the garden of Eden that afternoon. I pushed air through my lips and sound came out. Tutankhamun wouldn't recognise me when I visited him tomorrow. I hoped he wouldn't be angry that I had benefitted from Beano's death, pushing the thought back into a locked cupboard in my head.

I WOKE UP TO bird song. A blackbird was perched on the roof of the shed, calling to its friends to get up and start catching worms. They replied, a cacophony in the tree above me, as I lay on the camp bed looking up at the inside of the cedar tiles which separated us, pondering the balance of the worst and best days coming together – one breaking, the other building. I stared, too, at the shelf and the things I would put upon it. My body screamed in pain, muscle after muscle stretching and screeching, unused to physical exercise. The shed still had the faint smell of bleach from the floor which I had scrubbed along with the walls and the insides of the cedar tiles. The slipped tile had been re-pinned and the doubled over, lilac candlewick bedspread gave off the sweet smell of lavender from Heather's washing powder. All signs of damp had been eradicated, the green, mouldy books consigned to the bin. I had left the pastoral scene with heather on the wall, a nod to the real Heather, her generosity and purple hair.

The alarm went off a moment later, the two bells piercing the birdsong and the morning. I jumped and hit my head on the window ledge, knocking it out of place. A drop of blood landed on the candlewick and I sucked at it so that it wouldn't stain. Putting on my underwear and anorak, I rushed down the path to the toilet and ran the hot tap. I washed with a little bottle of shower gel which Heather had left with a note that after a week I would have to buy my own. It seemed more than fair as I splashed hot water on my body and washed using the flannel which Heather had also supplied.

It seemed more than fair, also, that I was allowed a full English of my own for every shift I worked. Heather gave me Saturday, Sunday and Monday with room-cleaning after breakfast. She had regular clients in her six rooms, business men with dreams larger than their wallets or too shrewd to spend their earnings, labourers from Poland who had been there a year, and what she called 'occasionals' like myself.

"I like that," I said.

"What?"

"I'm an occasional."

"You're not now, so get your head down and listen." She winked so I didn't go red but I did listen a little more intently.

"I'll show you how to do breakfast. Let me know when you've watched enough times and are ready to do it yourself." I nodded hopefully.

She began her routine by turning on all the flames on the range cooker, dropping the grill door and turning on the oven. I watched, spellbound as she went through the body memories from a dance she had done for decades, cracking eggs, slicing black pudding, stirring beans and catching toast as it shot skyward from the industrial toaster.

"Take these plates through to the dining room for me," she said, "Table three."

"I can't," I said. "I don't know how."

"Don't be ridiculous," Heather said. "Just take them through and put them on the table and don't rise to anything they say."

I took them, my hands shaking. "I thought I'd be back-room, cooking and cleaning in the shadows where no one could see me."

"It's part of the job," said Heather, folding her arms across her ample bosom.

The plates shook in my hands as I backed through the kitchen door. The room fell silent for a moment. Then, "Morning darling," said one and they all began. "Heather had good plastic surgery overnight." They laughed.

"And lost three stone."

Almost dropping the plates on table three, I turned and ran to the kitchen.

"Ignore them," said Heather.

My heart raced. Heather said, "Ignore them and they'll stop. Give 'em an inch and you know what they'll take. Straight face and off you go."

I went, juggling three plates this time, laid on my fingers by Heather who was taking no nonsense from me, opening the door with my back as I delivered the food and returned with pots of tea and coffee. Heather smiled as I struggled, giggling to herself when I almost dropped a tray of teapots, flailing arms to catch them. Seven plates and seven teapots were delivered, the redness of my face the only sign of my discomfort to the braying pack of workmen in the dining room.

"Good job," she said as I brought the last empty plate back to the sink. "Hardest part facing people when you've been avoiding them for so long." She winked and disappeared into her parlour leaving me with a devastated kitchen.

I surveyed the scene, greasy pans and plates and cups, piled by the sink, a forlorn bottle of washing up liquid waiting for me. By ten, it was spotless, rays of sunshine flashing off the buffed draining board, pans and saucepans stacked inside each other in the cupboards and on top of the cooker. Taking the caddy of room cleaning stuff, I trudged up the stairs with the keys she had left me and opened the first door. Three beds with candlewick bedspreads of different colours met me, crumpled and empty, the detritus of men's lives strewn around the floor. A porn magazine, hair products, spare high-vis vests and thick, black socks. I left their personal items where they were, as instructed made the beds and cleaned the bathroom, replacing the towels and placing extra toilet roll on the stand. The next room took less time, less pondering about the people who stayed in it. The third was occupied by a business man and was neater, cleaner and easier. I flew through it, piling his belongings onto the nightstand so that he could see I hadn't stolen any, cleaning the mirrors with extra effort as he was sure to be checking his appearance in them. Carrying the rubbish and caddy down the stairs, I met Heather, watching with amusement.

"Harder work than you thought?" she said.

"Different," I said.

"What did you expect?"

"I don't know. But it's not bad work. In fact, it's quite interesting."

She laughed. "You'll lose interest quite quickly, but as long as you do it well, that's all that matters." She adjusted her lime green turban. "I'll be checking the rooms and I'll make a list of anything I want you to do differently. Don't take it as criticism."

"I won't," I said, although I wasn't sure. "Could I have some beans on toast?" I asked, hearing my rumbling stomach.

"Of course! Sorry, I forgot to do your breakfast." Heather slapped her own wrist. "Clear up after yourself, mind."

I ate quickly, watching the kitchen clock, my mind already on the next task of the day.

By one, following Tutankhamun's advice, I was en route to The British Library with a new pen and two pads nestling in my rucksack along with the nail file, comb and tissue which I had replaced from a box in the kitchen. Beano's dolphin leapt and frolicked in my ear and the new red jumper flapped around my knees, keeping out the early, spring chill.

With reverence, I entered the cathedral of knowledge, the height of the domed ceiling feeling like no ceiling at all. Books lined the walls, as high as ten men, with ladders and floors and staircases reaching the thousands of books which graced the shelves. Breathing in the heady scent of old knowledge, I found a desk away from anyone else, placing my rucksack on top with ceremony. Mesmerised by the vastness of it all, I took a moment to drink it in, letting it slip down my gullet like fine wine, full and heady with old oak. Behind the central desk were three middle aged women, huddled over a huge tome. I kept them in my eye-line as I pulled out the pad and began to draw.

With my eyes tightly shut, I could see clearly the figure which had adorned Beano's back.

I opened and closed them as my pen flew across the page.

A goat face peered out; the figure with breasts and a snake for a phallus, with wings and the moon and the pentagram. I could see her skin as clearly as if I were staring at it; the pen took on a life of its own, shading here, redefining there. Through squinted eyes I saw Beano's body and the images upon it, copying them onto the paper with notes about where they were and how they looked. It was exhausting, overwhelming. It forced me to see her again, as I had never seen her before. It forced me to see how little I knew of the girl I loved and whom I had killed. It forced me back into the railway arch with its stench of death, rats and filth – the place I would have called home had it not been for the good fortune she had given me.

When it was done, it was as true a representation of the beast as I could have managed. I recognised it as the tattoo covering Beano's back. I retched, covering my mouth, eyes darting to make sure no one had seen, then turned the paper over so I didn't have to look. It was real now, more real than washing up or cleaning bathrooms, more important than living in comfort. After a moment concentrating hard on my breathing, I took it to the desk and the three twin-sets looked up.

"Can you help me please?" I said in my best working woman with a home voice.

"Yes,"

I showed them the picture. "Do you know what or who this is?"

"Baphomet," they said in unison, their toning twin-sets touching as they all jinxed each other for speaking at the same time.

"Baphomet? Who is he?"

"Different things to different people," said one.

"The occult or a Pagan God," said another.

"Bad news or good news depending on your view," said the third.

"Are there any books on him?" I asked.

"Plenty," said the first woman, touching the picture with a manicured finger. "some you can borrow, over there," She pointed at the vastness.

"And read only. You can't borrow them," said the second, nodding to her comrades. "Peter will show you." She called the name and a young man in a corduroy jacket and jeans appeared from behind a bookcase.

"Take this lady to Baphomet please," she said and smiled at me. I was distracted by being called a lady and Peter disappeared before I realised where he had gone; the second twinset had to point to an aisle.

"Here you are," he said as I rounded the bookcase. "Everything on Baphomet from the occult influence to the pagan celebrations. It's all here. Writing a book?"

"A life story," I said before I thought about it. "I'm researching a life and this is all I have to start with."

"Weird thing to start with but, hey, plenty of weird people about." He smiled and a mop of sandy hair fell over his right eye. "So, I'll leave you to it, then."

"Thank you."

I picked up the first volume, "A history of Baphomet," opened it on the first page and tried to read. But the words moved and joggled on the page so that I could neither read nor recognise them. Tucking it under my arm, I pulled three other books from the shelf and took them to the desk where I put them down, laying out the contents of my rucksack in a safety net around me.

Apparently, the whole world knew about Baphomet apart from me. There were authors and academics, religious leaders, historians studying the Knights Templar and modern Satanists who all knew the powers of the creature that represented everything.

I found a picture which looked almost exactly like mine and underneath it said "Sabbatic Goat" image drawn by Eliphas Levi which contains binary elements representing the "sum total of the universe" (e.g. male and female, good and evil, etc.). The words swam around my head, good and evil, male and female – how could one thing be all those things and look like a goat? It didn't make sense.

Peter tapped me on the shoulder. "It's a bit of a long shot but I found this. Baphomet's big in the tattoo world." He handed me a book on the tradition and representations in the subversive art of tattoos and smiled, a lopsided grin which balanced the flop of sandy hair and made him look like the boy he had been.

"Thank you," I said. "It was a tattoo I saw."

"Wow. Big one?"

"It covered her back. But there were others too."

Peter crouched by the desk. "Fascinating stuff this. So, this life story, whose is it?"

"My best friend," I said staring at the cover of the book and Baphomet, the man-woman-goat thing which graced it. "She had this on her back and others all over her. Even bees flying from some internal bee hive between her cheeks. And ugly demon type things and skulls and such like. I'm going to draw them all from memory." I showed him my version of Baphomet.

"Wow," he said again. "You can draw." I blushed a little.

"I don't know about that but at least you recognise him." I fiddled with the handle on my rucksack.

"I mean it. You have real talent. Are you an artist?"

"No." I swallowed. "I work in a B&B."

"Good for you," he said. "But you really should be an artist. Come with me and I'll show you the subversive tattoo section. It's more visual, less to read and more to learn from pictures, don't you think?"

"A picture speaks a thousand words," I said feeling more normal than I had ever felt even though my best friend had just died and I was discussing subversive tattoos with a stranger.

"Here you are," said Peter, running his hand along a row of books on the third shelf. I had to stand on tiptoe to reach and, a few seconds later, Peter supplied a sturdy little step to stand on. I smiled and thanked him and began to turn the pages of old photographs of tattooed women and men. These people were freaks, earning money simply by being different. Atlantic City freaks. I had heard of Atlantic City in America but never seen what it was all about. The designs were strange but not ugly. The models, for that's how I saw them, were in control of their bodies; the images their choice. Something inside told me that Beano wasn't one of these women. She wasn't proud of her tattoos. She hid them.

Taking the books back to the desk I began to draw, sketching each of the tattoos that I could remember from Beano's body, referencing with the tattoo books to see if I could find anything similar. Two hours later and the pages of the pad were fabulous with diagrams and drawings and explanations. I had named demons and angels and gargoyles and broken the vast amount of information on Baphomet into three lines.

1. Worshipped by Knights Templar in fourteen something
2. Pagan representation of everything
3. Looks nasty and is worshipped in church of Satan.

Beano didn't know about the Knights Templar; of that I was pretty sure. Pagans were weird but harmless people who liked gathering by stones and dressing up in crushed velvet. It seemed unlikely. The Church of Satan was still active and although it was just as unlikely as the others, something made me stop and consider the idea that Beano had been mixed up in something black and sinister. My breast bone vibrated and a voice by my ear said,

"This way." I looked around but Peter and the twin-sets were all busy and no one was near me. "This way," it said again and the page with my drawing of Baphomet curled at the corner. "This way," I heard a third time and the pen rolled until it underlined number three in my list.

"Tattoos? Baphomet?" I whispered, a statement and a question both at the same time.

"Yes," said the voice and a puff of air on my ear caused me to turn suddenly.

"Beano?"

The air was cold and directed at my ear so that it tickled. The pen rolled across the perfectly flat desk and came to a halt by a picture I had doodled of the comb with three teeth missing. A fine, long blonde hair floated from the heavens and settled on it and I knew it was Beano because she had used the comb and only she and I knew that.

Wrapping the blonde hair around my finger, I kissed it. "I'm sorry," I whispered before the weight of my lies pushed me back down into my stomach which lurched with lack of ease.

I clutched my rucksack, rocking backwards and forwards at the desk. "I'm sorry," I whispered again, "So sorry."

Another tap on the shoulder brought me back into the room. Peter bent down. "Are you okay?" he said.

I nodded my reply.

"Do you need a glass of water?"

I nodded again, glad when he turned and walked away. The blonde hair was still wrapped around my fingers but the cold air had gone. I breathed deeply.

Peter returned with water which he made me drink before handing me a card. "I love tattoos," he said. "That's how I know about Baphomet, saw one being done on a guy's chest once. I wouldn't have it myself but the work in it was amazing. I like Japanese stuff. This tattoo artist did my legs and sleeves." He pointed to the business card and rolled up a sleeve to reveal colourful Japanese lotus flowers and fish.

"They're not keen in here so I have to keep them covered."

"They're beautiful. I saw a fish like that, but not on Beano. On someone's arm," I said.

"Aah, a leaping koi. It represents triumph over adversity. I like that."

"Me too," I said, nodding thanks for the card.

"He might not be able to help but you never know."

I thanked him again, tucking the business card into the pocket of my rucksack.

"So why are you doing all this?" he asked, watching as I packed my things into the bag.

"Because she died and she was a street girl so no-one cared but me. And I promised." I left out that I had killed her."

"Oh. How did you meet her?"

"It doesn't matter," I said, standing up to end the conversation. "I did meet her, that's what matters."

Peter took the pile of books from the desk. "I'll look out for some others for next time," he said. I smiled, thanked him and took the tattoo book to the central desk, asking if I could borrow it. A twin set nodded and held out her hand.

"Your library card?"

"I don't have one."

"Fill this out then. It'll only take a minute." She handed me a form which I filled out with a home address which was both strange and exciting at the same time, then handed it back. A moment later she came back with a library card and told me that the book was due back the next week.

"I'll be here to worship before then," I said and they smiled as I turned and strode out of the cathedral with my book and a pad full of drawings.

I TOOK THE BUS to the British Museum, because I could. Tutankhamun rose to meet me as I sat down next to him, greeting him as usual before telling him all that had happened at the B&B.

"Strange how things turn out," he said.

"I don't deserve it," I said.

"But you've got it. That's what matters, and what you do with it, of course. What you do with it is everything."

"I won't screw it up, if that's what you mean." Indignation pulled my shoulders back.

"I'm sure you won't," he said. "But all this nonsense about not deserving it will ruin it for you if you're not careful." I felt his breath on my neck. "You have an opportunity to change everything," he continued. "Don't let past mistakes hold you back."

"I won't," I whispered. The security guard who I had seen and been ignored by a thousand times, nodded in my direction. My eyes darted back to the relics, disturbed.

"Everything changes," Tutankhamun said. "You'll forget me eventually."

"Never," I said, louder than I had intended. "Never," I repeated, lowering my head on to my hands. "I don't even know what it is I've been given. It's all so weird."

"You'll work it out."

"I went to the library, like you said. I started drawing the tattoos and did research. Baphomet. That's what was on her back. Baphomet."

"Aaah, everything and nothing. Good and bad, male and female. Pagan and Satan."

"How do you know? Am I the only person who didn't know?"

"I know everything. I have the Universe at my fingertips. You are merely mortal and you hadn't read about it because... why would you?"

I couldn't disagree. Why would I? I'd spent many formative years seeking food from bins and a dry place to sleep.

"Draw them all," he said after a deep silence. "Draw the pictures you saw on her body. Keep a record and continue along the road until you find a signpost. Be vigilant. Be courageous."

"Beano sent me a sign today, a blonde hair and reminder of our time together." My temple tingled and I scratched at it with a filed nail.

"Good," Tut said. "That's the kind of sign that means the most."

"Thought so," I said, and the place in my stomach where doubt had settled felt peace.

THE ALARM WENT OFF at five thirty, shattering the sleep I had so deeply fallen into. Beano's blue eyes shone, looking up at me from the mattress in the railway arch, smiling and happy from the best day of her life. She faded. I caught the sob in the back of my throat and shoved it back down into my gut where it could fester before dressing and dodging fat raindrops down the path to the house. I washed, a lick and a promise really, in the toilet basin, combed my short hair and cleaned my teeth. Anyone who has been on the street will tell you that teeth cleaning is the greatest pleasure.

Minty and fresh, I met Heather in the kitchen, wrapped a pinnie around my waist and offered to do bacon and tomatoes.

She smiled, ruffling my hair so that I felt childlike and ridiculous.

"Watch and learn. Tomorrow you're doing the lot. You're bright and quick and you'll be much better off getting on with it without me." She smiled, adjusting the floral turban scarf which had caught on a large, gold hoop earring. "You'll do a better job if you're left to your own devices."

"Did you?"

"Yes. Made a mess; cracked a few more eggs than I needed, burnt some bacon. Within a week, I was doing a decent job."

"And now it's a dance."

She looked at me, a quizzical look on her large features, orange lipstick bleeding into the lines around her mouth.

"You dance around the kitchen with moves you've performed a thousand times. When I watch,

I see someone totally comfortable. That takes years," I said.

"A dance! I love it!" she said, pouring two cups of coffee from the filter machine.
"Kitchen choreography!"

We laughed and the sound of my own gurgling amusement surprised me.

"You're quite clever, aren't you?" said Heather.

"I don't know about that," I said, positioning myself at the side of the stove to watch her begin her routine.

She began cracking eggs and asked, "So, where did you go to yesterday after work? You were gone hours."

"The British Library."

"Oh?"

"I'm doing some research."

"On?"

Not knowing how much of Beano's life I should share, I hesitated, blushed and tried to straighten my ruffled hair.

"It looks better scruffy," she said, "More feminine."

The belly laugh came from deep within me. "Feminine?" I managed through guffaws. "Me?"

Heather remained straight faced. "Just because you've been on the street doesn't mean you're a tramp. Homeless is not the same as being a tramp. Homelessness is a circumstance and being a tramp is a lifestyle choice. There's a big difference; I should know." She wiped her forehead with her pinnie. "Violence at home, being thrown out because of step parents and lovers and everything coming before you. I've been there."

I didn't speak.

"Some of us had to put up with all sorts and the streets seemed like a better option than what we had. A better option, eh? What a fool I was. So why are you homeless, then?"

I shuffled my feet and stared at the new trainers which pinched my toes a bit. "I couldn't cope," I said, making it clear that the conversation was over. Or so I thought.

"Couldn't cope with what?" she said. "Life, men, family, what?"

"Please," I said. "I don't want to talk about it."

Heather set her mouth, wiped her hands on her sweaty pinnie and hugged me, her ample bust almost cutting off my air supply. "I'm sorry, sweet, I shouldn't be so bloody forthright and nosey. You can tell me in your own time."

Tell her what? I thought, the past, too well-filed, had become a blank which filled a space in my brain. I lied and promised that one day, I would confide in her. This placated her and she flicked the tea towel over her shoulder, juggling pans on the already lit stove.

My shift flew. The guests were more polite this morning as I placed their enormous breakfasts in front of them; the rooms which needed changing had had nothing out of the ordinary happen in them. The bathrooms shone. The carpet pattern jumped as the vacuum swooshed over it. The washing machine jolted into life, the last of my chores, filled with sheets which I would hang over the Victorian airer later. With a thoughtful eye, I checked the list which Heather had left, making sure to empty the waste paper baskets which I had forgotten the day before. She hadn't criticised, just left a list of 'reminders' which I both appreciated and agonised over. Rubbish dumped, I returned to the shed and pulled on my red jumper, running for the bus which would drop me near the British Library.

The twin sets had been replaced by two women in blouses and skirts. I made myself comfortable at one of the desks furthest away, so that I wouldn't be interrupted by their whispers and took out my drawing pad and pen. But my hand wouldn't draw and the pictures in the books which I had spread upon the desk didn't look like Beano. I laid my head on the pages, my body slumped, my brain unable to stop the myriad images of the khaki hood which swirled within. Four days had passed since I happened upon the B&B, four days of events so enormous that I struggled to comprehend. Even Tutankhamun's words were different from the gently encouraging ones I had heard before, full of purpose and shared determination, not shared by me. I lifted my oversized head.

The pen hovered over a clean sheet of paper before touching it, tentatively at first, then with bold strokes. A tendril of hair, an eyebrow, the shadow cast by a pretty, turned up nose. From some consciousness, Beano appeared from the page, bright eyed and full of wonder. Her lips curled into a slight smile, Mona Lisa-like, enigmatic and distant. And from her beautiful face, a slender neck, sculpted collar bone and tiny breasts. I carried on downwards, remembering the rib cage which, if I had pressed hard, would have snapped under my fingers and the tiny waist, smooth skin taut across it.

The paper finished here. I took another sheet and, lining it up with what I had drawn, continued downwards, penning tiny floral knickers for modesty, moving down with sweeping strokes to take in her long thighs, knees, slim calves and small feet.

Here was Beano before the tattoos, her skin as white as the fresh clean sheets I had placed on the beds at the B&B. She stood before me in the knickers I had given her, one tiny hand on her hip, the other hanging freely. Taking two more sheets of paper, I began to draw again, her back view this time, the line of her vertebrae clearly visible as it travelled down her spine to a small, firm bottom. I stopped here, remembering the bees which seemed to nest inside her, fleeing their cavernous nest through her rectum and across her buttocks. I shuddered, sliding the picture under her front view until the image in my head had receded, then, taking a deep breath, continued until I had all of Beano on my paper.

With a pencil and a light touch, I began to place the tattoos I had seen on her body, Baphomet covering her back, the demons, the bees…

The shaking began in my fingers, travelling up my arms into my jaw. Teeth chattered, the hairs on my body standing to attention as the trembling gathered momentum. Down my legs it went, the chair underneath vibrating with the movement. Snatching up my paper, I placed Beano inside the pad once more, slipping an elastic band over it to keep her safe. The book of tattoos bounced off the desk as I grabbed at it, flinging it towards the shelf for returned books before fleeing from the cathedral of knowledge and back into the ignorance of the world. Breathing fume-filled air as deeply into my lungs as I could, I stopped and sat on the steps for a moment to gather myself. Staggering to the nearest tobacconist, I bought cigarettes, discarding the cellophane as I rushed to light one. Calming smoke filled my deflated lungs; I sat on the steps once again, concentrating on the in-out, in-out of smoke as people walked by, unencumbered by guilt and the enormity of change. I sweated underneath the acrylic fibres of the red jumper, feeling my lifeforce trickle down my spine, tickling, leaving a cold trail behind it. My hand reached into the rucksack; nail file, tissue, comb, touching the sliver of card which Peter had given me. Now it played with the dolphin in my ear, Beano's dolphin. Stubbing the cigarette out on the step, I took the business card between still shaking fingers. The name, "Dave the Vampire", written in script filled the top portion, an address and a telephone number underneath. I put it back, unsure what it meant and headed for the park, alighting on a bench where I could feel the freshness coming off the water. It cooled my skin and, familiar, deadened the pictures flooding my brain. Cigarette after cigarette was lit, smoked, discarded.

I WAS GETTING QUICKER. The rooms were clean and sparkling by eleven thirty, skirting boards washed, bedding changed and the baths scrubbed. Without being asked I scraped lime scale off the taps, cleaning all the windows so that the sun could penetrate the rooms. I vacuumed the floors with ancient, juddering machinery, and the window sills and the corners of the room by the ceiling where tiny spiders with long, spindly legs liked to make their homes. The kitchen worktops gleamed, the stainless-steel cooker bore no reference to breakfast. I danced with the mop and the bucket, over the encaustic tiles in the hallway and rushed to put all my cleaning equipment away as soon as I could.

It was important, I had somewhere to go. Peter had given me my next direction. With no phone, a visit to Dave the Vampire was my only option and I didn't feel much like walking all the way to Soho. My funds were diminished and I would have had to go dipping to earn the fare had Heather not blocked the path as I came out of the shed.

"You off again?"

"Yes."

"Where to this time?"

"I'm doing research." She didn't need to know more.

She held out a twenty-pound note. "Thought you might need this."

I took it, thanking her profusely, delighted not to have to go dipping. The urgency left my limbs.

"You've been doing a good job," she said. "The kitchen was spotless this morning and the rooms are more than adequate for the clientele." She laughed and the sound of it travelled up the back of my neck. "Anyway, I thought you could do with it and as you're not rushing off to buy drugs or cider, well, have a treat on me."

"Thanks Heather. Really. I am so grateful."

"I don't need your gratitude. Someone did it for me and now it's your turn. One day, I hope, you'll do it for someone else."

Suddenly I didn't want to rush to Soho. Heather's purple cardigan and turquoise trouser combination smelled and felt like home. I stuttered then, "Would you like to come in?" I said, pointing at the shed door.

"I tell you what," said Heather, "You come to me. I've got a kettle and a couple of chairs we can sit on." Her smile lit the rhododendrons and bounced off the wings of a worm-grappling blackbird.

As I followed, Heather talked about the house and the woman who had owned it before her.

"Set a precedent, she did. No charity nor nothing like that. Just that knowledge that someone would come to the door at the right time needing a bit of help and here we are, both of us turning up and both of us getting helped. The world turns and in it there are thousands of private people not making a fuss about the fact that they're saving lives and giving people second chances."

I nodded even though she couldn't see me.

"And all the time these charities send money to evil people and the people who need it don't get it and they put these aggressive collectors out on the street and when I nip up to Seven Sisters, they lunge at me, grinning their false smiles and demanding I set up direct debits. Direct debits! Like I'd let them have my bank details. Next, they'll be taking money contactless from all our pockets, you mark my words." She took a meaningful breath.

I laughed and she turned. "Not laughing at you," I managed between giggles, "But I know what you mean."

She rustled through the kitchen, opening the door to her private parlour, pushing me in front of her so that I entered first.

It was everything I hoped it would be.

A frilled standard lamp shone a dim glow over the gold Draylon sofa, cross stitched cushions scattered over three seats. In another corner, a patchwork knitted blanket was thrown over an arm chair and an old television blinked. Patterned red carpet and floral green wallpaper clashed with the yellow and blue striped curtains which were drawn against the road outside. A dusty chandelier hung, oversized from the middle of the pink ceiling and Heather ducked beneath it, settling herself on the gold Draylon as she pointed at the armchair. I sat down, taking in the gold framed prints of Highland cattle which dotted the walls.

"Tea?"

"Please."

She reached over to the Regency style side table and turned on a Teasmade. "I don't want to go into that kitchen in the evening. Too breakfasty."

"Don't blame you," I said, pulling out a tapestry cushion of two kittens from behind my back. A collection of dolls sat on a mid-century sideboard, peering out from beneath velvet bonnets as they judged me. Heather saw me looking.

"Do you like my collection?" she asked. I nodded although their haunted expressions sent shivers down my arms. "I've collected them over the years," she continued. "Never had dolls as a child so I thought I'd make up for it now."

"They're lovely," I lied.

She handed me a china cup which I took and thanked her for. Sipping the sweet, hot tea relaxed my bones and I leant back and crossed my legs.

"It's taken many years to collect them all but it's worth it. So, what about you? What's all the research about and what are you going to do with it?"

Taking a deep breath, I drank in the cacophony of colour before taking my time to reply, choosing the words I wanted, carefully.

"The girl who was my best friend," I said, "Was covered head to toe in tattoos. She had no one to mourn her, so I thought I'd find out who she was and why the tattoos were there."

"How strange. All over?"

"All over."

"Very strange. Poor girl. Why do you think she had them done?"

"I don't know. But she always kept her parka on so she can't have been proud of them. She never showed me and people who love their tattoos show them off, don't they?"

Heather put her cup down and leaned in, conspiratorially. "Do you think someone did it to her?"

"I don't know. I don't know anything about her at all, but I owe it to her to find out."

"That's the spirit," said Heather. "Of course, you don't owe her anything at all but if we don't help each other out, we'd all have to rely on the do-gooders in the soup kitchens of the world."

Nodding, I drained my tea. "So, I went to the British Library and found out about one of the tattoos. It's Baphomet apparently."

Heather bowed her head but made no comment and I deduced that she, like me, had never heard of Baphomet before. The Highland cattle stared at me from the wall.

"Sometimes," I said, "I like to go to the British Museum and talk to Tutankhamun. Is that weird?"

"Spectacular, considering he hasn't been there since 1972", she said, laughing heartily.

"He is there," I said, suddenly uncomfortable.

"No, love. He was there for a special exhibition in 1972. I went to it. I remember seeing all the gold and turquoise and those hyro thingies but then he went back to Egypt. My cousin saw him on a holiday about five years ago."

I changed the subject back to the dolls and switched off while Heather regaled me with stories of where each had come from and how much she had haggled, while I thought about Tutankhamun and how, if he were in Egypt, someone was impersonating him. But he spoke like a king and gave good advice like a ruler and I was sure that if his body had been shipped back, his soul had remained because it liked the British Museum and the friends who came and talked to him. Heather was wrong on this one. She was kind and loud and colourful but she could also be wrong.

"And the last one came from a day out in Stratford in 1997. It was the third year I'd had this place and it was doing well so I treated myself. She's German bisque."

"Very nice," I said, trying not to sound cross about Tutankhamun.

"What will you do when you find out about the girl with tattoos?"

"Beano. Her name is Beano."

"That's not much to go on."

"No, except I did wonder if she had a name like a character and called herself the comic instead."

"Like Dennis the Menace?" Heather laughed.

"Well, no, but…"

"Sorry, it's a good idea. If you go to the local library, you can use their computers and they'll help you if you ask them nicely."

"I might do that."

"I would. Closer than the British one and they've got computers. You can Google what you want these days."

"I will do that. But I love the British Library. It's so vast, cathedral-like and full of the most beautiful light which streams down over the books."

"I prefer the dolls."

Heather was tired. She stretched and yawned and I took the hint, thanking her for the tea and the chat. Maybe I hadn't been interesting enough but she seemed as happy to see me leave as she had when she met me on the path.

Back in my shed, I wondered if I'd ever truly want a room bloated with fabric and pictures and chairs and stuff. The simplicity of the shed was magnificent. I liked the wooden walls and the candlewick bedspread and although a shower would have been nice, the shed was good just as it was.

Bone tired, I curled up on the camp bed, imagining Beano and Tutankhamun dancing a jig in the halls at the British Museum, sticking two fingers up at Heather the heathen and all the non-believers.

AN OWL HOOTED AND the percussion patter of rain made background music to my night. I had woken at three and stayed awake listening as damp crept up through the chipboard floor. My body ached and my head wouldn't keep still. No time to waste it said over and over again. Get up and go and find her.

I didn't heed the advice but remained curled up in lilac cotton, watching a drip of water come through the gap in the cedar tiles which I thought I had fixed, relentless yet softly splashing on the floor. The mug which had contained tea last night caught the drips. The wind-up torch shone a beam at my rucksack: nail file, tissue, pens, paper. I had dropped the comb down a drain as I struggled to reach a pen in my bag at Seven Sisters market. It seemed fitting, a comb with teeth missing having no place in my life now. I bought a new one, red and shiny and perfect.

The picture of Beano was still hidden between the pages of the pad. I took her out and laid her on the bed, naked and beautiful in the torchlight, wanting her to rise from the flatness of the paper and become my friend once more. Taking a pencil, I drew some more of the pictures which adorned her body, the graphite stroking her imaginary skin until skulls and goat heads covered her shoulders and the all-seeing eye sat staring from her chest.

Dawn arrived, her bluish, ethereal light spreading over Beano, casting shadows. She seemed to smile at me, the corner of her mouth reaching upwards towards a glinting eye.

"I promise I won't let you down," I said, finding the twenty pound note that Heather had given me in my pocket. "I'm going to see a tattooist today."

As the sun rose over Islington, I washed in the scullery, cleaning my teeth, using my new comb to arrange my short locks into some semblance of neatness before dressing in my new jeans and red jumper which I pulled over my knees as I ate toast and sipped coffee in the shed like a normal person.

I met the Polish labourers on the street as I left. They smiled and waved and joked in heavy accents about my eggs and how I didn't deserve a day off because I hadn't been there five minutes. I told them they were ignorant.

"You need more practice," one said.

"I'm working tomorrow so if you don't want me to gob in your eggs, I'd shut up!"

They laughed and slapped me on the back as I passed, and I could hear them talking quickly in Polish, no doubt slagging off my eggs once more. I was glad I'd bitten back. I couldn't do it in the confines of the dining room, but on a pavement in the open air it was second nature.

The bus came quickly, the journey taking half an hour as it wove its way between commuters and rickshaws and motorcycle couriers, clipping a cyclist, the driver and rider shouting obscenities as they went about their business. I watched them all speeding past, rushing here and there to reach jobs they didn't like, to earn money to pay for flats they couldn't afford and drink to dull the pain.

By the Queens theatre, I stepped onto the pavement and looked around. Vampire Dave's

Tattoo and Piercing Parlour lay on Frith Street in the heart of Soho, surrounded by posh eateries, a vintage clothes shop and a triple x rated, blacked out window emporium. My heart pounded as I stood and stared at the hand drawn images which filled the shop window, fairies and skulls and daggers and biomechanical aliens. The bright colours reminded me that Beano had been decorated in shades of black and grey. There was no colour on her body save her skin. I stood and stared past the images until raindrops fell out of the sky and bounced off the back of my neck, bringing me back to Soho and the crowds jostling for space on the pavements. And then I opened the door and walked in.

"Can I help you?" A large man with facial piercings, a waxed moustache and a massive amount of body art looked up from the thigh of the woman he was tattooing.

"Are you Dave the Vampire?" I asked, although his blonde hair and blue eyes made me doubt.

"Vampire Dave? He'll be in at twelve. Have you got a booking?"

"No. I have a question, maybe several questions."

"He'll be working then. You might have to come back when he's not got a client.

I turned to leave then stopped. "You see, Peter from the British Library said he might be able to help me find out about my friend."

The man wiped down the thigh of the young woman on his chair. "Peter? Oh yes, the book guy. Got his favourite books all over his back. Said

Dave would tattoo a library on him." He laughed. "Pretty cool actually. And pin ups on his arms. Has to keep them all hidden at work. Must be awful."

I stepped forward, leaning on the counter between me and him. "Peter said Dave may be able to help me." I pulled the picture of Beano from my bag. "Have you seen her before," I asked thrusting the paper over the counter. He looked.

"Pretty girl," he said, "But I don't recognise her. I think I would. Is she missing?"

"No. She's..." I hesitated before finishing, "...dead."

"I'm sorry." He stepped towards me, apologising to his client for the interruption. She sat up and looked at the picture too.

"Beano, that's her name, died and I didn't know anything about her except her name and that's not real. She was covered in tattoos, from head to foot. And this." I showed them the other drawing of her back and Baphomet and the bees which buzzed from the paper.

"Weird," he said. "Dave might know the style of the tattoos; he might even know who did them if they was done in London. He knows everyone. Look, he's always here by eleven and he hides in the back with his accounts for an hour. You might be able to interrupt him. Come back at eleven. I'll tell him, clear the way for you."

"Thanks."

"Eleven."

"I will. Thank you." My eyes rested on the girl having script across the top of her thigh. "Sorry I interrupted," I said. She smiled and I left, turning left then right outside the shop, stepping forwards then backwards. I had a lead.

Buying a steaming cup of coffee in a cardboard cup, I wandered down Old Compton Street and through to Leicester Square, leaning against a bench as I watched the tourists gather outside the cinema and the Swiss centre, loud and excitable. I remembered the nights I had tried to shelter in a doorway before being moved on by the police to trudge, unwanted, until morning. I shuddered and thanked Heather in words that sounded like prayer for she might be an angel. And Beano, losing her life that I might find her. The unfairness translated into fat tears which rolled, unfettered down my cheeks.

Eleven o'clock rolled by slowly. I tried to look at the familiar streets with new perspective but the anticipation of meeting Vampire Dave was too much to contain. I bought another coffee, sitting at a café, filling time in a city which had none to spare.

"On the dot," said the waxed moustache, as I entered the studio. "I told him about you. Hang on."

He disappeared behind a black beaded curtain; the sound of male voices drifted through, rustling the beads. The hairs on the back of my neck stood up, straining to hear the words which were being spoken. A moment later the waxed moustache appeared from behind the curtain and beckoned me in.

Dodging the desk and ducking under machinery, I followed him into a tiny vestibule off which was an office. Dave was sitting behind a desk covered in receipts and a large calculator, a skinny man in his forties. He wore a black T-shirt and black skinny jeans, his skin covered in brightly coloured Japanese designs. Cherry blossoms collided with a Hannya mask and three leaping koi travelled up his muscled arm. His face was thin and pale, the widow's peak which shot like an arrow down his forehead the obvious reason for his name.

"Vampire Dave?" I asked, holding out my hand. He shook it and nodded.

"And you are?"

"Jay," I said, sitting down where he motioned, gently moving a deck of cards which laid out the odds of me finding Beano's artist.

"Guy said you needed my help. Said Peter had referred you." His north London accent was pronounced, his eyes dark, almost black as they searched mine.

"I do," I said, a tremor in my voice. "I met a girl, well, she was my best friend. She died next to me in a railway arch but I'm not homeless anymore." Don't judge me my eyes said. He didn't. I told him more than I'd intended, about the celebration of my plan but not that it was a lie. About the stinking mattress on which Beano had passed. Shame flushed my cheeks red and sweat pushed itself from every pore. I wiped my forehead, lowering my head until I could see only my knees. He waited until he was sure I had finished speaking, handed me a box of tissues for the tears which he had seen and I hadn't felt, then took a deep breath.

"Well," he said in a strong, clear voice, "That's all been a bit shit." He paused, "But what can I do to help you?"

"The pictures; the tattoos. They're my only clue as to who she was. Would she have asked to have her body covered and if so, would someone have done this for her?" I laid the pictures I had drawn over the calculator and the receipts, the front view closest to him in the tiny floral knickers which I was glad I had placed there, the back view closest to me where I could keep my hand across the place where the bees gathered.

"Only she and the artist can know that," he said. "We don't judge what people want inked on their skin. We don't do Swastikas or anything to do with Hitler or the Holocaust. I might refuse to do a Donald Trump because he offends me but I'd respect the idiot client's right to have it and recommend someone else who will. Have you got photos?"

"No. A camera isn't a priority when you're squatting in a railway arch."

"I guess not." He smiled and leaned back in his chair. "Who drew these?"

"I did."

"From life?"

"From memory. I didn't think to draw a corpse." The harshness in my voice was a shock. "I told the ticket seller at the station where to find her. I saw a cordon afterwards so I know they did."

"So, you drew all this from memory?"

"Yes."

"How can you be sure it's correct?"

"Because what I saw that day is burned into my eyes." I rubbed them. "I loved her, you see. She was my best friend. My soulmate. My only companion. I remember every detail, every needle mark, both drug and tattoo related. I remember her body like a map of her life, something she left for me to follow."

He nodded. "Your drawing is very good. Did you train?"

"No."

"Very good indeed. You have style and flair and your Baphomet is extraordinary. Lovely detail and pen work. And a true representation of what you saw, you say?"

I nodded, irritated that he seemed more interested in my penmanship than finding the person responsible for turning Beano into a freak show.

"I've seen work like this before," he continued and my ears strained. "At a convention in Birmingham. Can't remember who did it but it was all very occult. I remember because it felt more like a black mass than a tattoo session. All candles and chanting beforehand. Woman, I think, yes. The German, that's my wife, pulled me away and told me she was giving me sexy eyes! Ha!" He raised an eyebrow in my direction and the glint in it was impossible to miss.

"What was her name?" I asked.

"I don't remember. She wore black and had a black baseball cap and the German got very angry. Oh, I remember that all right, and the row we had on the way home. Got those motorcycle helmets with radios in them and she gave me ears a battering all the way home. Fuck's sake, I remember that!" His face creased into a thousand lines as he laughed. "God love her, my wife's a crazy bitch."

"Are these tattoos normal?" I asked, manoeuvring him away from Germans and crazy wives.

"Unusual to have them all together. Mostly it's men who like these occult things. Think it makes them look hard. Between you and me I think it takes a real man to rock a cherry blossom." He ran his illustrated fingers up his arm. "Any bloke can wear a skull. Baphomet is usually occult or pagan related. In your case," he pored over the drawings, "I would say this is definitely occult. Although the bees could be pagan."

"Coming from inside?"

"Mmm. Maybe not."

"Are there clubs for this sort of thing?"

"I don't know. It's not my thing. Is it yours?"

I shook my head. "Shame because you're very good. Have you ever dreamed of tattooing?"

I shook my head. "I don't have dreams," I said feeling disingenuous towards Heather.

"It's not a dream, really not. Wrong word. I meant ambition. It takes a lot of time and patience and not earning any money." He crossed his arms and leaned across the desk on top of Beano. I snatched the paper from underneath him so as not to crease her.

"How about," he said after a while, "I give you some drawings to do and I'll have a think about that woman in black. Don't tell the wife, though!

Do the drawings and bring them back on Friday?" He handed me a sheet of paper which he had pulled from his desk drawer. On it were written in list form, explanations of pictures. The first said, a fairy with large wings hovering over a lotus flower. I looked at him, quizzically.

"These are all tattoos we've been asked for. There are twelve of them on there. I don't want the finished article but a sketch of what you might do for each one. You don't need to colour them unless you want to."

"I don't have any colours," I said.

"Black and grey will be fine. Just do them and bring them back on Friday. At eleven, if you're free? I'll make some enquiries and rack this brain of mine until I find something about your friend or her tattoos."

"Is it payment for finding Beano's tattooist?"

"No. If you don't want to that's fine. I'll still have a think about your friend. But why not, eh? What have you got to lose by doing a few drawings and bringing them back?"

I couldn't argue with his logic. "I'll have a go," I said.

BACK ON THE STREET, before I realised what I had agreed to, I took the bus to Bloomsbury, alighting near the home of my dear friend, rushing in and taking up the bench next to his mummified body which probably wasn't him because Heather had said he'd left in 1972.

"Did you go back to Egypt?" I asked.

"Aah, someone burst your bubble." He sighed deeply. "Only the bit I don't need went back to Egypt," he said. "The mouldy, dried up bits that aren't relevant anymore."

"So how much of you is still here?"

"My essence is here with you, my friend. The important bit."

"Tutankhamun, King of Egypt, can I ask you something," I said.

"You can always ask."

"How did you die?"

"An accident. My body was fragile, not well made. I had always wanted to drive a chariot but didn't have the strength." He sighed and I felt his breath on my neck. "So, I asked my man servant and good friend to take me out for a ride, thrilling and uncompromisingly fast. But I fell and broke my leg."

"And?"

"That's it, modern girl. We had nothing to fight infection and infection began at the break which pierced my sensitive skin and travelled through my body. I felt it spread, coursing through my veins until it reached my head. Like closing shutters. Like a blind being drawn over me. I was forced out of my body. But I don't miss corporeal weakness."

109

"Is that what it's like to die?"

"It's what it was like for me. I can't speak for anyone else."

"So why did you stay here after 1972?" I asked.

"I am everywhere, child. Everywhere and anywhere I wish to be. I knew you would come and speak to me and acknowledge my existence. I knew you would come."

"But how? How could you know that when I wasn't even born then?"

"Because I am everywhere, in all time, and I can be wherever I choose, whenever I choose. Pick a century! Paris, 1764, I can be there. London 2047, I can be there too."

I didn't understand. "I don't know what to think. I don't understand how?"

"Because you are earthbound, for now, but one day you will fly too."

Not sure that I wanted to fly across all time and space, I brought the conversation back down to earth; Vampire Dave and how kind Heather was and that I had drawing homework to do although I didn't know if I should be doing it. He told me to go with the flow and accept that sometimes, people are nice and don't want anything from you except a day's work or a few sketches. My shoulders began to relax, my arms to drop onto my lap. My head rolled and the sound of my neck crunching was like rustling paper.

"People need people," he said. "Maybe you've found the right ones."

HEATHER WAS IN THE kitchen when I entered. She held an apron for me to put on, placing the battered frying pan on a ring, scooping cooking lard into it from a cracked butter dish.

Neither of us spoke as I tied up the apron and began laying strips of bacon in the frying pan, my heart pounding with the weight of expectation. Tinned tomatoes were poured into one saucepan, beans in another, black pudding under the grill along with chipolatas, three each, as the usual fat sausages had run out. I made my own dance, less co-ordinated than Heather's, as I cracked eggs, separating the scrambled from the fryers, dolloping more lard into a pan until the eggs swam the breast stroke in the fat. Bacon under the salamander, bread in the bacon fat. Sizzle, splash, the beans were boiling and the scramble sticking. Heather remained calm, stepping back when she should have stepped forward to help. I spread hot plates all over the work surfaces and began to pile the food onto each plate, ticking off each element as it went.

Wiping my hands on my apron, I used it as an oven glove, taking the food through to the dining room and the Polish labourers first. They grinned and pointed and said, "well done" and were happily eating when I returned with plates for the salesmen and occasionals who had filled the dining room.

Food served, I returned to the kitchen and began to clear the surfaces, Heather leaning where I wanted to clean, not speaking. She smiled once, when the surfaces reflected the light from the small window over the sink. Her arms were folded across her bosom which heaved each time she moved. She puffed and panted as though she had run a marathon.

"You've done good," she said, "I'm off for a lie down," and she disappeared into her parlour and shut the door.

I stared after her, the closed door, informed. With the cleaning caddy in my hand I took the stairs two at a time. I changed one bed from the one occasional, vacuumed and polished the bathroom, checking twice for any rogue hairs which may have attached themselves to the suite. I was beginning to find a routine in the work, allowing my brain to concentrate on Tutankhamun and Beano and Vampire Dave instead of the brushing and scrubbing and dusting.

By twelve, I had folded the last duster and returned to the shed, checking my rucksack for the nail file, tissue and pens which nestled in the bottom of the canvas. They were all present and correct, along with the list of drawings which Vampire Dave had given me. I had found a ball of used BluTack in the scullery; now I worked the putty until it was soft and malleable, attaching it to the back of the pictures of Beano before sticking them on the walls of the shed, opposite the camp bed. They filled the space, her face looking down on me with faith that I would see her right. I stuck the list up too, next to the bed like homework. I wasn't sure why Vampire Dave wanted me to draw his list, but draw it I did, my pencil flying over the sheets as butterfly wings and pin up girls took shape on the paper.

And as I became increasingly absorbed in the task, the afternoon faded along with the light and I found myself squinting over blackened paper and shaded images, determined to buy some kind of light to make my work less painful on the eyes.

SEVEN SISTERS MARKET GROANED with the weight of people next morning, shoulder to shoulder at the fruit and veg stall. I bought the fruit which Heather had requested, four apples and two pears, and pushed my way through to the electrical stall where there were battery operated lights with sticky bottoms. I bought six at a pound each and two packs of batteries so that if they ran out I wouldn't be plunged into darkness again. I also bought a cheap and cheerful duvet, a sheet and pillowcase set and a pillow.

Heather had offered the old paint stored in the cupboard off the scullery; I had chosen white for the maximum light and, by the light of the torch, had splashed a first coat of paint. It would be dry by the time I got back, dry enough to replace the pictures and arrange the lighting.

I was excited as I struggled back with my unwieldy purchases, tripping and stumbling over the uneven pavement on the Holloway Road. Heather was hanging out washing when I opened the gate, an array of bright headscarves, trousers and tops clashing colourfully on the rotary line. She stopped, placing her hands on her hips as she stepped back to allow me to pass.

"Show me when you're done," she called. I said I would, opened the shed door and closed it behind me to ensure she had the full 'wow' factor when she visited.

The white emulsion had done its work; the shed seemed double the size and although I knew I would have to seal the floor, the whiteness of it was captivating. I unpacked my new possessions, laying

115

plastic bags on the floor to protect my paintwork, moving as little as possible so as not to scuff the walls. I made my bed, throwing the lilac candlewick bedspread over it, allowing it to hang down to the floor, making a perfect storage place where nothing was seen. My rucksack went underneath, as did the anorak which I hadn't yet replaced but which looked incongruous hanging on the nail in my spotless new pad.

Beano went back on the wall and I was sure she winked at me as the BluTack pressed into the wood. Then I stuck three lights in a line above her, two at the side of the bed and one over the door. I turned them all on but the white and the sunshine rendered them pointless so I saved the batteries and turned them off before standing back and admiring my work.

The clean, white box was so far removed from the railway arch in which I had slept next to my dead best friend that it overwhelmed. As I hugged myself, rocking backwards and forwards, shaking, Heather knocked on the door, opening it onto me, catching my hip with the handle. She scooped me into her arms and onto her lap, cradling me like the child I was. We stayed like it for some time, until my hysterical breathing calmed and my shaking limbs were once again under control.

"It'll happen now and again," said Heather. "Life can be overwhelming at times."

"I think I know how to do it and then…"

"I know, I know." She stroked the back of my head. "A lot's happened."

"I found a man who might have an idea who tattooed Beano."

"That's wonderful."

"He asked me to do all these drawings."

Heather slid me off her lap and began to look at the pictures of Beano and fairies and skulls with daggers through them. "Why did he want these? Does he want you to work for him?"

"No, why?"

"Because... You did tell him you'd got a job?"

"Of course. And I don't think he wants me to work for him; more that he wants something in return for the investigating he's doing for me. It's more than fair."

Heather shrugged but I could see she was unconvinced. A cloud pushed the sunshine out of the white shed; I shot up and switched on all the little lights. The full effect was extraordinary, like an art installation. Shadows bounced up and down the walls, across Beano and the fairies and the lilac bedspread.

"What do you think?" I asked.

"It's beautiful," said Heather, nodding and rubbing her hands together. "It looks like a little white church."

I laughed and pointed at Baphomet. "Not his type, though."

"Certainly not," said Heather, standing and opening the door. "I was bringing you this when..."

She handed me a white laminated shelf with black brackets, approximately eighteen inches in length, perfect for my small, personal items. We tried it in several places as I thanked her in several different ways. She had brought a screw driver and a spirit level, doling out advice as I fixed it to the back wall, placing toothpaste and the new comb upon it.

"You can use the bathroom in number four for the rest of the week. Have a good soak in the bath. Guests arrive Sunday night so make sure it's spotless when you're done."

"Thank you."

"And stop saying thank you or I'll stop being nice."

"Thank you, okay, thank…"

The sound of her tinkling laugh followed her back to the house and, as I settled on the bed which resembled a dawn sky with clouds and streaks of lilac, I remembered someone telling me a story about a fairy godmother. You never know what's true and what people have made up. After all, most people don't believe in Tutankhamun. And no one would believe that Beano dropped a long blonde hair on the comb. But she had.

IT TURNED OUT THAT I loved routine. Five days a week now, I got up at five, cooked breakfasts and cleaned the rooms. I was always done by one o'clock, ate lunch and then went to Seven Sisters Market or to the British Library or to the British Museum and today, I was going to see Vampire Dave with a pad full of drawings.

I arrived at two, having explained about my work and not being able to do eleven, dodging the rain which ran off my new plastic raincoat in rivulets. The man with the waxed moustache smiled as I entered, putting down the machine which he was adjusting.

"I didn't think you'd come back," he said. "I've just lost a tenner."

"I'm sorry," I said, not sure whether I should be or not.

"Don't be. My mistake, never underestimate a woman."

I smiled in reply.

He parted the beaded curtain and I passed through; Dave waved me into his office and pointed to a chair. I sat. He was on the phone, berating a supplier for late, overpriced, shoddy goods. I wondered how much was true. Finally, and with a flourish, he put the phone on the desk.

"Show me what you've got!" he said. I stared back at the widow's peak, wondering if he'd completed his side of the bargain.

"Show me what *you've* got!" I demanded, banging the rucksack down on the table.

"Whoa!" He said. "No attitude in here."

Reddening, I apologised immediately, clutching my rucksack to my breasts. He laughed.

119

"I hoped you'd have found Beano's artist," I said.

"These things take time. I can't just go through my black book of Baphomet artists, 'cause I don't have one. And if I did I'd hand it to you, wouldn't I? Or copy down the names – easy." He laughed again, sweeping a hand through his coal-black hair, catching my eye with his piercing black ones.

"How long will it take?" amazed at my own boldness, wondering if I was picking it up from the walls.

"I can't do this for you," he said, suddenly serious. "But I thought, if you were a good enough artist, you could do it yourself."

"How?"

"Let me have a look at your drawings."

Uncertain, I pulled the pad from the bag and laid it face down on the desk. I didn't have the words to articulate how disappointed I was so I let my face do the talking.

"May I?" he asked, taking the pad in his hands. I fiddled with my fingers, nodding permission.

I watched as he leafed through the papers, his eyebrows arching and flattening although I couldn't read his expressions. Finally, he laid his tattooed hands on the paper and looked at me.

"They're good," he said, "Very good in fact. You have a natural talent. The only thing I would say is that these aren't tattoo pictures. There's no outline, nothing to contain the ink."

"I didn't realise I had to," I said.

"You didn't. I didn't ask you to. I just wanted to see if you could really draw, and you can."

I remained silent, the grasp on my rucksack loosening just a little.

"I'd like you to do them again," Vampire Dave had stood and was pacing the room. "We get lots of kids with a bit of talent coming in here and asking to be an apprentice. I tell them there's no money attached and they last a week. I'd like to mentor someone, to have the chance to guide someone through to a career in tattooing, to keep the real art alive so that when the fashion is over, the true artists will still have a place."

I imagined him talking to a room of suits, his pleas unheard. I listened, not really taking in what he was saying, loving the way he said it.

"I'd like you to try the list again, but this time draw like a tattoo artist."

"Peter from the library showed me a book about the subversive art of tattoos in the nineteen twenties. They were beautiful but nothing like these." I pointed to the illustrations which covered the walls.

"Outlines," said Dave. "Start with an outline and work in. Come back next Friday with them and we'll talk again."

"What about Beano?"

"If you take the opportunity I'm giving you, you can find out for yourself."

"What opportunity?"

"Apprenticeship. I'm offering an apprenticeship."

"But I can't leave the B&B. It wouldn't be fair."

"You don't have to. I can't pay you. Stay and work at the B&B. Come here next Friday and we'll talk about a schedule for you to come in and learn. You'll be sweeping floors and cleaning, making tea and watching. Watching is how you learn this game. Come and watch me."

I thanked him and, still uncertain about what I had committed to, left the shop with an idea that I could just not turn up next Friday and nothing would be lost except a lead to find Beano's artist.

The streets were full of people, bumping and hurrying, reminding me of the endless days with nothing to do and nowhere to go. I found Soho Square, sat on a bench and watched pigeons squabble over sandwich crusts. Not long ago, I would have fought them and won. But with Heather's money in my pocket and a belly full of breakfast, I let them fight it out, glad when the smallest bird put up the better fight. With his prize in his beak he flew off, leaving the other hungry and battered.

A girl like Beano walked through the park, slender and pale with blonde hair and blue eyes. I was sure she winked at me.

"Who were you?" I asked. The girl didn't look but walked faster. "Who were you?" I said louder, breath swelling my chest, the image of a naked and dead Beano filling my head once more. I didn't want to talk to anyone or hear another opinion so I sat on the bench until the sun began to dip behind the roof tops, clutching my rucksack and my future in my hands.

There had been kindness, too much kindness in fact. Even if the B&B and Dave the Vampire and the British Library all went up in smoke, Beano's influence would keep me safe. I thanked her, raising my eyes to the heavens where she lived.

The decision came easily to do as Dave had said. After all, he was the only link I had.

MY SCHEDULE FILLED UP. Wednesday through to Sunday I worked for Heather, cooking breakfast for the labourers and occasionals with whom I now had a rapport. Cleaning the rooms became easier too, with a routine in place nothing was missed; Heather grew more relaxed often inviting me to share a coffee and a chat with her before I clocked off.

On Mondays, I went to the library and began to draw everything I could find in tattoo books from 1810 to 2010. Two hundred years of design. I learned that most of the royal family had small tattoos, particularly the women, small animals or butterflies to be found by a husband, a lover. It occurred to me that a lover, knowing the tattoo, could make it very difficult for a married lady if he wanted to. And I was sure that many a "happy marriage" had been ruined this way. It lit my imagination and I read on.

I learned that freak shows in America, relied on their tattooed stars and that they, in turn, made a fortune out of being different, deviant and drawn upon. It was a culture all its own, sucking in people from all walks of life, some flamboyantly showing off their art work, others hiding it from anyone but their closest companions. I learned too, that women had always been proud wearers of body art and that the highest earners in the freak shows of Atlantic City had all been women, the shock of seeing an illustrated woman far more alluring to visitors. I imagined Beano caged in a carnival show, people staring at her illustrations without seeing her at all.

On Tuesdays, I went shopping in the morning, stocking up on the toiletries I couldn't remember ever having. Shampoo and shower gel; buffers, loofahs and sponges all made it onto the little shelf in my shed. I bought clothes too, adopting a one off, one in the wash approach to work and play clothes. And shoes; a pair of blue suede lace up shoes with crepe soles because I could; and a new coat, not a donated anorak but a sharp black coat with brass buttons and pink lining. It cost me forty pounds, the most I could remember spending. But on cold days and sunny days and grey days, I wore the coat because it had pink lining and it made me feel better about life.

Wednesday and Thursday afternoons, I drew and drew until the walls of the shed covered my shoddy painting and on Friday, I went to Vampire Dave's Tattoo Parlour and watched the master at work.

He liked my drawings so much that he gave me a set of coloured pencils and several pads of cartridge paper. "This is your university degree," he said, "And you must have the tools. I've started you off and now you're on your own but you can use the shop discount if you want to order stuff." Overwhelmed, I stayed late sorting out the store room which was desperately in need of some tender loving care.

The studio was a warren of tiny rooms, but the main event, Vampire Dave, worked to the right of his office in a room with a black leather treatment lounger and black, shiny worktops and cupboards. Drawings covered the white walls, some brightly coloured with pin up girls strutting their stuff; others black and grey, daggers, skulls, roses, butterflies with metal wings, tribal and Celtic designs, scripts and dragons. There was a Japanese section which I particularly liked, a melange of koi carp and cherry blossom trees, Hannya masks and waves, their colours bright in orange and turquoise and green.

Paper towels and Vaseline and little bottles of ink scattered the work surfaces, the tools of the trade. Dave had said that one of my responsibilities would be to look after his gear, clean his machines and wash the ink from the needles. His nimble fingers had flown over the bottles, mixing and shading as he worked and I thought it would be many years before I could do the same.

Having scrubbed the parlour until my fingers bled, Dave sent me home with more homework, ideas for designs with butterflies which he said he would put on the wall in the front office if they were good enough. He explained how the designs were copied in ink which could be transferred onto the skin, allowing the artist to fit the picture to the body, using natural curves to bring out the best in both.

I drew and coloured butterflies in various positions, overlapping and dancing together, orange, purple and pink shading on the wings, some with fairies riding their backs.

And as I drew, I lost myself in the process and the hours disappeared as Beano and Tutankhamun and I made art in the shed, happier than I had ever been.

I HAD BEEN AT the B&B for six weeks when Heather offered me a room in the attic. She took me there after finishing the rooms, to a place in the house I had not been before, up a flight of stairs behind a door which I had thought was a locked cupboard.

It was pretty, in the eaves with sloping ceiling and a tiny en suite shower room. A pink candlewick bed spread covered the single divan and floral wall paper evoked an abundant flower bed. There was a wardrobe and a dressing table with a kettle and a cup and saucer on top and a mirror in which I caught sight of myself and was surprised.

My cheeks looked rosy and full; I had put on weight and my short hair had grown, tiny strands curling over my ears. The street-lines and grey skin had vanished. I touched the tiny dolphin in my ear.

"So, what do you think? It's where I slept for three years."

"It's like the countryside," I said a little overawed by flowers.

"Would you like it?"

My mouth opened and closed like a goldfish. "What about my lovely shed?" I said at last.

Heather laughed her high, tinkly laugh. "I said the same!" she said, wiping a mirthful tear from her eye. "But honestly," she said, "It'll get cold again soon and there's no heating in that shed and there's no insulation or anything and I know, sometimes you wake up with ice on the inside of the window and your feet frozen to the camp bed. You'll be right in here."

"It's beautiful," I said, unconvinced. "It's a truly lovely room and there's a shower and everything and I'm most hugely grateful but…."

Heather lowered her large frame onto the bed and adjusted her purple paisley turban. "I know," she said. "It's a bit much?" I sat down next to her placing my hand on hers.

"It is."

"Of course."

"When the cold weather comes, I'll be ready. It's just that…"

"The shed is the first home you've had in a while."

"Yes, yes that's it exactly. And I'm not ready to leave it just yet. I made it my own."
Heather placed an arm around my shoulder and pulled me to her.

"You and I are very alike, you know." I nestled my head onto her bosom. "I made that rag rug and wouldn't leave it, brought it up here and sat on it for days while I tried to get my head around why I wasn't ecstatic."

"I know I should be," I said.

"Let's make it easy," she stroked my hair, playing with a curl in the nape of my neck. "Let's make a date for you. How about the last day of October? You'll be feeling chilly out there by then and, if you like, you can decorate this room for yourself before you move in. I put all these flowers in here to remind me where I grew up."

"Did it?"

"No. It reminded me of my Granny's bedroom which is probably why I put it all up in the first place. She was a good woman. You can do it all modern and you can have a cork wall for all your pictures. And get rid of that old bedspread."

"No! I love the bedspreads," I said. "I love candlewick and the colours remind me of Edinburgh rock."

She smiled, pushing me away just enough to hold both hands. "My Mum ate Edinburgh rock. I never liked it though."

"I remember once someone went to the seaside and brought me back sweets which looked like pebbles."

"I remember them too. Felt weird putting them in your mouth." Laughter bubbled up in her chest, bursting out of her mouth with such force that I was swept away by it. "Once, I remember giving some to my brother and then convincing him that the dog shit in the garden was made of the same stuff and he ate it and chucked up all over the garden. I was in awful trouble." The gurgling laughter died away and she stroked the side of my face.

"You never talk about the time before."

"The time before what?" I asked.

"What happened to you? Why were you on the streets" she asked, suddenly soft.

"Nothing," I said, tight lipped.

"Why was a pretty little thing like you out there?"

"I couldn't cope."

"Is that your stock answer or the truth?"

My lips remained pursed.

"I don't want you working for that Vampire man," she said, pushing herself off the bed, oblivious that her words would have the opposite effect.

Closing the door on the pretty room in the eaves made me stronger because the shed was home for now. I could rely on it to be there, the white, drawing filled walls and little shelf now laden with toiletries and the battery-operated lights, my safe haven of peace and quiet and rhododendrons. I walked to the British Museum, arriving late as the last visitors straggled through the doors to be amazed by the ancient exhibits within.

Tutankhamun was pragmatic. "If it's warm and safe and comfortable why turn it down?"

"Because I don't feel like I'm ready to go mainstream in a house with plumbing."

"Too comfortable?"

"I like the shed. It's a space between being normal and being me."

"Stay there, then."

"But in the winter, it'll be really cold and I can't do that again. It nearly killed me last time."

"Then take the room."

"You're really not helping."

A security guard wandered past, watching as my hands flew to my head in a re-enactment of me pulling my hair out.

"It sounds to me like you feel you don't deserve the room?" Tutankhamun whispered so that the guard wouldn't hear.

"I don't know what I deserve. It's been six weeks since Beano died and I haven't found anything out except I'm good at drawing. And I've got a job and an apprenticeship with Dave and the

offer of a room and I've done nothing for Beano."
A tiny white feather fell from somewhere above me, landing in my lap.

"When you see a feather, it's your guardian angel," said Tutankhamun.

"Is it Beano?"

"Only you can find that out," he said.

He wasn't helping. I left and walked and walked until I came to the twenty-four-hour Italian where Beano and I had eaten pastries and drunk coffee. I ordered the same, two coffees and two pastries, carrying them out of the shop to a bench. I laid one pastry out on a napkin next to me, inviting Beano to join me. The tiny dolphin earring felt hot. I touched it and was relieved to find it *was* hot. A sign. I ate the pastry in my hand and chatted to Beano about all the things which had happened since she died and how I felt guilty because none of it would have happened is she hadn't died; eventually I heard her whisper, "This is the right way," and all Tutankhamun's prevaricating, floated away on the breeze.

A couple of benches down, someone like me was covered by newspaper, sleeping off cheap alcohol from the night before, his heavy snores reverberating around the park. I laid the extra coffee and pastry next to his shoulder so that he wouldn't miss it, hoping that he'd wake up before the coffee got cold.

I carried on walking, up Holloway Road to the university crowds and the railway arch beyond, not stopping until I rounded the corner and found the arch straight ahead. A "for sale" sign hung from the door, a telephone number emblazoned upon it.

There was no sign of the cordon or of the horror which had taken place here. The buddleia pushed its way through the roof, heavy with buds dipping low over the doorways. A cat meandered past, then stopped and rolled in the dust.

I stood, immobile as the smell of the mattress drifted back and I coughed. A memory. The needle. Beano's body. Tattoos and more tattoos and one I'd missed? On her ankle, I could see it as clearly as I could smell the mattress, a coat of arms with a dolphin and a serpent. A coat of arms on her right ankle, the dolphin and the serpent in the only colour on her body, the dolphin green and the serpent blue. I had missed it, hidden in plain sight, hidden by ugliness, their colours clearly obvious to me now.

And there she was, the girl with beautiful eyes, pointing at her ankle, smiling at me as she approached the door. I clung to the brickwork as she ducked, opened it and walked through. "I'll be here waiting," she said, disappearing into the darkness.

THE POLISH LABOURERS practiced their English with me every morning. They said they could understand me because I had no accent. I didn't know what they meant because I spoke English like everyone else I knew, but they preferred to talk to me, they said, and had begun bringing a new word to the table every morning.

"Flamboyant!" one of them said.

"A great word," I said.

"I am flamboyant!"

"No, you are a labourer. Julian Clary is flamboyant."

"Who?" I explained to three blank faces, as simply as I could, about flamboyance and how we used it today. They nodded and left the dining room calling Heather flamboyant which I thought was accurate so I didn't correct them. Having said the word so often in such a short space of time, it became nonsense on my lips and I giggled as I made the occasionals' beds and wiped down the skirting boards ready for the next customer.

It was library day, and the drawings I had made of the coat of arms were fresh and bright. Peter saw me arrive and waved a corduroy clad arm in my direction as I set myself up at the usual desk and felt in my rucksack for the nail file, the tissue and my pens. I laid them next to each other at the top of the desk, largest first, so that they made a pleasing shape as they waited to be used. He watched my ritual from a distance before joining me at the desk, leaning his slight bottom on the wood next to my pad.

"What are we doing today?"

"Coats of arms." I pointed at the pictures and he picked one up, studying it closely. "I don't know how I missed this on her ankle but I did. And I didn't, if you know what I mean. It was a shock but it wasn't a surprise so I must have recorded it in my mind but not on paper." My eyes remained fixed on the little image. "Am I making sense?"

"To you perhaps." He smiled and I knew he wasn't judging me.

"I thought you might think I'd made it up."

"No one makes up stuff like this. No one has an imagination twisted enough if you ask me. It has to be real."

Confused, I turned back to my drawing, casually swiping a finger across the dolphin on the page before touching the one in my ear.

"There are books on heraldry," Peter said. "I'll show you where, then you can see if you can find this one, although it doesn't look familiar to me. It's not one of the old families' crests but there are so many these days. And of course, it may not be a real crest at all. It may be a bit of artistic licence."

"Nothing was accidentally drawn on her body," I said. "There was a reason for it all."
He nodded, leading me to the shelves with heraldry books, he selected three and gave them to me. "Start with these," he said and I carried them back to the desk.

There were dolphins and serpents aplenty, on red shields and with trees of life and with axes and daggers. There were serpents too, slithering and curling around lions and griffins and white horses with unfeasibly long manes. But I couldn't find

Beano's coat of arms anywhere, no matter how many pages I pored over, no matter how hard I tried.

The minutes passed as my head bent over pages, then hours as my frustration grew. Dejected, I put my head in my hands and the images flashed in front of my eyes. Peter tapped me on the shoulder.

"Don't worry," he said. "Sometimes you can't find the answer in books." I looked at him, confused. He continued. "Sometimes you just have to go out there and talk to people."

"I don't like talking to people very much." I said.

"You talked to me," he said, "Talk to Dave. He might know more about coats of arms than Baphomet. You never know." He winked before slipping away to re-shelve a pile of books left by a group of students.

My hands pressed the book closed but I remained, leaning on it, pushing it into the old, oak desk, hoping to follow it through a trap door into a world I could understand, where sign posts pointed the way down a serpent like path lined with the pictures I had seen on Beano. I was sure of my memory, sure now too, that it was in the subculture of tattoos that I would find whatever it was I was searching for.

I had no idea how much time had passed in contemplation when one of the twinsets was announcing the library was closing in ten minutes. Gathering up my things, I went out into the evening, new trainers bouncing on the pavement, my feet only lightly attached.

"RECKON THAT BOY IN the library is sweet on you," said Heather as I told her what had happened. The kettle boiled and she poured water onto two mugs, squeezing the tea bags until the liquid was dark brown and held a teaspoon to attention.

"Why?"

"The way he helps you. Reckon he thinks you're cute."

"No! It's not like that at all!" I protested.

"You mark my words," she said. "He's sweet on you and there's nothing to be ashamed of. Except, of course, if he thinks he's going to lure you away from here."

"Heather, I have my own mind."

"Men have a way about them. First that Vampire Dave and now this library boy."

"It's nothing, Heather, nothing at all."

"Why do you keep going then?"

"I'm going to ask Dave about the coat of arms on Beano's ankle," I said, following her into the parlour where the television was belching out baking fumes.

"Why? Is he an expert on heraldry now?"

"He knows all the artists in London. Well, most of them. And others he recognises because of their work. He's a source of really good information."

"That bloke just wants to steal you for himself."

"No, he doesn't. He told me to stay with you and work around what you need. He's not like that at all". I felt tired. "He thinks I can draw."

"And so, you can, but drawing doesn't keep people fed or clean or pay the bills. It's hard graft that does that, over a stove or with a mop in your hand."

I didn't argue. "No one is going to tempt me away from here," I said, laying a reassuring hand on her arm as she and Peter had done for me. "But there's no harm in spending my time off over there. I'm thinking of going more often. Maybe someone will walk in. I'll know it's them but I won't know if I'm not there talking to people, like Peter said."

"He'll steal you, tempt you with fame and money and being an alternative artist or something."

"Heather please!" My temples pulsated, blood pumping, unwanted around my head. "I promised you. I don't break promises."

She stopped then, wiped her nose and looked at the TV screen on which a large chocolate cake with four layers was being scrutinised by a panel of judges.

"But I can do both," I whispered so that she wouldn't hear me over the joyful winner's music.

VAMPIRE DAVE WAS DELIGHTED with my new enthusiasm, meeting every iota of keenness with his own.

"See how the colour changes on different coloured skins?" he asked. "Very pale skinned people like yourself should be covered in colour because it stands out so well. Dark skins look wonderful in black and grey with white highlights. You'll learn all about this by watching and taking in what you've seen. Write notes if you like, or go home and keep a book of tips. I did that."

He allowed me to stand close to him as he worked on the living canvas, as the needle juddered and vibrated art into skin. The customers were happy to have me there; some wanted to talk about the minutiae of their lives, sharing shopping lists and bucket lists and relationship rules. Others were silent. Dave was a consummate professional, making clients feel at ease as he pushed and pulled their skin into the right position for his needle. I handed him Vaseline and paper towels and bits of cling film and tape to cover new designs. I made tea with lots of sugar in it for the clients who felt light headed after having work done and I kept a supply of sweets in the desk drawer to offer his longer session clients.

I saw the designs take shape from freehand drawing to finished tattoo, and as Dave invited clients to check the positions of indelible art in a huge mirror, I saw myself in it, strong, well-fed and healthy, with a full bust and proper thighs, a woman I hardly recognised.

As Dave's shadow, I cleaned up his work station, placing used cling film and foil in the bin, wiping the surfaces and preparing him for the next client by filling tiny vessels with coloured inks, sticking them on blobs of Vaseline so that they couldn't be knocked over. Country music streamed out of the speakers attached to the ceiling, the plink plink of guitars soothing on the soul.

In the front of the studio, working mainly on walk ins, wax moustached Guy chatted endlessly about his girlfriend and his boxer puppy and I wasn't sure which he loved more. Sometimes Dave sighed as he heard for the fourteenth time the story of the puppy getting stuck in the waste paper basket, pushing the door of his little workspace until it cut out some of the noise. He would wink at me and roll his eyes conspiratorially.

Dave spoke little and concentrated hard, his life's work exhibited surrounding him. I noticed that he always wore the same black leather waistcoat over band T-shirts, country stars mostly, groups I didn't know. He squeezed his legs into too-tight skinny jeans which looked strange on the ends of his long body. His hair was slicked back to make the most of his widow's peak and therefore his name, his skin pock-marked and tanned, stretching over high cheek bones and impossibly small ears in which he wore three earrings. His nose was pierced too, like an Indian bride or a teenage wannabe. But it was his hands I loved most, hidden in black latex gloves while he worked, it was a treat when he took them off. Long fingers, tanned hands, white nails, slim knuckles; they were artist's hands and they moved with grace and ease.

Sometimes, I couldn't tear my eyes away from them as they grasped a cup of tea I had made, so swift and confident were their movements. He wore a wedding ring on his right hand, underneath which The Cat in the Hat saluted. The different suits of playing cards graced his knuckles and on the inside of his thumb a name, Sarah.

I wanted to ask who she was and if the wedding ring was attached to her but the words got stuck in my throat and I found myself smiling benignly instead. And then, one afternoon when a client hadn't shown up and I had cleaned all his equipment until it shone, he invited me into his office for a chat and a cup of tea.

Placing the mugs on the desk between us, I sat down, crossing my legs, wrapping them around each other until I could feel my muscles tightening.

"You're doing well," he said. "And you have natural talent for drawing, for design actually. I can see a strong sense of design in your work. I'm impressed." He opened a file in which he had put my drawings, spreading them across the desk.

"I like this one very much," he said, placing a finger lightly on my butterfly ridden by fairy. "You've got the outline down, the shading's good too. I like your colour palette. I'm going to start getting you fruit so you can get the feel of the machine.

The sentence scrambled in my head and I looked for my rucksack which was hanging on the inside of the kitchenette door.

He continued, "Melon is good. Grapefruit is good too but melon is bigger so you can get more practice on it."

I wondered what Tutankhamun would make of practicing on melon and fiddled with the dolphin in my ear.

Dave was smiling, his head cocked slightly to one side. "Are you following me?"

"No," I said, afraid that he was going to sack me for stupidity, even though I wasn't employed.

"It's the next stage," he said, flashing white, even teeth in a wide smile. "I'll lend you an old tattoo machine and you can draw on a melon."

"Oh. Oh, I get it now. Instead of a person. I did wonder. I'm such a fool." Redness rose up my neck.

"No, not at all. I haven't explained. Drawing on paper is markedly different to skin so, when we start out, we practice on fruit and then on pig skin, pork belly is good, and then, once you're confident and sure, we let you out on the general public."

"You mean I'll be a tattoo artist?" I hadn't got beyond parlour junior, making tea and sweeping up, listening and learning to reach my goal.

"Of course!" he said. "Why do you think you're here?"

"Because of Beano."

"That's what brought you here and no doubt you'll find your answer and be a tattoo artist to boot. What do you say?"

"I say, I love drawing," Thinking of Heather and how she was right and not right at the same time.

"You need to build your confidence though. When you speak, you're fascinating but you don't speak much, do you?"

I shook my head.

"So, I'm going to put you on reception so you have to talk to people. Three to seven, Wednesday through Saturday. Is that okay?"

My head nodded but my heart raced and the words I would like to have spoken got stuck in my throat again. I coughed.

"Tell me it's okay."

"It's okay," The words came out.

"Good. People training starts Wednesday and in the meantime, I'd like you to start on these."

He handed me another hand-written list of pictures to draw, Japanese themes with lotus flowers and koi carp, cherry blossoms and a simple Hannya mask.

"If you don't want to draw the Hannya mask, it's okay. I don't expect you to start with scary stuff even though it's not really scary, if you see what I mean."

"What is the Hannya mask," I said.

"It's a lucky charm, supposed to protect the wearer from evil. But actually, it's used in that Japanese theatre where they wear masks and stuff. It represents a jealous woman, a woman scorned. It could be my wife when she's mad." He laughed. "Mad bitch she is but I love her."

"I love Japanese tattoos," I said, changing the subject.

"I noticed. Thought you might like to have a go at it. I don't have a Japanese specialist. I love the old school style and Guy loves his biomechanics and shit. Japanese would be a good place to start."

I thanked him, realising that he must have put a lot more thought into this conversation than I had.

"Don't thank me," he said. "Just get good and express yourself. It's about the outline and your freedom of hand. Waves are much harder than you think. Fish scales are nothing without shading. Cherry blossoms can look like cartoon flowers if you're not careful."

"Who did yours?" I asked, bravely, pointing at the fish tail disappearing up his sleeve.

"Had them done in L.A. when I was working there. Jesus, that guy was a genius." He pulled up his sleeve. "See how it looks as though it's diving in the water and there are shadows and depth." I nodded.

"Shading. You can learn a lot from my arm." He winked. I blushed and looked away. "Jay?" I looked back and met his eyes.

"Yes?"

"Don't worry. Just come in on Wednesday and I'll show you how reception works."

I fiddled with the hem of my T-shirt.

"Start with a koi," he said. "The curves are much harder than they look. It'll teach you a lot."

I nodded.

"And it represents triumph over adversity which is quite fitting, I think. Don't you?"

I nodded again.

"Say yes," he said.

"Yes," I said, the corner of my mouth turning up in a smile.

HEATHER SEEMED PUT OUT when I mentioned, in passing, that I was going to be an apprentice tattooist. She was watching me fry bacon for the Polish labourers who had come downstairs with the word "discombobulated", their laughing easily heard through the kitchen door.

"What are they going on about?" she asked.

"They're saying discombobulated," I said. "They try a new word out every day."

"Well, they should be more quiet," she said. "And I hope you remember who gave you a home."

Piling the bacon onto plates, I turned and smiled at Heather, uncomfortable and tongue-tied.

"I love the shed and the B&B," I said presently. "And you."

"You'll be tempted away by these people. They're not like us."

"But that's the thing, Heather. They're exactly like us. They may look different but they're just the same." Marginal was the word that sprang to mind.

She made a strange noise in the back of her throat and reminded me to scrub the sausage pan. I served breakfast, changed one bed and vacuumed the dining room, before returning to my shed for an hour of drawing.

The koi carp on my sheet of paper did not leap from the waves. It straddled weird curves as if trying to escape, a startled expression on its face. Orange scales and blue water jarred, unshaded and brash. My disappointment in the creature was evident in the black outline which confined it. How was I to draw an outline which flowed?

Shoving the page underneath a pile of other unworthy drawings, I began again, allowing my hand to flow in one movement along a new creature's body. This time, my hand took on its own life, curling and swooshing with the shape of the waves, making tides and winds to blow the water into a white froth. When I had finished, it looked more like the one on Dave's arm, shadowed and shaded into three dimensions. With a feeling of accomplishment settling in my chest, I put the drawing in to my rucksack and walked to Soho.

Summer had arrived, bathing London in a hopeful, orange light. A slight breeze was all that kept me from wilting as the sun burned a red stripe onto the back of my neck.

Dave and Guy were smoking on the pavement outside the shop as I turned the corner, both waving as they saw me approach.

"How goes it?" Guy asked, stubbing his cigarette out on the window sill before chucking it in the gutter.

"It goes well," I said, standing between them.

"It's a walk-in day," said Dave. "It's warm."

"What Dave means," said Guy, "Is that when the sun shines, the kids get their skin out and then realise that it needs decorating. We've had three butterflies and an Arsenal badge."

"When are you going to have your first one?" asked Dave.

"I don't know," I said.

"But you will have one, right?"

"I guess so," I said realising that I hadn't thought about it at all.

"That's your next bit of homework," said Dave. "Design a tattoo for yourself. I'll do it for you, whatever you want. It'll be like a bonus for working hard."

I blushed, thrust my hand in the rucksack and pulled out the koi. "I did this," I said, handing him the piece of paper.

He looked hard, turning the paper around several times before speaking again. "It's good, the outline is your best yet, curving and confident. I'll show you how to draw foam a little more effectively but, actually, this is as good as anything Guy has drawn." He handed the paper to Guy with a wink. The waxed moustache twitched.

"Actually, it is," he said after a while. "Very good. Looks like we've got us a Japanese specialist.

"That's what I thought." I watched as the two men swapped facial expressions, a silent, secret language to which I was not privy.

"Good work, Jay," said Dave, opening the door of the shop, allowing a waft of stale air out of the cramped space. "Now let's show you the reception ropes."

It wasn't complicated. Dave and Guy really wanted someone to answer the phone so they weren't interrupted when in full flow. They needed me to record appointments in a large black book and take deposits for those appointments. 'No shows' were the death of many a small studio, Dave said, and by getting a deposit, clients were much more likely to turn up. There was a computer programme which would do everything for them

149

but, like their art, they preferred a hands-on approach to business, the book and pens being vital.

I sat on the stool behind the little curved desk, doodling on a piece of scrap paper, until the telephone rang and I nearly leaped off the stool into Guy's lap.

"Good afternoon. Vampire Dave's Tattoo Parlour. How may I help you?" Dave had told me what to say.

"An appointment for piercing?"

"Our piercer comes in on Thursdays only," whispered Guy.

"I can do Thursday at eleven," I said, wrote it in the book and returned the receiver to its cradle. My heart felt as though it were going to leave my chest. My hands shook. I hadn't used a telephone in as long as I could remember.

"Well done," said Guy enthusiastically as he cleaned the last of his machines in preparation for his next appointment.

"I did it," I murmured, checking my rucksack for my nail file. The phone rang again, a supplier this time, needing Dave to pay a bill or place a larger order. I transferred the call to his office and my cheeks flushed with pride as I switched on the kettle, making my strongest cups of tea.

The strains of country and western music drifted from behind the beaded curtain, Johnny Cash bemoaning "A little thing called love". And a young woman opened the door, waif like and blonde and wearing a parka over shorts. My heart stopped. It couldn't be…Beano?

"Can I make an appointment?" she asked. I coughed, spluttered and slid off the stool, jangling the beads as I fled to the loo. Sitting down on the lid, I leant my head in my hands as the shaking subsided and clarity of thought returned once again. It wasn't Beano. It couldn't have been Beano. Beano was dead. Shock turned to misery as I sat contemplating my future in the cramped lavatory.

A knock on the door brought me properly to my senses.

"You okay?" It was Dave.

"I'm sorry," I said through the door.

"It's okay. Open up."

I leaned forward and unbolted it, pulling it open from my seat. "I'm sorry," I said again.

Dave reached out and took my hand, pulling me gently from the toilet and into his office where he closed the door. "What happened?" he asked.

"I thought she was Beano. She had a parka and her hair…"

"I see," he said. "Well, that would screw you up a bit, wouldn't it?"

"I'm so sorry," I sat on the chair opposite his desk, clutching my rucksack and my knees together.

"It's easy to forget what you've been through," he said, twiddling a pen with agility. "I thought that pushing you a bit might help."

"You weren't wrong," I said, suddenly aware of what I might have thrown away. "I'm really grateful to you."

"I don't want your gratitude, Jay. I want you to be a good tattoo artist."

His eyes shone non-judgementally. I stared at the floor, willing it to split open and swallow me up; for Tutankhamun to burst through the beads and whisk me away to Egypt; for Beano to take my hand and lead me to heaven. I took an exaggerated breath, trying to build up momentum to push the words out of my mouth.

"I managed the phone and I was going really well and then I saw that girl and I don't know what happened but I couldn't stop it."

"Are you okay now?"

"Yes."

"The German says you should have bereavement counselling? Have you got a doctor?"

"You talked about me?"

"She's my wife, Jay, and my best friend in the world. Crazy bitch. She didn't judge, just said it's a hard thing to deal with without professional help. She's a counsellor. She knows about these things."

"I don't need counselling. I just need a lead. I've wasted so much time."

He swivelled his chair, running his long fingers over a stack of magazines which sat on the shelf behind him.

"You should look at these some time," he said, flicking through pages of designs and interviews with top tattooists. "But what they're really good for," he turned and caught my eye, "Is conventions. All these pages," he flicked again, "Are full of listings of conventions all over the country." With a flourish, he closed his eyes and planted his finger on a page. "Look, here's one in Somerset next week!"

"I couldn't go to Somerset," I said.

"Why?"

"Heather would be upset if I weren't there to do breakfasts."

"Fair enough. Can't piss off the landlady."

"She's more…"

"I know, I know, I was joking. She sounds like a good woman and no, you don't want to be pissing off good women. I should know." He winked. His finger jabbed the next page. "You could get to Shoreditch, though." I nodded. "On Monday?"

"Yes."

"Well, that's fixed then. Meet me here at ten and we'll go from there. I haven't been to the Shoreditch one in ages. It's a trade show, really, but there'll be artists and a competition for tattoo of the show and there'll be hipsters from East London with big beards and tourists who've come for shows. It'll be a laugh. Go and see if Guy wants to come, and," he stopped, placing the magazine on the desk. "And stop worrying. If you steal from me or wantonly break my stuff, I'll sack you there and then. If you feel wobbly because you're still grieving for someone, just say and we've got your back. Guy just shouts, "Man down". It usually does the job."

I didn't know how to thank him, so I told him that I didn't know how to thank him and he said that making him a cup of tea would be thanks enough.

Guy was deftly drawing a tiny butterfly on the ankle of the girl with the parka. I started to apologise but Guy butted in. "It's okay, Jay, she knows all about your dodgy bowels!"

Reddening, I took my place at the desk and waited for the phone to ring again.

I TOLD TUTANKHAMUN ABOUT the convention.

"Things are moving," he said.

"They are," I agreed, smiling at the security guard who no longer kept an eye on me now that I wasn't homeless. He smiled back, a toothless grin which told of adventures and pub brawls.

"You're happier now you're busy?"

"I am."

"But still…"

"Yes?"

"The search gets lost in all the responsibility."

"Yes, but it's just people. I'd forgotten how cluttered life is when there are people. They won't stop me finding Beano's family."

"Have you thought that they may not want to know?"

"Someone did the tattoos. I need to know why."

"Finally, honesty. I'm very proud of you."

My forehead scrunched.

Tutankhamun continued. "Your motive is selfish, not the selfish you're thinking of now. Your motive is not altruistic, to give her back to her family. *You* want to know. This is the most important step you've taken so far. *You want to know*. Remember that from now on."

Something shifted in my head, the tightness leaving my jaw. I did want to know what had happened to put the girl on the street, but more importantly, I wanted to know because I had been the reason she had died that night. Everything, ultimately was about me.

155

Half an hour later, I ordered coffee and a pastry to eat in at the all-night Italian. Through the large glass window, I watched men and women and children and dogs pound the grey asphalt, sweat pouring from pores which hadn't been hot for months. They were the same people that I had watched before or, at least, the same kind of people with lives and purpose, hurrying or sauntering to the next part of their day. Once, I had not understood their urgency, for I had none of my own. Once I had been envious of their busyness. Now I was one of them, stopping for coffee amid tasks and responsibilities.

As an elderly woman with a shopping trolley filled with all her worldly goods shuffled by, I wanted to tell her that there were people in the world like Heather and Dave and that she, too, could have a shed and a cooked breakfast. But she talked to herself loudly enough to shut everyone else out. I recognised her hostility and fear, shoved a five-pound note in her pocket and ran away before she had a chance to shout at me.

DAVE WAS ALREADY LEANING against the window of the shop when I arrived at five to ten on Monday morning, Heather's admonishment still ringing in my ears.

"Don't be falling under these people's spell," she had said, "And make sure you're on time for work tomorrow."

He acknowledged me with an arched eyebrow and gestured for me to sit on the window sill. I tried not to listen to his call but the chuckling got me and I was hooked. I lit a cigarette.

"Don't say that. No! No I didn't! Did I? I've got to go. Jay and I are heading off now. Yes. To the Shoreditch Convention...." He laughed. "Not the Shawshank Redemption, no!"

I tried to imagine what the German, Dave's crazy bitch of a wife, might look like. Dave interrupted my thoughts:

"I brought the wife's car," he said. "She's six months pregnant so we'll have to get her a bigger car." He stopped in front of a Smart car, tiny and shiny and black, which was parked on the pavement next to the shop. I hadn't noticed it before and now I wondered why.

Instead I said, "Pregnant? That's nice."

"It's a boy," said Dave.

"Lovely," I opened the car door and sat down. "Do you have a name yet?"

"Yes, but I'm not supposed to tell anyone so if I tell you, and you tell, I'll have to kill you."

"Don't tell me," I said.

"Cash," he said.

"I don't need cash to keep quiet!" I said, indignation creeping up in a red cloud across my face.

"No," Dave said, a smile creeping past his eyes, "Cash Lennon Burgess will be his name."

"Oh." I blushed. "Oh, I'm sorry. It's a great name, a name to grow into, two Johns come together."

"Two Johns?" Dave looked perplexed.

"Johnny Cash and John Lennon. Does she like the Beatles?"

"Yes."

"And you like Johnny Cash so it's more than fair."

He laughed again, snorting and struggling with his airway for some minutes as we drove towards The Shawshank Redemption, slightly too close to each other in the tiny car.

His arm brushed my leg as he changed gear; "It's a good name though," he said. "Different without being weird; cool without being hipster, alternative wouldn't you say, Jay?"

"Alternative is good," I said. "What's good about being like everyone else."

"Quite. So where does Jay come from?"

"A bird. At least that's what it is to me. Maybe once I was Jessica or Jennifer or Jaime. I don't really remember."

"You don't remember your own name?"

"I don't remember why it's Jay. It's not a name, right? It's a letter."

"It's your name."

"And it's the only one I've got."

"Exactly," he said and, with a smile of settling on his chiselled jaw, we drove in companionable silence until we drew into a car park at the back of a supermarket. "Although you might have to think about the rest of it when you're properly legit, with a bank account and everything. Debit cards. Credit cards. Mortgage."

"No," I said. "I don't need any of that stuff."

"You might."

I knew that I wouldn't, so I changed the subject back to Dave and his family.

"Why do you wear your wedding ring on your right hand?" I said, staring at his hand.

"My wife's German," he replied as if this were an explanation.

OUTSIDE THE WAREHOUSE where the convention was being held, a red Corvette had pulled in a crowd of illustrated men. I walked close enough to Dave to feel the electricity coming from his skin.

"Can't stay too long, I'm afraid," he said. "The wife wants me to take her maternity dress shopping this afternoon."

I nodded, following him through the door to the desk where a woman in black leather and a full facial tattoo ripped him of the forty-pound entrance for both of us, smiling with filed teeth as she stamped our hands. I began to protest but Dave put his finger to his lips and winked.

The noise hit me first; a rockabilly band was playing, the bassist throwing his instrument around as he twanged at the long strings. His fellow musicians clapped and cheered and picked up their guitars and joined in. An audience of sorts swayed along with them, the music rising above the people to reverberate around the ceiling.

A smell of antiseptic wipes drifted on what air there was; a feeble attempt at a breeze from a floor fan caressed my neck. It was overwhelming, so many people crammed into the space, colour and noise painting the room with rainbow colours. Keeping a close eye on Dave, so as not to get lost in the crowd, I followed him from station to station, nodding as he introduced me to people with patterned faces and piercings which made them look like aliens.

Not far from the Rockabilly band, a Harley Davidson, all chrome and flame paintwork, had drawn a crowd of its own, men in scarves and black leather with old school tattoos and abundant facial hair. They were the Rockers, bearing T-shirts from heavy metal bands, their jeans stained with oil from the bikes parked outside. They swayed to the music too, talking engine sizes and exhaust pipe circumferences, comparing badges on their faded, denim waistcoats. I liked the look of them, grey hair tied back in straggly ponytails, weathered faces from too much time spent outside talking bikes. I liked the bike too, peering through bodies to see the highly polished work of art which seemed much more at home on the pedestal than it would have done on the road.

Around the edge of the room, tables and leather couches were littered with figures being inked. Needles buzzed and men high fived and everyone was shouting, laughing or slurping on cardboard coffee containers. I wondered how they could concentrate with everything going on around them, their outlines perfectly drawn. My head buzzed, jealous of those who could enter the 'zone' at the drop of a hat. Dave knew everyone; stopped to talk at every station; laughed and joked and slapped the backs of almost twenty men in just a few minutes. He introduced me to some as his apprentice and although I was flattered, the term sat uneasily in my own mouth.

Tired of smiling and shaking hands with people I may never see again, I saw a way to grab a few minutes to myself. Telling Dave not to move, I joined the queue of a tea vendor, taking in the cacophony of colour and sound as I waited for the drinks. It was hard to focus with so much going on, hard to choose a place to look. Without realising, my eyes settled on Dave who was making himself comfortable on a stool not far away, recognition calming my trembling hands. I bought the teas and picked my way through the crowd to reach him again.

"And this is my new apprentice," he said, thanking me for the tea with a nod of the head. "She's got a taste for Japanese."

"Take her to Kurt. He's here today."

"Oh, that's a great idea; hear that, Jay?"

"I did."

"Let's go and find Kurt and leave these rogues to their work."

"Let me know when the sprog comes. We'll buy him a drum set and a trumpet!" They laughed and Dave slapped a hand on my shoulder, pushing me back out into the tide of people moving as one. More visitors were piling in, pushing the walls outwards to accommodate them all, leaving me with the feeling that, if they didn't stop, there would be one huge, amorphic tattoo leaving the show at four.

"Kurt!" Dave darted through the crowd, grabbing my arm as he went. Kurt rose from his stool, pulling Dave towards him for a man hug and three slaps on the back. On his face, a perfectly symmetrical Celtic design in blue. His eyebrows had been shaved off and replaced with thin blue lines reaching from the bridge of his nose to his ears. Black ink as eyeliner, like Tutankhamun's, accentuated the blueness of his irises and the blackness of his tattooed whites. He had blue lips, drawn wider than his own, and red flashes which picked out the finicky blue ones. His ears bore stretchers, revealing the frailty of stretched skin, and studs adorned his top lip, nose and chin. His bald head bore a second and third set of eyebrows before they splintered into a dagger design, dripping with red ink down the back of his head and onto his neck. Strangely beautiful, Kurt stuck out a hand decorated with black checkerboards, each white space filled with a small red star. I took it and met his grip with a firm one of my own.

"Good start: a firm handshake," he said, looking at Dave.

"This is Jay," said Dave. "She's my new apprentice and she likes Japanese style which would be good for my business. Could she sit with you a while?"

"Of course. Any exponent of the Japanese style is a friend of mine." He ran black painted nails through my hair. I froze.

"Looks to me," he said, winking, "That she doesn't have any of her own?"

"Dave asked me to draw one that I can have as a bonus for working hard," I said and as soon as the words had left my mouth I regretted sounding like a school girl with a crush.

A look passed between the two men.

Dave spoke first, "Jay was on the street and came to me for some help. But she turned out to be so talented I couldn't let her go!" Kurt laughed deeply and nodded knowingly; silently, I both thanked and hated Dave.

"She hasn't started on fruit yet," he said, "Still on paper, but I've ordered melon for Wednesday."

"Let's see if we can get you really interested," said Kurt, pointing to a stool next to his. I sat on it, checking my rucksack for the nail file and the tissue which I used to wipe beads of sweat from my forehead.

"This is Casey," he said, pointing to the model who lay on the couch in a tiny T-shirt and polka dot knickers. "We're doing a koi from top of thigh to knee. I made the drawing and the stencil last week. Now I've got to fit it to her rather lovely leg." Casey blew a huge pink, bubble-gum bubble which burst across her face.

Kurt took the drawing, wrapping it around her leg, pressing the picture onto her skin before rubbing with a towel. He peeled it off again, revealing purple line work which filled Casey's thigh.

"Look here," he said, motioning me to bend with him. "See how it doesn't fit here and here and over here?"

I nodded.

"I'm going to freehand these bits in purple Sharpie. It stays on when you're working and, because it's the same colour, I don't get confused."

I nodded.

"I'm dyslexic and I'm on the autistic spectrum," he said. "People find me a challenge."

"Aren't we all?" said Casey.

I didn't know if I was or not but there was something about Kurt that I liked so, ignoring Casey, I leaned in and watched him work. The pen flew over smooth skin with grace, a curl here, a flourish there until the koi and its stormy sea were perfectly in tune with the shape of her thigh.

"Amazing," I said, unable to keep the word from escaping. Kurt smiled again and I was glad that his teeth were even and white and not filed to aggressive points.

"Thing is," he said, "This is family. A convention is a big family party. You stay in the industry and you'll have all the family you've ever wanted."

I looked into the blacks of his eyes.

"I was a children's home kid," he said, testing the buzzing machine as he loaded black ink. "Dave was adopted. Chris over there, he's been in and out of hospital with sclerosis of the liver and Andy was kicked out as a child, living as a rent boy until Gary found him and gave him a job. And Alma has lost two husbands and one child, although it hardened her."

"Really?" I said.

"Of course, not every tattooist has a story. Some just like drawing and fall into it. Others, those that come from good homes and good schools, start getting ink as rebellion and end up loving it so much they become part of this family, leaving their own behind."

I nodded, although Kurt was looking at Casey's leg and didn't see me.

"You see," he continued, "People like to judge us because we choose to look different. They shy away, like to think that we're hard and nasty. Perhaps they should judge us on the money we raise for charity or the people we save from themselves. Perhaps they should learn not to judge a book by its cover."

"Amen to that," said Casey.

"Who's Alma?" I asked, intrigued by the name.

"She's here somewhere. A rockabilly chick, bright red hair. She's been on the Camden circuit for years. Very messy life. I went out with her once. She scared the fuck out of me to be honest. I never went there again." He shuddered. "Very, very good at pin ups. Pin ups are definitely her thing."

"Like Dave?"

"Very different to Dave but old school nonetheless. Guy didn't come then?"

"No."

"Bit too hip. Thinks we're dinosaurs with his beard and his wax. Would have fitted in perfectly here, though." My head followed his as we took in the array of ginger bearded men in cloth caps who were filing into the warehouse.

"Right, I'm ready to outline."

"Does Dave know Alma?" I asked.

"Don't think so. Not his type. Are you ready Casey?"

The girl nodded, blowing another unfeasibly large, pink bubble. Kurt stretched the honey-brown skin taut and began. His hand and arm moved together with definite, confident strokes, wiping away the excess ink after each line. Casey didn't twitch, plugging in headphones whose leaking beat added to the general cacophony. Working upwards from the tail of the fish, he pulled and stretched and wiped and pressed his needle into perfect skin, following the purple lines of the perfect koi carp.

"Not many artists get paid for what they do. We should count ourselves lucky," he said, taking a breath before diving in again. I nodded, not wanting him to stop, hanging on every line, every fish scale and seventh wave crashing over the honey-coloured canvas.

The band changed, the Rockabilly double bass making way for heavy metal, guitars bashing out tuneless noise while a hairy man screamed on the makeshift stage. I stuck a finger in the ear closest to them and leaned closer to Kurt. Time passed and the outline grew, curling winds suggested by gaps in the outline. The scales reached further up her leg, nudging her groin as they formed the leaping fish. It was magic, like watching something appear from nothing with no reason, except there was a reason. Kurt stopped, wiped his forehead and sipped a diet Coke.

"The judges get the sitters to parade at four. I'm not sure I'm going to be finished. I should have started yesterday but I'd promised this guy a Hannya mask on his chest and I couldn't renege."

I liked his use of the word renege.

"I know about the Hannya mask," I said. "The jealous woman."

"Yes," said Kurt, his drawn eyebrows raising. "And they ward off evil spirits too. Well, they're supposed to. Don't know if it works or not." He laughed.

"What happens if you're not finished?" I asked.

"Casey here can't show the judges and I don't win!" he said.

We didn't move, Kurt and Casey and I, not for another two hours. When Dave approached the station my back was stuck and I couldn't uncross my legs.

"I've got to go now," he said. "The German called."

Kurt laughed. "How's she doing?"

"We've picked a name." He winked at me. "But I'm not allowed to tell and she needs maternity clothes because, for some strange reason, she can't seem to get into her size eight jeans."

"What's Junior's first tattoo going to be?" said Casey, pulling out an ear bud; none of us knew she'd been listening.

"My son won't have tattoos until he's eighteen. I'll pick his first artist and design his first ink." Dave sounded serious.

"I'd have 'fuck cops' tattooed on his knuckles when he's five," Casey said and laughed, a high, brittle laugh which broke half way through.

"Classy," said Dave, then, "Do you want a lift back to Islington or do you want to brave another hour with Kurt?"

I looked at them both and thought about Alma. "I'd like to stay."

"Great," said Dave. Kurt will look out for you."

"Stay and watch a bit of colour," said Kurt. "It all comes alive with colour. I'll put you in a cab home later."

"I don't need a cab," I said.

"Of course you don't," the men said together. Dave chipped in a twenty-pound note which I also tried to refuse.

"Think of it as your university," he said. "I'm paying your tuition fees for today. I want you to learn. It's not charity or kindness; it's commercial sense."

"Don't knock it," said Kurt, peering over his shoulder.

"Thanks," I said to Dave.

"You can learn a lot from Kurt," said Dave. "The best Japanese artist I've seen, anyway."

"I'd blush but you wouldn't notice," said Kurt winking at me.

"Enjoy yourself, Jay. I look forward to seeing how your art changes after this."

I smiled and thanked him again and was admonished for doing so again, and then found myself alone with Kurt and Casey, the interminable death metal and a thousand illustrated people.

Kurt took a lunch break soon after, bending and stretching his portly body until it straightened.

"Be prepared for a bad back," he said, rubbing the base of his spine. "Do you want anything?"

"I'll have a look around and get something, thank you."

"Casey?"

"Spliff."

"You'll have to wait for that," he said, disappearing into the crowd. I didn't stop to talk to the canvas I had been staring at for hours, but slipped away after Kurt, away from the band, towards the smell of warm sugar which I took to be candy floss. I bought a stick of sugar and a burger, eating them the wrong way around because I couldn't put the candy floss down. I downed a bottle of water and bought three teas, taking them the long route past work stations where I stopped to see how different artists tackled the same subjects. There were more Japanese and pin-ups; a guy doing old school swallows, like on the sailors in the books Peter had found me to read. There were Vikings on calves and wings on backs, fairies riding dragons across shoulders and a vine wrapping itself around someone's thigh. Everywhere I looked, needles buzzed and art emerged and sweat dripped from the canvases and artists alike.

IT WASN'T HER CRIMSON hair, extensions piled high in a beehive on top of her head or the lace dress which barely covered her ample bosom. It was something in her eyes, something I read but couldn't understand, something ethereal and beautiful yet tragic and broken. A black raven stared out from her arm, threatening and protective of its mistress, in its claw, a string of rosary beads and a key.

The woman who'd caught my attention was strong and tall, half her face tattooed as though the flesh had been torn from it revealing muscle and bone and sinew underneath. The ripping continued down one side of her neck, settling on her shoulder where another image held it back. The body of an octopus, coloured orange and tan and intense, covered her right breast, its tentacles reaching across her chest and up to her left shoulder. I couldn't see anymore, hidden by black lace and a circular skirt. She wore dirty, red Converse trainers, the crimson matching at the top and bottom of her body.

The rest of her skin showed signs of age as it stretched over fabulous cheek bones. Her eyes wore the flick of fifties liner, her ears stretched with the weight of gold hoop earrings of differing sizes. She had a ring through her septum, bull-like and proud. Piercings travelled from the bridge of her nose down, to the top of her lip and below, gracing her chin with silver baubles like tiny bells.

I stared for some time, transfixed, excited and afraid. "Are you Alma?" I said eventually.

She turned, her neck straight and long, her shoulders even and not weighed down. "Yes, why?"

"I was watching Kurt," I began.

"Freaky bastard. Got a checkerboard dick, you know?"

I didn't.

"I like your tattoos," I said weakly.

"Thanks. Don't have any yourself, I see."

"Not yet. But Vampire Dave is going to do one for me."

"I've heard of him. Soho studio? Old school pin ups, like me but not as good," she said and turned away. A tiny bee sat on the nape of her neck, so realistic that I wanted to swipe it away.

"I'm looking for someone…" I said, listening to my voice fading as I spoke.

"Better get going then," she said.

"No, I mean…"

"I've got a client now," she said. "Take a card. Come and see me if you want a little glamour in your life." She looked me up and down, appraising everything I was in less than a second and I knew why Kurt was scared of her. Picking up the card, I placed it in my pocket.

"Thank you," I said.

Her eyes bored into me, accusing me of something I wasn't sure I'd done. I walked away, the pieces of a puzzle I didn't understand, falling into place in my mind. I had come to this place to meet Alma; Tutankhamun could have told me why if he hadn't been hiding in the British Museum.

"SHE LET ME TAKE a card," I said, as I returned to the blue man with the three, now tepid, teas.

"She's touting for business, love," said Casey. "Nearly had my stomach today but Kurt here won, didn't you, darling?" He continued mixing colours.

"Anyway, I might go and see what her studio is like," I said, not knowing why.

"You won't learn any Japanese from her," Kurt said. "But I do love the octopus. Done in LA when she was there with her then boyfriend. He was big on the circuit there; she thought she could get big on his coat-tails." He threw a knowing look and I wanted to be in on the gossip.

Casey's koi carp was emerging from her thigh, thrusting itself out of the water which splashed and swirled around her endless thigh. Kurt worked, consumed by the waves as he coloured and shaded and wiped ink and blood away from her skin. I leaned around him, watching his black latexed hands move with precision. A siren sounded, something left over from the war, heralding the end of tattooing for the artists involved in the main competition. Kurt wiped sweat from his forehead with a wad of kitchen towel and shrugged.

"I'm not finished, I'm afraid," he said.

"No competition parading?" asked Casey, looking across the room as several new canvases made their way onto a makeshift stage.

"Not today, Casey. Sorry."

"Well, stop then. I want to see who's won."

Kurt wiped her leg with Vaseline and let her go, out into the crowd where a man with a Viking

175

across his back was flexing his muscles to show how the tattoo worked with his body. Casey was already at the edge of the stage, whooping with excitement as the four remaining artists showed off their work.

"I hate not finishing," said Kurt. "Lets down the client."

"Casey seems happy enough," I said.

"I would have won too." He shook his head and wiped his brow again.

"You would have won," I said, nodding, helping him tidy the work station of ink and foil and tattoo machines. In silence we tidied, listening to the cheers for the winning design which wasn't the Viking but a yellow cab speeding through a New York night, a sleeve of energy and excitement in a style I hadn't seen before.

"Where's the outline?" I asked Kurt.

"New wave artist," he said. "They think they can rewrite the rules of tattooing but just you wait; in a couple of years you won't have any idea that it was New York and a yellow cab. It'll just be a big smudge." I noted the distaste in his voice. "You shouldn't mess with thousand-year-old art. There's an outline for a reason." His sulkiness pushed out his bottom lip, reminding me of a painted baby.

"There are plenty more conventions, though," I said. "I'm sure you'll win the next one."

"Let's hope I have the time to do it justice," he said, sweeping used tissues into a black bin liner. "I should have gotten on with it quicker but Casey..." His voice faded. "Anyway, it's a beautiful piece. I'll see if I can get it in a magazine or something."

"You definitely should." I said.

KURT CALLED ME A CAB on his mobile when the work station was spotless and Casey had returned to thank him. She confirmed that several people had told her she would have won if it had been finished and Kurt snorted in disgust. As we waited under a fan which pushed the stale air around the room, my eyes travelled over the kaleidoscope of colour, resting momentarily on the space occupied by Alma and her crimson beehive, which had slipped a little on her head.

It was as I shook Kurt's hand and he pulled me in for a hug that I noticed it, peeking out from the top of Alma's Converse, a tiny coat of arms, a dolphin tail just visible. I saw it and still it took a moment to register. With Kurt's arms around me, I froze, staring at the tiny spot, one tattoo in a disharmony of colour.

Eyes still fixed on the prize, I felt Kurt push me gently away from him, turning to see where I was looking.

"It's a coat of arms," I said. "One I've been looking for."

"On Alma?"

"Yes."

"Good luck with that."

"I just want to ask her about it."

"Like I said, good luck with that."

The taxi pulled up outside, the driver yelling "Jay" to be heard over the Harley engines and tannoy.

"Can I have a minute to ask her?" I said, feeling the pressure of Kurt's hand on my back.

"Come to the studio and watch me finish Casey off," Kurt said. "And watch out for Alma." He laughed as he closed the door of the car and waved, smiling from stretched ear to stretched ear.

But I didn't really hear him, my eyes and mind stuck on the tiny coat of arms on Alma's shapely ankle. Nor did I hear Heather call me as I walked the garden path to my shed, or the Polish labourers call "frangipani" from one of their windows. I fiddled with the dolphin earring, checked my bag for the nail file and replaced the sweat-covered tissue before wrapping myself up in the candlewick bedspread. I closed my eyes in the hope of not seeing, but the image had burned itself into my retinas. A sense of dread, which I couldn't explain, rose up from my toes and settled, rock-like, in my stomach. Opening one eye, I noticed a tiny, white feather fall from the uncluttered ceiling.

YOU CAN TAKE CUTTINGS from buddleia. I remember watching an old man crouch over tiny flower pots, carefully cutting the tips from branches before placing them, two at a time, in a hole in the soil he made with a pen. It was probably my Grandfather, hiding with me in the greenhouse to escape lumpy rice pudding. We had spent many Sunday afternoons safe, behind glass, with plants and cuttings which didn't answer back or insist you took out the rubbish. He told me that in a few weeks there would be a hundred plants where once there was one and this was the power of the gardener, to split and reproduce plants, playing God over where and how they grew.

And so I found myself outside the railway arch, kitchen knife in hand, cutting the tips of straggly branches on the plant which proved it was possible to survive anywhere. The cordon was gone. Gone too, a doorway which would open, replaced by planks of wood and six inch nails, barring my way to the place where Beano died.

Placing the cuttings in a damp piece of kitchen towel which I had brought specially, I plunged them into my pocket, sat down and leaned against the door. We could have been safe here, Beano and I, could have turned the arch into something cool and interesting, lined the walls with pictures by Dali and Matisse. Could have stayed together forever on the filthy mattress, covered in quilts. I'd have brought in a camping stove and a sofa from outside the charity shop on the high street, and Beano could have stolen a wind-up radio to listen to on cold winter nights when we sat around a roaring fire.

The coat of arms bore holes in my retinas. A man with an Alsatian turned the corner into the courtyard in front of the arches, stopping when he saw me.

"This is private property," he shouted, the dog straining at the lead. "It's all for sale and it's my job to keep it tidy. Off you go!"

I stood, brushing down the bottom of my jeans, checking for the cuttings in my pocket and the nail file in my rucksack, walking without direction until the man and his dog were the size of toy soldiers. I didn't look back, placing one foot in front of the other, Alma and her coat of arms leading me somewhere I hadn't yet fathomed.

It was much later that I turned up the stairs of the British Library, unsure why but determined to make the most of all the information I had.

Peter smiled and waved when he saw me, rushing in my direction with a pile of books under his arms.

"Where have you been?" he asked, slightly out of breath. "I've missed you."

"Working and stuff," I replied.

"I found several books which might interest you. I've put them to one side."

"Thank you."

"You look great by the way. Really healthy and…"

"Thank you," I said again, wordless in my world of pictures. Placing the rucksack on my usual desk, I sat on the edge of it and tried to smile but the edges of my mouth were stuck in a straight line and my jaw clamped shut.

"So, what have you been doing?"

I inhaled as deeply as I could through my nose, letting the hot breath out the same way.

"Working in the B&B and at the tattoo parlour."

"You work there?"

I nodded.

"Are you drawing?"

I nodded again.

"That's just great!" he said excitedly. "I knew you were good. I bet Dave was pleased to have you. He'd said he needed someone to help out because of the baby and everything." My brain jolted back into my world, away from the mystery of the coat of arms.

"Why does he wear his wedding ring on his right hand?" I asked. "He said it was because his wife's German."

"That's right."

"Why?"

"Because the word for left in Latin is sinistre, or sinister. A lot of eastern Europeans wear theirs on the right hand so the marriage isn't sinister. She probably came from East Germany as it was in the old days before we were born." He laughed.

"Oh." It was a proper answer and it deserved a proper response but I didn't have one. I blushed at my own inadequacy.

"I'm glad for you," he said.

"Thanks. I went to a convention yesterday," I forced myself to say.

"Wow, that's so cool. I've wanted to go to one for ever. How was it?"

"Loud."

"Cool. And I bet there were great bikes there."

"Harleys, mainly," I said, sounding cooler than I felt. I paused, picking my words. "I saw the coat of arms on a woman's ankle."

"Wow! What did you do?"

"I ran away." Peter stared at me. "But I got her card." My hand slid under the cover of the rucksack to where Alma's card nestled in a pocket; I pulled it out, brandishing it like a deadly weapon.

He bent over and looked at it. "Do you want me to come with you?"

"Where?"

"When you see her, of course."

My stomach flipped. "Oh, I don't know. I don't know when I'm going yet."

"Jay, you don't have to go alone. I'm just saying that maybe, just maybe, it would be a good idea if you didn't. Here." He handed me his own card, his name, Peter McKinley, printed in black letters, a mobile number underneath."

"I don't have a phone," I said.

"But the B&B does and Dave does and there are many phone boxes in London which haven't been turned into homeless shelters." He blushed, pushing a lock of floppy blond hair away from his face. "I didn't mean any…"

"It's fine." I nodded, placing both cards in the pocket in my rucksack. "I'll let you know about coming with me," I said.

"And in the meantime, you might like to look at these." He produced a stack of books from a low shelf behind him, piling them on my desk, still talking with real enthusiasm about what I might find in them. "Maybe not the heraldry one now, although you never know; you might find the actual coat of arms you saw and it may fill in some gaps. Or not!"

His voice filled every corner of my mind, keen, interested and pushing me forwards when I wanted to stay ignorant for a while longer. I continued nodding, half smiling and looking as though I was listening while I sniffed buddleia and walked through a purple, butterfly-filled garden with Beano. I watched him from a safe distance as he planned and made diagrams with his hands, all the time blocking out his words so as not to be influenced by them.

"Anyway, I'll leave you to it. But don't hesitate to call me if you need a hand with anything at all, from books to brick work, I can turn my hand to most things." He sounded like an advertisement for the perfect boyfriend. I nodded, turning my head to the pile of books, leafing through the pages of the first one, my cathedral becoming mundane under the sound of his voice.

"Thanks," I said again, hoping he'd leave me to it.

"I'll leave you to it," he said and before he had the chance to speak again I leaned over the book in perfectly acted concentration.

Nothing leapt out from the pages, nothing except Alma and Beano's faces, one stern and haughty, the other pretty and vulnerable. I took out my pad and drew them together, looking for similarities or clues as to why they had matching tattoos. Their faces didn't tie, didn't merge together into one, didn't give me any more clues than I already had.

Without speaking, I got up from the desk, slung my rucksack over my shoulder and tried not to run outside, down the many steps and into a side road where I could breathe and make my own decisions and no one wanted to help me or save me from myself.

HEATHER WAS STANDING BY the shed as I reached the garden, looking intently at something in one of the rhododendrons.

"I've got buddleia cuttings," I said, pulling them out of my pocket. "Six of them. I thought I could put a couple near the shed for the butterflies."

"You can," she said. "I think these have got some kind of disease."

"And I thought I'd plant the others near places that Beano and I went to so that they could grow in place of her."

"That's nice," said Heather. "Fancy a cuppa?"

"Thanks, but," I said. "Peter from the library talked too much and scrambled my brain."

"Fair enough. Pop in later when you feel better."

Her vast behind, swathed as it was in purple and pink silk, swung as she navigated the path, her orange head scarf swaying with her, until she disappeared back into the house. I shut the door of the shed, scrambling under the lilac candlewick from which I had emerged earlier, clutching my rucksack and the card which held all the clues I needed if I could just find the courage to use it.

THE MELONS ARRIVED IN a crate, eight of them, large and green and not at all like skin.

"It's for the shape," Dave said, "More than the skin thing. We'll get pork for that. No, this is for the shape, so you can get used to drawing on something that isn't flat and designed for drawing on." He laughed. "Get on alright with Kurt after I left?"

"Yes thanks."

"Find anything useful?"

"All of it. He's a great artist and I loved his shading."

"Makes a difference doesn't it. You can't tell it's shaded but if it weren't it would look wrong."

"Yes," I said. "I understood when I saw it being done. Casey was a good canvas."

"She's trouble, that one. Hangs around all the conventions trying to find a man to pay for her expensive drug habit. I know a few who got stung."

"I didn't know."

"Why would you?" he said.

"What about Alma?" I asked, surprising myself. "What do you know about her?"

"Nasty bit of work by all accounts," he said, smoothing his hair back from the widow's peak. "Kurt went out with her a couple of times and then she put pictures of his dick all over social media. We all knew it was Kurt's because it was blue, and checkerboard. Quite cool actually."

"Not a very nice thing to do."

"No, Jay. It wasn't."

I hesitated, unsure about how much to say, then blurted, "She's the clue to Beano."

189

"How?"

"She has a coat of arms on her ankle the same as Beano's. I noticed it as I was leaving."

Vampire Dave stepped back, juggling a melon between his hands. "Are you sure?"

"Yes."

"Well, I don't know much about Alma, except that Kurt dated her of course. She's old school I think."

"She is, likes doing pin ups."

"Competition, eh?" The melon rose and fell in his long fingers.

"I've got her card so I thought I might book a tattoo, something small like the butterfly you were going to do for me so that it won't take long and I can suss it all out."

"Don't want a Vampire Dave original on your skin?"

"Of course I do!" I blushed deeply, crimson cheeks flushing.

"I was joking," he said, reaching out to touch my arm. "You can get tattoos from anyone you like."

"I only want to go to her because she has the same coat of arms as Beano."

"It's okay, Jay. I'll do something else for you."

He smiled and his eyes creased in kindness and once again I found myself at a loss to know what to do with the emotion which rushed through my veins, disabling speech.

He continued, "Now this afternoon's task is first to draw a cherry blossom tree on this melon and tomorrow you're going to tattoo it. Crack on!" he said, throwing the melon at me so that I had to jump to catch it.

"With a tattoo machine?" I asked, a strange butterfly wing sensation in my stomach, pulling me out of my stupor.

"With a machine," he said, winked and pushed through the beads to his office.

ALMA'S ASSISTANT CHARMED me as I telephoned for an appointment. Alma was busy, very busy in fact, but she could fit me in for a small butterfly on the nape of my neck next Thursday at five. It would be between forty and sixty pounds depending on the size and colour and a deposit of forty pounds was required to make the booking. I had no bank card and was about to replace the receiver when Dave, who had been listening from his office, ran through with a credit card.

"I'll take it off your wages," he said, snatching the phone.

"I don't earn wages," I said.

"Well, you probably should. And you can do a stock take and a tidy up to make up for it."

The appointment made, I felt better, proactive, strong instead of compliant. Thinking of Tutankhamun and what he might say about it, I drew butterfly after butterfly on the melons, filling each one with Sharpie designs in black and grey and colour, struggling to place my hand on the curve of the fruit. Sometimes I wiped the images away before they were dry; others I kept. Picking my favourite, I drew it out on a piece of paper, placing it in the pocket of my rucksack with Alma and Peter's cards. At barely two centimetres across a black outline with shades of orange on the wings, I reckoned it wouldn't go over my forty-pound budget and would be my initiation.

The butterflies I had drawn settled in my stomach, fluttering with anticipation and nervous excitement. I didn't want a body like Beano's, covered in abominations, but a scattering of pretty images over my pale skin might make me look more interesting. It would certainly make me fit in, an idea which attracted and repelled me in equal measure.

I PLANTED THREE CUTTINGS of buddleia around the shed, filling the spaces where Heather had hacked back the sickly rhododendrons, imagining the small building completely concealed by purple blooms and butterflies in a couple of years, no longer a shed but an artist's retreat, safe and white and beautiful in its simplicity.

On a walk around the pulsating city of London, I found a patch of dirt near Tate Modern, sticking one of the little twigs into the ground, watering it with French mineral water because I had forgotten to refill my own bottle. Matisse would have been delighted to know the work I was doing and maybe Dali was pleased too, dancing with Beano with clouds beneath their feet.

I wandered until I found a similar space near the twenty-four-hour Italian, a patch of forgotten dirt around a dying tree, making a hole for the cutting with my finger, pressing the earth around it gently. A child stopped to watch me, shouting to his mother that I was "plantin". I told him that one day, when he was big, the plant would be taller than him and would bow its purple flowers to him when he visited. His mother pulled him away.

Underneath a picture of a tattooed woman, which had been painted on a wall in Islington, I found an abandoned flower bed, full of fire weed and dandelions. Pulling out some of the unwanted plants, I made room for the buddleia as close to the wall as I could, both to give it shelter and to hide it until it was ready to burst through the fire weed.

I knew that my cuttings would thrive, knew that they would reach skyward for the sun, making refuge for the city butterflies trapped in diesel fumes and fetid breath. I had honoured Beano's corporeal self, planting the seeds of beauty in a filthy city, a haven in a dangerous world. I thought about the butterfly I had seen the day she died, struggling out of the arch into the brightness beyond. I had loved her more than any human being, my best friend. And in me she had placed her trust. I promised now, with a whisper, that I would nurture the plants as I would have done her, allowing her to fulfil her potential and bloom in the sunshine.

EVERYONE HAS AN OPINION. This is something to rejoice, unless, of course, they all have differing opinions on something that has nothing to do with them and won't keep them to themselves. Thus, the days leading to my first tattoo were filled with voices, warnings, and scaremongering.

"I just don't understand why you want to mark such lovely, line-free skin," said Heather.

"Make sure they're scrupulously clean," said Peter. "Check the equipment, poke around in corners. If you see dirt, scarper!"

"She's a good artist, just a bit weird," said Dave.

"Weird? Fucking crazy!" said Guy.

I wished beyond all wishing that I hadn't mentioned the coat of arms to anyone and, by the time Thursday came, I couldn't wait to slip out of Dave the Vampire's Tattoo Parlour and across town, alone.

Alma's studio, Scaramouche, was in Camden; I had passed it a hundred times without seeing it even though the paintwork was scarlet. A white, painted face stared from one side, a long moustache and pointy beard reminding me of the faceless Occupy movement. His checkerboard onesie with ruff seemed innocuous enough.

With shaking limbs, I opened the door and stepped inside. The space was dark and crowded with pictures and taxidermy; midnight blue velvet cushions jostling for space on a black leather sofa occupied most of the space. A girl behind reception looked up.

"Five o'clock?" she asked. I nodded. "Fill this in please." She handed me a clipboard with a standard agreement and disclaimer clipped to the top. I filled it in, still enjoying a frisson of pleasure as I wrote my address. The girl took the form and said Alma would be a few minutes. I settled into the sofa, crossing my arms as I noted the weird and the strange exhibited on shelves of varying heights. There were jars with tiny, malformed creatures; a lizard with two heads, a snake with three. Taxidermy birds were fixed to the purple ceiling and an owl watched them from a corner shelf. In between, heavy gold frames surrounded pictures of tattoos, demons, skulls, ravens and spiders, beautiful and ugly at the same time.

The buzz of a needle machine caught my attention and I noticed, for the first time, a young man in the corner, tattooing his own thigh. His head was bent over, a bead of sweat travelling down his just visible forehead, dripping onto the other thigh as he drew and wiped, drew and wiped.

Claustrophobic and uncomfortable, I stood, about to make a quick exit, when Alma appeared through a side door. She was wearing a blue dress, the low neck perfectly framing the octopus which straddled her breasts. The tight waist accentuated her own, small one, and grey converse high tops grazed the bottom of the tattooed coat of arms I had seen at the convention. Her hair still red and extended but loose, cascading down her back in ringlets, at odds with the piercings and the ripped skin effect across her face.

"Next," she said, turning her back.

Rooted to the spot, I watched her, unable to speak or process the thoughts which rushed around my head. "Are you coming?" she said. "I'm very busy."

As though I'd been smacked, I jolted into life. I was here for Beano, after all, and I followed her through the ubiquitous beaded curtain and into a black painted room with more taxidermy and jars with strange things in them. The black skewed the walls, making it impossible to tell where they stopped and I started.

"Have you got a picture?" she asked, loudly enough to be heard over the old-time jazz which emanated from wooden speakers.

"I have," I said, my hand shaking as I handed her the scrap of paper.

"Did you draw this?"

"I did."

She looked at me, her head tilted, her eyes fixed. "Oh, I remember, you're the one who's started at Vampire Dave's in Soho. Apprentice?"

"Yes. Just on to melons."

She laughed and the lightness of it surprised me. "Well, I'd better do a good job," she said. "Where d'you want it?"

"Here," I pointed to the nape of my neck.

"I'll be five minutes transferring this. Maggie will get you a cup of tea and you can read a magazine if you like."

"Thank you," I said, not taking my eyes off the coat of arms on her slim ankle.

She returned, as promised, in five minutes and was amused to find that I had neither moved nor ordered tea. She told me I needed more confidence if I were going to succeed in the game and I nodded, hoping that it would be sufficient.

"You really don't talk much, do you?" she said, positioning the purple copy on my neck. "And you look like a boy. Is that a style choice? Or are you into girls? Or maybe you're just lazy and can't be bothered to put mascara on every day." She laughed again. I remained silent.

"I reckon you're into girls."

"I'm not gay," I managed.

"I didn't say you were. The world is far more psychedelic than straight or gay, black or white. It's possible to be into someone just for who they are."

I tried to remember a time when I had been into someone but the picture was vague and covered in mist so I left it there and joined her in the blackened room.

"You're cute, that's all. Cute but you don't love yourself."

I shifted uncomfortably on black leather. "How do you know that?" I said.

"Because your hair is cut by a barber and your clothes fit but aren't saying anything about you and your trainers are not fashionable or cool and neither are you. But you're cute, very cute." She ran a finger along my jaw bone, catching my eye and holding it with her own.
"Do you like the position?" she asked, holding a mirror up so that I could see the back of my neck."

"It's perfect," I said, my stomach turning somersaults.

"Good." She ran her finger over it, murmuring to herself. I tried to make out the words

200

but they were, in fact, a chant or mantra and I fell under its spell, my body eager to feel the pain I knew she had in her power.

"Tattoo virgin," she said at last. "It's a while since I had one. It excites me." She ran her tongue over her scarlet lips as she pulled on black latex gloves. "I'll make the first line and ask you how it feels. Are you ready?"

I nodded, unable to speak. The needle caressed my skin, then harder, scratching and scraping. She stopped.

"Okay?"

"Yes," I said, breathless, the pain fresh and stimulating.

She continued, deftly and swiftly, making tiny noises in her throat as she worked which travelled through the back of my ear like erotic art. The world disappeared with the pain on my neck, weaving a pattern which I tried to follow with my mind's eye.

"Outline done," she said. "I'll mix some colours." Shades of orange littered the black workbench, red and yellow too. She mixed them, a drop of this and that until there were eight different shades in tiny plastic cups.

"Ready?" she asked. I nodded. "Some people say this is the easy bit and others that it's the worst. She began and the vibration of the needle went down my spine. My knees shook. Skin tore on my neck as she went over and over the same spot, shading and colouring the part of my body I couldn't see. The pain was invigorating, chosen, but awful too.

Alma dipped and shaded and murmured, exhaling hot breath onto my body in the stuffy room. The vibration stopped. She placed a tiny kiss on my shoulder blade.

"You're mine now," she said, barely audible over the strains of jazz.

The minutes passed, dreamlike in the blackness. I turned to see what was happening as Alma, beads of sweat on her breasts, licked her lips and then her even, white teeth. "It's beautiful," she said, "The first of many I hope I will do for you."

"Thank you," I said, panting, my spine still carrying vibrations down into my pelvis. She pulled at the neck of my T-shirt, down past my shoulder blades then up again. "I have plans for your lovely back," she said. "Come over one evening and we'll discuss it."

A head appeared through the door, the receptionist asking if she had time for a walk-in. Alma waved her arm in the direction of the girl who abruptly disappeared. The bubble burst; I stood, asking for the mirror in which I could see her art.

It was indeed beautiful, the butterfly seemingly having landed on my neck for the briefest of moments, caught in ink, delicate and strong, orange and black and larger than the picture I had shown her. Shading suggested its three dimensions.

"Thank you," I said again. "It's more than I wanted."

"That's the idea. Take a picture and turn it into something more," she said, removing the latex gloves. "You can go now. But come back. I can turn you from cute to unbelievably beautiful." She touched my cheek. "Dave was lucky to find you," she said.

And I was on the muggy street again, cling film stuck to my neck with sticky tape which rustled as I walked, blurred images of what had gone before replaying behind squinting eyes. So different to Dave, her manner enveloping, claustrophobic. She had touched my body and kissed my shoulder; had promised to make me beautiful by telling me that I wasn't. Unprofessional, I thought, the space between my legs tickling. Confused and sore, I passed the all-night barber on Frith Street, darting in for a short back and sides to show off my first tattoo.

Dave was still working on a sleeve when I returned to the studio; he stopped shading and put down the machine, suggesting a break for himself and his canvas.

"How did it go?" he asked as he stepped outside.

"Fine," I said, turning my back so he could see the butterfly which had landed on my body.

"Lovely work," he said. "You've got to hand it to her; small but perfectly formed but then again, it was your design and she only had to copy it."

"She wants me to go back and have more done," I said.

"And what did you say?"

"Nothing."

"Did you find out anything about your friend?"

"No."

"Then I guess you'll have to go back," he said.

"I guess I will," I said, fiddling with the zip on my rucksack. "It's not like here."

"No? Alma's one of the 'hip' artists, studies style magazines rather than industry ones. That's what I heard anyway," said Dave.

"She's not like you. She doesn't make people feel comfortable."

"Kurt isn't a fan. Mind you, why would he be? Having your dick plastered all over the internet would put anyone off." He lit a cigarette. "Kurt liked you, though, said he'd be happy to have you at his studio whenever you like. Very impressed that you helped him clean down."

I shrugged.

"You're becoming a good apprentice, Jay. Other artists will want to steal you away from me. Just remember who gave you a shot."

"I'll never leave," I said, rather too enthusiastically for my own liking.

"Good," said Dave, stamping out his cigarette with a suede boot. "But I don't mind you learning from Kurt. He's a good guy. Even our lot find him a bit scary. It's the eyes. But he's a good bloke and you can learn a lot from him. Just don't let him poach you."

"I won't," I said.

HEATHER SAID IT WAS a shame to mark such fair skin and why couldn't they make them semi-permanent so you didn't have to live with a mistake.

"It's not a mistake," I said. "I love it."

"You can't see it," she said.

"Exactly, but I know it's there," I said to put an end to a pointless conversation.

"They'll steal you away into that weird world, away from here."

"Why does everyone think I'm going to leave?" I asked. "Why can't I stay here and there?" I chuntered, plodding up the path to the white shed. I closed the door, calming myself in the whiteness and the drawings of Beano before climbing under the lilac candlewick.

The skin on my neck was raw and sweaty. I peeled off the cling film and held a hand mirror over my shoulder so that I could see it. It was perfectly beautiful, better than my drawing, deeper somehow and more real. I looked at the delicate shading under the wings, turning my head so that the mirrors reflected it perfectly. Trying it on one of my own pictures, I was amazed to see the image jump out of the page. The touch of pencil underneath allowing the image to dance. I had learned something from Alma.

With Baphomet looking down on me, I started to draw the next piece Alma could tattoo on my body, a tree of life, a back piece, a masterpiece. I needed time with her, time to understand how she fitted into the tapestry of Beano's life - and my own. Her touch lingered on my skin, stimulating nerves which had long been asleep. It was wrong, unprofessional and reportable. It was intriguing too, and the remaining sensations ensured that I would return to her lair.

HEATHER HAD STOPPED TAKING occasionals, preferring migrant labourers who required less attention. The sign had been removed from the front window and the 'posh' bedding put away in the airing cupboard on the landing. My friends, the Polish men, had been joined by Romanians and Albanians who didn't understand our word game but watched as we giggled.

"Expunge", one of them said as I placed bacon and eggs in front of them. "Paraphernalia," said another. I smiled, correcting their pronunciation slightly until an Albanian man with a good command of English joined in, annoying the Warsaw nationals who wanted to keep the game for themselves.

"Two new ones tomorrow," I said, smiling at all the tables of men eating the breakfasts I had prepared. It still gave me a buzz to feed people. It's the kind of buzz which comes from knowing times without food, bin diving and waiting outside the back of fast food restaurants to pinch the out of date food at the end of the day. It fed me emotionally as I ripped through the cleaning and changed all the beds.

The reduced workload gave me an extra couple of hours to practice on the melons and Dave was pleased with my progress, purchasing more, giving me ink and more projects to fulfil. Guy, too, encouraged my art, often asking me to draw out something for a client which he might or might not use as his own. Dave said it was because he was too lazy to draw his own but there was a thrill in seeing my designs on skin no matter who did them. The sun shone from a cloudless blue sky and the buddleia cuttings by the shed pushed out new shoots with strong stems.

And I called Alma.

The appointment was made, my promise to Beano secreted somewhere in the layers of reasons I was visiting Scaramouche – the hours and days stretching out towards the day I would feel Alma's hands on my skin once more.

SHE MET ME IN purple gingham, stretched over her curves until the seams groaned. A petticoat flashed white broderie anglaise, catching my eye above her purple high tops, the tail of the dolphin just visible.

"Come in," she said, lightly brushing my shoulder with her fingers. I shivered and goose bumps rose on my skin and the octopus across her chest wrapped its tentacles around me. I could hear the shallowness of my breath, smell the incense which burned in reception.

"I knew you'd come back," she said.

I followed her through to the black room where the stuffed owl judged me from its ledge. A million questions rattled in my head; I sat on the edge of the couch, flicking my feet against each other, listening to Alma shuffle papers and move ink bottles.

"Have you got a drawing?" she asked, her voice husky and low.

I pulled the sheet of paper out of my back pocket, unfolding it on the black leather. The tree of life, animals and flowers peeping out from the branches, the trunk and roots reaching down towards water. Cherry blossoms filled in the gaps between squirrels and birds pecking at already ripe fruit.

"It's bland," she said. "But quite pretty. It could be a lot more interesting but if it's what you want…I'll do most of it freehand." She scratched her head, tilted it and held the page up to my body. "Take off your T-shirt."

It wasn't bland. It had taken me hours to draw, the beauty of nature and female strength represented by the cherry blossom. I had put a lot of thought into it. I remained silent, shivering as I peeled the clammy cotton from my skin, covering my breasts with shaking hands.

"Don't blush," Alma said, laying cold fingers on my hot back. "You have a beautiful little body." A flush of heat followed her fingertips up my spine, touching the butterfly which I knew rested there.

"Tell me who you are," she said, standing back, leaving my skin screaming for more of her touch.

"Jay," I replied. She laughed, throaty and deep.

"Okay, we'll play a game. Tell me what you love," she said.

The word "you" caught in my throat. I panicked, coughing it out. "Drawing," I said. "I love drawing."

"Not a person?"

"Drawing," I repeated.

"Have you ever loved or been loved?" It sounded like a challenge.

"Of course," I lied and she could smell my lie.

"Desire, lust, love. Maybe they're all the same thing. What do you think?"

Searching the words which tumbled in my head, I caught three. "I don't know," I said.

"You're not very good at this," she said. "Maybe you just don't have the experience."

My silence gave her all the answer she needed.

"Okay, let's try this one. What are you most afraid of?"

The question caught me unawares, t̬ "you" rising in my throat once more, threatening expose me for the coward I was. "Insects," I said, "Spiders and beetles and cockroaches."

Alma laughed. "Your Room 101 is bugs?"

"I hate scuttling things and things that crawl on your skin without being invited." But not your fingers, I wanted to add.

Alma laughed again, a low, throaty laugh which vibrated through her own body and into mine.

"Yes, I hate the way spiders move. And wasps. I'm afraid of being stung and going into anaphylactic shock and having locked-in syndrome and people thinking I'm dead and burying me though I'm still alive. The Victorians used to be buried with a bell in case they woke up." Pursing my lips so no more words would burst out, I pretended to have an itch on the back of my neck, scratching it to distract her.

"You know some very weird things," she said, running one finger down my spine as the hairs on the back of my neck stood to attention.

"I am weird," I said.

"Yes, you are, little one. Spiders and beetles and wasps and cockroaches are more afraid of you. But you know that."

"I do." I thought of Tutankhamun and how I missed him. "I've often wondered," I said, "If we feel their energy and that's why we feel afraid. That it's their fear and we're just picking up it up out of the atmosphere." I closed my mouth, clenching teeth together, then took a deep breath, "How about you? What do you love and what are you afraid of?"

Alma sighed, leaning away from me so that I could feel the air between us. "I love this place, my studio and my work; I love making love; I love sensations that stagger the mind." She paused. "I'm afraid of nothing." Fingers touched my arm, pulling me round to face her.

Intensity in her blue eyes met mine, pupils dilated. Tiny lines framed them, in contrast with the girly, full breasts which seemed to fill the room. Her breath hot on my skin, she leant forwards, kissing my ear, my temple. I shuddered. Alma's hands encircled my body as she pulled me towards her, hungry lips landing on my own. I responded involuntarily, mouth open, tasting her and all that she had to offer. Allowing my arms to wrap around her neck, I caressed the place where it looked as though her skin had been torn apart.

Maybe we kissed for hours, maybe for a moment. I didn't care, so lost in the sensation that I didn't want it to end. When she finally pulled away, my heart was pounding and my eyes were running with tears I didn't know I was shedding.

"I'm not gay," I whispered as she gently pulled the clasp of my bra open, letting my small breasts bounce free.

"Neither am I," she said, pulling at the button at the top of my jeans. I lay back, letting her seduce me, unable to run, the sensations in my body both yearning and vengeful. Her tongue skipped over me, down, down to where no one had been; stomach churning with anticipation. When she reached that secret place, I came immediately, shattering my body into a thousand pieces which leapt into the universe far beyond my control. She lay me down, pulling my jeans off fidgeting feet, caressing inner thigh with tongue and fingers. Our clothes now scattered over her desk, the ink and machines of her trade a backdrop to our own art form, our bodies writhed, our breath shortening and lengthening in unison. Sweat trickled between my breasts, rubbing onto hers, sloshing and slapping as we ground our bodies into each other, panting, lost in the moment. Straddling me, she pushed my hands away, bringing herself to orgasm as I watched, feeling my own rise repeatedly. She screamed. I gasped as her weight dropped onto my chest, her wetness a hot mess between us.

It was over as swiftly as it had begun; Alma dismounted, handed me my clothes and disappeared into another room. I sat on the couch, my legs dangling over the sides aware of my skin, inside and out, the blackness of the walls closing in. "What have I done?" I whispered to the glass eyes judging me from within glass domes. "What have I done?"

Alma returned, a business-like manner settled on her shoulders.

"Come on, get your clothes on," she said. "Let's go to the pub."

My T-shirt stuck to the place she had come. My jeans skidded up the clammy trail where her tongue had been. Running my fingers through my hair, I bit my lips and followed her out of the studio, past the assistant who squinted at me.

At the bar, she ordered a gin and tonic and stared at me.

"Coke, please," I said. "I don't drink anymore."

She placed the drink in front of me. "Of course you don't," she said.

I sipped and the bubbles went up my nose. I snorted.

"The tree of life thing," Alma said, "Are you sure that's what you want? Nothing edgier? Pin ups?"

"Dave said you were very good at pin ups."

"I am."

"But I want something more natural."

"I suppose you're one of those New Age hippie types? We're all one in the Universe crap?"

"No," I said, her words stabbing the love swelling inside. "It's the opposite of the city. I like that idea, that I'm more than the city."

"No one is more than this city. It's my life blood. Can't you feel the energy that comes from it? You should celebrate that rather than fight it." She downed her drink and got up to order another. The dress swung around her bottom, a glimpse of her strong legs offered to the men sitting at the bar. They knew her. She said something and they laughed and turned and looked at me. My eyes dropped down to the place of my own shame. I stuck my hands between my legs in the hope of hiding it.

"How did Dave find you?" She asked as she sat down again.

"I kind of found him," I said, turning my own glass around in my hands. "I was looking for someone. It's a long story, but someone gave me his name."

"Did you find the person?"

"Sort of …"

"You either have or you haven't?"

My teeth bit the glass. "I may have found them. I'm just not sure what it all means. I just want to be sure and then I can take it from there."

"You speak in riddles, which would be fine if you were a spy or a terrorist or something vaguely interesting. But there really doesn't seem to be much substance to you. A little lost girl in a big bad city, looking for someone you may or may not find. I don't believe there's much to you at all." I looked out of the window at the happy people. She continued, "So why did you come and speak to me at that convention. You weren't looking for me, were you?"

"No," I said too quickly.

"Cause if you were, you"ll be disappointed again. I've got nothing to give you other than sex and fantastic tattoos. And you have absolutely nothing to offer me."

"I could prove you wrong."

She laughed. "No, you really couldn"t."

"So, I'm cute but not pretty, my drawings aren't edgy enough, I've got nothing to offer you and I'm not interesting. But it didn't stop you fucking me on your leather couch."

She laughed and it sounded like the jazz she had played at Scaramouche.

"No, it didn't." She turned and looked at me. "Feisty now. I like feisty. You can bring feisty to the sex we're bound to have. I love a challenge." She raised her glass. "And if I become even slightly interested, learn something about you that sets you apart from everyone else, I may help you to find the person you're looking for."

"So far, all you've told me is what you don't like about me. I wouldn't trust you to help me." I regretted the words immediately as Alma's shoulders stiffened and her jaw set.

"Fair enough," she said and, swinging her bag over her shoulder, slid out from the bench. My eyes followed as she swerved and ducked out of the front door. I watched the gingham disappear as it closed behind her.

"Piss off the ogre?" said the barman, snatching up her glass and wiping where she had been.

"She's very rude," I said.

"She is that."

I smiled my best smile, handed him my glass, which was still half full, and stepped out onto the street looking left and right, a glimmer of hope fading. Alma had disappeared. I was alone again, the memory of her touch still twitching in my knickers.

HEATHER MET ME IN the kitchen the next morning, a mug of tea in her hand. She stood next to the fridge, watching as I cracked eggs.

"It's about time I had a holiday," she said. "I was thinking of Dawlish in Devon."

"That's nice," I said.

"I'll see if Irene wants to go with me. You're doing a good job here. You won't mind looking after this place? It'll only be for a week."

"I don't mind," I said, keeping my face turned away in case she could see what I had done the night before, etched on every feature.

"I'm a bit worried about you, though," said Heather. I stopped what I was doing, heat rising. Did she know? She continued, "This tattoo thing is taking up too much of your time."

I breathed a sigh of relief. "It's not interfering with my work," I said.

"No, that's not what I mean. It's all those strange people with piercings and attitude."

I looked at her purple headscarf, pink cardigan and floral, green trousers. Her nails were blue and her jewellery based on Disney characters.

"It's just how they express themselves," I said.

"It's a cult, I reckon," she said, shaking her head so her earrings rattled. "And you're going to get dragged into it."

"It is not a cult," I said, harsher than I had intended. "They're just people who choose to look different."

She ignored me and continued. "Exploiting you, no doubt. You get paid at this job so you can afford to work for nothing there. It's not right. I'm paying you so you can give your time free there. And I really don't like you working for someone with Vampire in his name. I mean, what kind of a name is Vampire Dave? Sucking the life and breath out of you for no reward."

"It's just how it works," I said, flipping bacon rashers. "Apprentices don't get paid. You have to bring money into the studio by being good enough and you don't learn to be good enough unless you're in a studio in the first place." I took a breath. "And he paid for my tattoo and the cab back from the convention, and he buys me tea and sometimes food and he's a decent man. Like he and you have both said, he doesn't ask me to do anything he hasn't done himself."

"Hmmph."

"And I love drawing and it's not as if it's stopping me from working. He always says to fit it round you."

"Well, it's wrong if you ask me, which you don't anymore." I moved the frying pan off the heat and caught her eye.

"Don't think I'm not grateful for all this, Heather. I am, truly grateful. I love my job and the Polish men and even frying bacon…" I said. "But I also love drawing and learning about art and tattooing is art. I'm very lucky to have you and to have both opportunities."

"This place was always enough for me," she said.

"Maybe I'm different."

Heather sighed, waddling over to where I stood, roughing up my hair with a hand laden with rings, the claws of which got stuck and pulled. "I just miss you, that's all. And you got home so late last night…"

"I went out for a drink with someone." I regretted the words as soon as they had slipped out.

"Oh, that nice young man from the library?"

"No."

"Well, don't forget him. He's clearly sweet on you. And he doesn't have Vampire in his name. What do librarians earn? Come and have coffee after you've done the rooms, eh? But don't go and marry him and leave me in the lurch."

I laughed, shoving the pan back on the stove to finish the bacon.

SHE HAD THE BEST china spread out on a table when I entered a couple of hours later. And biscuits with chocolate on the top. I took one when offered, settling into the armchair with the antimacassars, allowing my eyes to adjust to the patterns.

"How are you?" Heather fumbled for words as I sipped my tea.

"I'm good," I said.

"You seem withdrawn."

"I'm really not."

I squirmed in the chair, staring at the row of unblinking dolls on the shelf above her head. She continued, "How about your friend? Any leads?"

"I've got a clue," I jumped in. "And I'm following it. Peter said to follow any clue until you're sure it's dead."

"And dead is what I worry you'll end up if you carry on with that crowd."

"They're nice people, Heather. They've all been kind to me." I blushed, remembering Alma's fingers on my breasts.

"Well, anyway, I hope the search for your friend goes well. It's what brought you here, remember?"

I did.

"And you were such a poor, lost little thing, all grey and skinny and street-tired." She rubbed her hands together. "I was thinking that you've been a blessing in disguise and maybe I haven't told you how much better things have been running since you came and..." She fiddled with a striped napkin, her blotchy face contorting. "Well, maybe it's my fault you're hanging round with those misfits. So, would you like to become my partner?"

Her features relaxed with the words, which she had clearly not thought about.

"Wow," I said, unsure what else to say.

"What do you say?"

"I…I don't know. What does it mean?" I wanted to continue, to ask why things have to change when they're going well.

"It means you'd live in and I'd show you the accounts and you could order the food in or buy it at the market. It means you'd have a share of the profits as well as a wage. It means you'd have input as to how we go about running this old place." She waved an expansive hand.

Why was she offering me this, now? Now that I had found Alma and made a small space for myself with Vampire Dave? It wasn't fair.

"Can I think about it?" I asked after some time.

Heather's eyes were devoid of emotion when they caught mine. "If you have to," she said.

"It's not that I'm not flattered…"

Heather snorted. "It certainly wasn't flattery."

"I haven't even moved out of the shed yet, and you said yourself that real life takes some getting used to."

She nodded and I pulled myself out of the chair, staring out of the window onto the street beyond. A woman with a pushchair was struggling up a curb. An early butterfly fluttered across the garden. Heather coughed. I turned back and sat down.

"You'll have to commit to something at some point."

"I have committed to you, Heather. I've taken on more commitment than I ever have in my entire life." I opened the parlour door, slipping out without another word.

Sitting on the camp bed in the safety of the shed, I checked for my nail file, mindlessly rubbing it across my thumb until blood oozed from it. Beano stared down at me, enigmatic, unhelpful. Things had been so easy when I had no clue and no home, the pressures of life kept at bay by the need to eat and sleep. A yearning for freedom crept up from my toes, the need to feel tarmac hard under springy soles, spitting rain on my face, the stabbing of sharp wind.

Tutankhamun was waiting for me. He said he knew I'd come. He knew about Alma too, the curse of being a divine king, I suppose. He didn't berate me, just told me to follow my path whatever anyone else said.

"Things happen", he said. "It's what you do with them that counts."

"I think I love her."

"Thinking is dangerous. You should feel more."

"I can't feel any more than I already do. I'm just uncontrollable feelings wrapped up in a miserable mess."

"Keep following your path," he said.

I didn't know what my path was anymore, didn't want to know. Tourists in shorts spoke in many languages, all of which he understood. They filed past him, not noticing me on the bench a few feet away.

"You're lost," he said during a lull in the footfall. "A detour, that's all. A crossroads, maybe. There are no right or wrong choices. And you're on your way to solving the mystery of Beano, aren't you?"

"I don't know."

"Then you'll have to decide what to do when you've got all the information."

"She frightens me."

"Then why did you make love to her?"

"Because I couldn't not. Does that make sense?"

"The truth always makes sense."

"She scares me but she makes my knees weak. And I'm not gay. I've never thought about making love with a woman."

"No one needs a label. Everyone is just a different shade. Shades. Not one thing or another thing."

"She said that. But it scares me 'cause I don't know what's going to happen."

"Who does?"

"Well, you knew that you were going to be buried in a huge pyramid with all your worldly possessions and that people would always respect you and look after you."

"I did? I remember thinking that the girl who served me water was the most beautiful creature I'd ever seen, knowing she was a slave and I couldn't marry her."

"How old were you when you married?"

"We married at thirteen or sooner if the girl was ready for pregnancy. My wife was fourteen."

"I think marriage is weird. Why would you want to attach yourself to someone for the rest of your life?"

"Because you love them. Like you loved Beano and would have stood by her through anything."

The vision of Beano in her oversized parka blurred my eyes. "You're right," I said. "But that was a different feeling."

"Love comes in many forms."

The room filled with a second wave of foreign shorts, Asian this time, and a guide who talked Mandarin which pierced the atmosphere and broke my connection with Tutankhamun.

We waited in silence until they shuffled into another room.

"I think I love her," I said in the emptiness.

"Oh," said Tutankhamun.

"Alma," I said, hearing my voice speak words I didn't want it to. "You're angry with me, aren't you?"

"No. But be careful loving people who don't love you back."

"I think I could show her I was loveable."

"Perhaps you should start on yourself."

"I wouldn't know where to start," I said.

In the ladies, I replaced my tissue, splashing cold water on my face to cool off. Tutankhamun was right to be concerned.

ALMA FILLED EVERY BREATH, every thought, every nuance. I had hoped she would call me, inviting me for a drink in her local or for a pizza and a movie. I had no phone but the thought possessed me. Every time the studio phone rang I jumped, sure that it was her, disappointed when it was another booking.

After three days of waiting, I called Scaramouche on the office phone, asking the receptionist if Alma had an opening for me in her diary. She put me on hold, checked with the woman herself and came back to me that Thursday at seven would be fine. I wrote in the work diary that I would have to leave at six for the beginning of the Tree of Life tattoo. I didn't hear her voice but I could feel it in my spine.

Nothing else mattered, not the B&B nor my training on melons, not even Beano. Only the space between now and Thursday at seven. Would she want me, love me, take care of me? Would she run her fingers along my spine? Would I react, pulling her towards my eager lips? Or lie, motionless, waiting for her experienced hands to touch mine? My stomach did a full gymnastics routine, scoring straight tens as I set to work on a melon koi, my lines becoming ever more confident as I used the machine with ease, obsession with Alma replacing fear of drawing badly.

Alma's face appeared on the fruit; I traced the lines with the needle, sketching her face as it would have been without the tattoos which defined it. A wide smile looked back at me, even teeth and twinkling eyes devoid of menace. I scratched out the drawing so that no one would see it, then traced the lines with my fingers, horrified that I had disfigured her.

With each ring of the telephone I became more desperate to speak to her, to tell her that I loved her and hear her murmur the same. My eyes darted from melon to window, in case she walked by.

I didn't hear Dave speaking to me in confidential tones. He had to poke my shoulder, bringing me sharply back from my reverie.

"It's just a confidence thing with you," he was saying. "Don't worry," he said. "You're not in any kind of trouble."

"What?"

"Come with me."

He beckoned me into his office. I sat in the chair opposite taking the bottle of water he offered me. "In fact, I couldn't be more pleased with your progress," he continued, though I hadn't heard the start. "Your designs are becoming stronger and you're listening to everything I say so you're learning pretty damn fast. You're doing a good job, Jay. You should be proud of yourself."

I fiddled with the frayed edge of my T-shirt.

"It's just confidence you lack. And you have to have confidence when you're drawing something indelible onto a client's body. They need to feel your confidence. Do you see what I mean?"

I nodded, picking at the loose edges, managing to free a stubborn piece of cotton.

"So, what can we do to give you more confidence, Jay?"

"I don't know," I said, genuinely ignorant.

"Pig."

"What?"

"Pig flesh. I'll get you some pork belly to have a go on. You've done a good job on melons. You're ready for pig."

"Oh."

"In fact, let's go to the French butcher now. Come on!" He stood and I followed as he marched through the shop, waving to Guy who was placing script on a young woman's thigh. It read "never let your fear determine your fate."

I followed him out into the sweltering sunshine, around the corner and up towards the Berwick Street market. Through a muddle of sweaty bodies, he walked with purpose, me behind, barely keeping up, until he came to the butcher. Dave knew the men inside, talking to them about football and the weather, before introducing me. The youngest butcher disappeared and reappeared with a huge piece of pigskin. A small amount of money was exchanged, the flesh wrapped in plastic, and we were back on the street again. I lost him in the crowd for a moment, then spotted his shiny forehead talking to a man with half his face tattooed with Maori designs. My head swam, side-lining the people and the smell of sweat as I pushed through the market until a stall I hadn't seen before caught my eye.

On it statues and pictures of occult figures nestled with incense sticks and patchouli oil. And Baphomet, in all his glory, sat among them, his goat face unmoved by all that was going on around him. I stared into his eyes, searching for an answer to a question I didn't have, moving closer until the figure was in my hands and the man behind the stall hovered, in case I stole it.

"What's this for?" I asked.

The man shrugged. "Whatever you want it for, I guess." His accent wasn't London.

"Why do you sell it? I mean, who buys things like this?"

"People like you," he said and laughed. "I don't know. Hipsters, tourists, that kinda stuff."

"I saw one of these as a tattoo on someone's back once. It's Baphomet."

"Yeah. Them Wiccans and Druids and stuff worship him or summat. It's the world and everything in it. Or it can represent the dark side. Like Darth Vader." He laughed.

"How much is it?"

"Twenty to you."

"And to anyone else?"

"Twenty!" He laughed again.

"Do you know what bees mean?"

"There's flowers around." His laugh pierced my eardrums.

Dave touched my shoulder. "What have you found, Jay?"

"Baphomet."

"Perhaps you should try him on the pig skin," he said, thrusting the bag into my line of vision.

"I should be concentrating on her."

"Who?"

"Beano." Dave and the market vendor exchanged glances.

"Do you want this or not?" the vendor asked.

"She doesn't," said Dave, pushing me away from the stall, away from the sweat and the smell of burgers and the elbows vying for space amongst the goods.

"The German needs a holiday," Dave said presently. "I'm going to take her to Brighton for a few days. Get some sea air. And there's a convention, if you want to come down for a day."

"How soon will the baby be born?" I asked.

"Six weeks until little Cash Crichton comes along."

"You changed Lennon?"

"I did. Being named after two legends is too much for anyone. And anyway, Cash is a cool name."

"It is," I said.

The parlour came into view, Guy leaning against the window, a roll up languishing between his fingers.

"Dave?" I put my hand out to stop him. He looked at me.

"Yes?"

"Should I let Alma do a back piece on me? I've given her a picture of the tree of life that I drew but…"

"No doubt she's a good artist."

"But… I don't know if I trust her."

He swung around, clasping the bag of meat between his knees as he reached for my hands.

"You've got to trust your artist, Jay. If you don't, don't get it done. Or at least not by her. I'll do it for you, or Guy or Kurt. But if you don't trust Alma, don't go there."

"I've got to find out…"

"Not with your own skin!" He rubbed his temple. "You've got a lot to lose these days. Remember that."

I took the pig inside and put it in the fridge, busying myself with Dave's little pots of ink, his filing and the general mess which followed him. I did have too much to lose; the B&B and my shed-home, Dave the Vampire's Tattoo Parlour apprenticeship, Peter at the library and Tutankhamun, guiding and pissing me off from his place in the British Museum. From nothing, and because of Beano, I had all this to lose. Why, then, did it feel like nothing at all?

Leaving a note on the desk, I slipped out of the shop and caught the bus to Camden. A few minutes later I found myself outside Scaramouche.

ALMA OPENED THE DOOR in red Capri pants and a white, broderie anglaise top, octopus breasts heaving through the white cotton. My lungs expelled all their oxygen.

"I've got you booked in for Thursday," she said.

"I know. I just wanted to see you."

"I'm busy," she said, pulling the door to behind her. "Thursday at seven. Never without an appointment. Never." She stepped behind the door, closing it quietly but definitely until I was standing on the pavement, shame reddening my cheeks. I ran home, jostling pavement-users, elbowing an old man out of my way. I ran and ran, until the sweat dripped in my eyes and my back was sodden, down side streets and alongside buses. Finally, the path which led to the shed beckoned.

Collapsing on the camp bed, I cried, tears of frustration and shame and general misery which lasted well into the night, turning my pale, freckled face into a balloon of redness and swelling.

HEATHER WAS ANNOYED, HER face set in grim lines which reached her eyes. Two of the Romanian labourers had left in the night without paying. She wondered how I hadn't heard them as they must have made a racket. I wondered how she hadn't heard them, as close as she was to their room. My own, blotchy face didn't warm her heart as she paced the kitchen muttering under her breath.

"I need you in the house," she said at last. "If you'd been here, you'd have heard them and you could have stopped them."

I didn't reply but piled bacon into the frying pan. The Poles were singing "I'll stand by you," in the dining room, their deep voices vibrating my breast bone.

"And it's about time you stopped living in a shed and started helping me properly. If I can't rely on you…"

I froze and the bacon sizzled, releasing delicious aromas into the fetid air. She continued, "What I mean is, you need to move into the house. I don't feel safe in here alone with all these foreign workers. They could do anything."

I didn't mention that she had changed her business to accommodate these men.

"You're just not pulling your weight. I'm feeling more vulnerable than ever. And you've got all those weirdos on your side and I've got no one."

Words bubbled up from my chest, cruel, unhelpful words which I wouldn't release. Instead I said, "I don't want to live in a house."

"And that's your problem, my girl. Not ready for this and not ready for that. When will you ever be ready for anything. Life is just going to carry on without you. I'll find someone else to offer all this to, someone who'll be grateful."

The weight of her words settled on my shoulders. Tears oozed from swollen eyes. There were no words to express the familiar numbness which crept into my bones, the itch in my feet to walk and walk until I recognised nothing. Heather stopped, bending down to look at my lowered face.

"Now don't be making a song and dance about what I've said. You're a good worker but I need more commitment if we're going to make this a successful pension fund. That's all." She turned and the rustle of green silk on paisley cotton followed her through the door and into the dining room where the singing stopped abruptly.

I piled the plates with breakfast, delivered them to the subdued Polish labourers and ran to the shed, ignoring the two rooms which were scheduled for cleaning.

My drawings of Beano came down first, layered and rolled up and slotted down the side of my rucksack containing the nail file. Filling the pockets with toiletries, my scarf and all the new clothes I owned, it bulged, greedily accommodating six pairs of knickers and a spare pair of trainers. Before I had time to think, I was on the street again, walking towards a future which held nothing of Beano or Alma or Dave or Heather, a place where my mind could be free of obligation and gratitude.

Past Seven Sisters market, I walked, past the mosque and a synagogue, up the Holloway Road to an unknown destination, stopping now and then to check out possible sleeping sites, doorways and food options. Finding a half-finished carton of juice, I fished it out of a bin, enjoying the sweet juice until a wasp buzzed from inside. I dropped it, spat the juice across the pavement and continued until I didn't recognise the streets or the houses or the people who frequented them. Families with lives went about their business as my feet slapped the pavement, happy as the sun faded behind the trees in a park.

The cemetery was still open in Highgate, the great and the good looking down on the well-heeled. The gate creaked as I pushed it open just enough to squeeze through, the smell of damp earth like perfume to my sun-dried nose. Along gravel paths I ambled, admiring the stone mason's handiwork, the writer's inscriptions on the stones. Louise had been the loving wife of Arthur. Cedric, gone before his time. The cool air wrapped itself around me and I sat, leaning on a headstone, watching ants carry food back to their nest. A blackbird sang in a branch above my head and a fox scurried in and out of a thicket of nettles. London receded. People disappeared. I closed my puffy eyes, sheltered in the shade by a flint and brick wall which jutted into my spine. Birdsong fluttered down like raindrops, soothing my soul among the undemanding dead.

IT WAS KURT WHO found me, as he staggered back from a pub on the High Street with a girl who looked no older than sixteen.

"Is that you, Jay?" he slurred, waking me with beery fumes. He prodded my arm with his foot.

"Yes," I said through sleepy muscles.

"What the fuck are you doing in Highgate Cemetery?" The girl hanging on to his arm, giggled.

"I came to talk to Karl Marx," I said, suddenly alert, muscle memory returning to my stiffened limbs. Kurt laughed.

"No, Jay, what are you really doing here?"

"I'm on a break," I said.

"It's fucking two in the morning." He scratched his head. The girl was looking bored. "Come back with us."

"No thanks."

"Aww, come on. Dave'll be furious if I tell him I left you in a graveyard."

"He doesn't have to know." I brushed leaves off my jeans, parched like sandpaper, disintegrating under my touch.

"Of course he does. You're his apprentice, for God's sake. This family of ours is proper." He hauled me up off the ground, swinging my rucksack over his back. "Come back to mine. You can crash there and I'll take you to work in the morning."

"How come she gets to go on your bike and I don't?" the girl said, sticking out her lower lip.

"Shut up! It's a family thing." The girl sucked her thumb.

"Just leave me here," I said, dragging my feet as he pulled me towards the gate.

"Can't do that," he said.

"Please leave me here."

"Why?"

"Because…" Kurt stood me against the gate, pulling leaves out of my hair, patting dust off my jeans. He grinned and the patterns on his face contorted.

"You're running, aren't you?" he said. I didn't reply. He sighed deeply, drunkenness clearing from his features.

"Come on," he said, slipping his fingers through mine.

"Please don't," I said.

"Spend the night at mine. Make your decision in the morning. You're not safe here and I won't judge you if you run. I promise."

The hard ground had already bruised my skin.

"Okay," I said. "But you promise not to make me stay?"

"I promise."

It was only a five-minute walk to Kurt's flat, a spacious, high ceilinged, three rooms in a stucco fronted house. Depositing me on the sofa, he staggered to the bedroom, the girl still wrapped around him.

"See you in the morning," he said and winked.

Silence enveloped me, stifling my breath. I approached the door handle with stealth, turning it as quietly as I could but Kurt had met my kind before. The door was locked and the keys, no doubt, under his pillow. Admitting defeat, I lay on the sofa, staring at the ceiling rose with yellow stains that hinted at a leak upstairs. Tutankhamun's words went around in my head, chicken on a spit, over and over until they were perfectly roasted and served with a garnish.

"You've lost your way," he said. "You've just lost your way."

Pizza boxes littered the floor boards and the sofa was splattered with unrecognisable stains. I closed my eyes and imagined running and running and running until I ran out of road, slamming feet into sand, splashing out into the vast indifference of the ocean.

I WOKE AT SIX, the birds from the tree outside calling me up and into their morning ritual. I put on a pot of coffee and found some bacon and eggs which I tossed into a frying pan. As the familiar aromas filled the tiny flat, Kurt's door opened and the girl wandered into the kitchen wearing tiny knickers, her perfectly circular breasts bouncing with each step. Without speaking, she poured a cup of coffee and turned on the television. Piers Morgan's voice infected the already mote-filled air.

Putting the food on plates, I handed her one. She said "thanks" and "where's the sauce?" I ignored her, returning to the kitchen for Kurt's larger plateful. Knocking on the door, I entered immediately, ignoring the shapeless lump who had locked me in.

"Breakfast," I said.

The lump mumbled thanks. I returned to the living room to sit next to the girl who was watching women in their fifties modelling 'appropriate clothes' in various shades of blue. Her plate was already empty. She handed it to me and went to the bathroom where I heard the shower burst into life along with the pipes which groaned and creaked.

"Who did this?" demanded Kurt as he rushed from the bedroom with an empty plate and a towel covering his checkerboard dick.

"I did," I said.

"Great breakfast," he said. "Fancy moving in?"

"No thanks," I said and he laughed as he rubbed his temples and searched for paracetamol.

He sat down in the space the girl had left, leaning on his knees, his head low and purple.

"Why were you really in the cemetery last night?"

"I needed to get away."

"From Dave?"

"No!" I sighed and my legs turned to lead. "He's been nothing but amazing to me."

"Who then?"

"Maybe I can't do real life. Everyone wants so much from you."

"From you? Maybe." he said scratching a stubbly chin. "Talent, know what I mean? You've got it. Dave doesn't want to take it from you. Know what I mean?" It wasn't a question.

"I think I'm a bit lost," I said, repeating Tutankhamun. Kurt's blue skin soothed me, his eyes benignly reflecting my own.

"I think you are. Take it from one who knows, life in the family is a whole lot better than life outside the family. Know what I mean?"

Not knowing at all, I nodded, forcing a smile from the corners of my flaking lips.

"I've missed my shift at the B&B," I said. "Heather will be furious."

"You're going back, then?"

"I don't know what to do."

"What time would you be due at the studio?"

"Not 'til after lunch."

"Good. Come with me. I'm doing a little private job this morning, a woman I'd like you to meet." He stood up, stretching out his broad shoulders, his chest bearing an image of a Harley Davidson with all the accessories.

The girl emerged from the bathroom, kissed his cheek and left without a word. Kurt dressed, showing his even teeth the toothbrush, and his under arms some expensive cologne. He left the bedroom door open as he dropped the towel and I caught a glimpse of his white buttocks, devoid of tattoos and sunshine in equal measure. I washed up the plates and the pan and was ready by the door when he emerged.

"Come on, then," he said, opening the door onto a beige corridor which had not been decorated for many years. Kurt filled the morning with his voice, deep and strangely sincere.

"Trouble with life," he said, "is that it's shit. No matter what you've got, it's either too much or too little."

"Do you feel like that?" I asked.

"Look who I brought home last night," he said, shaking his head.

He handed me a helmet, unlocking a large black machine with too-shiny chrome. As the engine sprung into life I remembered the bike at the convention, belching out petrol fumes onto an adoring crowd.

"Is this a Harley?" I said.

"It is," he said, proudly dusting the already immaculate handle bars.

I clung onto his broad back as he kicked the bike into action, slipping past queuing traffic through the packed streets of Highgate. As we reached the A1, the bike roared and the houses stretched out, trees and gardens surrounding them. Kurt accelerated as the houses grew farther apart and the trees became the main feature of the landscape. I kept clinging until the bike pulled up outside a house with a drive and a selection of oak, ash and larch trees, providing welcome shade for the front of a Georgian farm house.

Kurt took off his helmet and unzipped one of the panniers, removing a travelling tattoo kit. Without a word, I followed him to the back door as he knocked and entered, calling out a name as he did.

"Joanie, I'm here. It's Kurt and a friend of Kurt's. Don't worry, she don't bite."

I followed him into a darkened room, heavy curtains still pulled against the burgeoning sun.

"Hey Joanie." He bent and lightly kissed the cheek of the woman who lay on the bed. She had no arms and stumps for legs, her face and body looking strangely large and ungainly as she smiled and said "Welcome. I'm Joanie and you are?"

"Jay," I said transfixed by her missing limbs.

"Birth defects," she said, "In case you were wondering. I'm not glamorous enough to have lost them in action in Afghanistan." She smiled. I looked away.

"So, Kurt," Joanie continued, "You've never brought anyone before." It was a question backed up by her expression.

"I found her in Highgate Cemetery at two in the morning. She's Dave's apprentice. She was copping out, going backwards."

"I was taking a nap," I said and the belly laugh which Joanie expelled was a force with which to be reckoned.

"I went to Highgate cemetery once to see the grave of Karl Marx," she said.

"Nice day out," said Kurt, setting up the tools of his trade on a pink table next to the bed.

"That's why I went," I said.

"Not a place to spend the night." Joanie raised her eyebrows. "Good job, Kurt." I watched and listened as they talked, two old friends with their own dialect; when Kurt brought out his tattoo machine I moved a little closer, careful not to nudge his arm as he checked the last piece he had done. Carefully, he removed the night dress which covered Joanie's modesty, folding it and placing it by her pillow with such tenderness that I wondered if they'd been lovers. Her large breasts flopped sideways, pooling on the plastic covered mattress.

Joanie was covered in Japanese patterns. Waves and koi and cherry blossoms travelled over shoulder and down breast; Hannya masks and more koi travelled up and down her spine, from neck to waist, where cherubs sprang, rejoicing in the spectacle. The colours popped out of her fair skin, aqua with crimson, gold and orange fish, conker tree trunks and shaded pink flowers. It was beautiful work, undoubtedly Kurt's, something I would have been immensely proud to display on my own body.

"You see," Joanie was saying, "My body is ugly and useless and I hate it, so I've turned it into something beautiful with the help of Kurt here. Don't you think?"

"I do," I said. "Very beautiful."

"And I want to go to a convention one day, when I'm finished, and people will look at me and

247

say what beautiful work and how sensitively done instead of turning away from me."

"You're beautiful, babe," said Kurt.

"Shut up," said Joanie, shuffling her bottom down the bed so that Kurt could reach the base of her spine and continue the decoration.

He worked for a couple of hours, the ticking of a distant clock the only sound to break the silence. And with the buzz of the machine, we journeyed to Mount Fuji, its magma bursting from its very top, surrounded by more cherry blossom trees. A crane stopped for a moment to catch the scene; Kurt drew its soul onto her delicate skin. And all the time the clock ticked and the machine buzzed and the morning sun grew hotter.

Joanie began to hum; Kurt put down his machine. "Had enough?" he asked.

"Yes. Thank you. That's enough for today."

He took the nightdress and carefully placed it over her head, covering the fresh ink with cling film before pulling the dress down and adjusting her collar.

"Shall I get the nurse?"

"Yes, thank you, Kurt. Same time next month?"

"Of course."

"With Jay?"

"Who knows?" said Kurt, packing his tubes and needles back in their carrying case. "We're all family now."

"Get a drink and some lunch before you go back," she called as I followed Kurt back into the cool, stone floored hallway.

The door Kurt opened led to a huge kitchen complete with fireplace, sofa and range. It was the most beautiful room I had ever seen, inviting and comfortable. It smelled of beeswax and sweet peas, a bunch of which had been placed in the middle of a large scrubbed-pine table.

I gasped.

Kurt turned, smiling. "Isn't it though?" he said. "I remember the first time I saw it. Thought I'd died and gone to heaven."

My jaw began to ache; closing my mouth I sat at one of the wooden chairs arranged around the table.

"Joanie had compensation. Very hard time, our Joanie's had. Won't bore you with the details but the family tried to get their hands on her compensation and somehow, they all ended up homeless and then Joanie had abusive foster parents. Well, you know the drill." I nodded.

"Anyway, she got her compensation. Bought this the day the money came through so no one can get their hands on it until she dies."

"Poor Joanie," I said.

"Poor Joanie, indeed. But she's happy now. Taking back control with her body art. Looks good though." This was a question.

"It's beautiful. The waves, the way they follow the curves of her body, accentuating the beauty in it. And the colours. I love the way you shade the pink flowers. And the wind, the way you leave bits out. Your Koi could be alive."

Kurt buried his face in his hands. I thought I heard him sniff and stared at a nick in the painted wall. After what seemed like hours, he lifted his head, blew his nose and gestured for me to sit up straight. Reaching over to the dresser, he rang a small, brass bell, placing it carefully back in the ring of dust from which it came.

Barely a minute later, an old woman pushed open the door, a floral pinnie over a floral frock.

"Mr Kurt. How lovely to see you."

"Doris, Joanie said you wanted to feed us."

"Well, of course I do. I'm a proper feeder." She winked at Kurt while raising an eyebrow in my direction.

"Meet Jay. She's an apprentice."

"Family?"

"Yes."

I saw the look which passed between them but couldn't interpret it and my attention was diverted as Doris began to dance around her kitchen the way I did at Heather's. And the enormity of running away felt like being punched in the gut. Remorse churned my stomach. I ran from the room, opening doors and retching until I found the right one, vomiting my guilt onto the white porcelain.

No one said a word when I reappeared, nor looked at me sideways. I ate the toast which had been placed on the table in front of me, sipping tea while Kurt ate more bacon and sausage and eggs and Doris chatted.

I listened to the litany of disasters that had followed Joanie and her strength shamed me. We were still talking about it an hour later as I climbed onto the back of his motor bike,

"Joanie became family then," he said. "We all need someone and if you ain't got someone, well, you know the drill."

"How could she have ended up on her own?" I asked.

"It happens, Jay. People are shit. Be grateful you got found, Jay. Know what I mean?"

"I do," I said.

Another hour and the Harley drew up outside Dave's studio. Dave, hearing the throb of the engine, rushed outside. He thumped Kurt on the back, thanked him and winked at me.

"Okay?" he said.

"Yes. I'm sorry."

"You weren't late for work so I've not got an issue with you. Heather's been here, though," he said. "You'd better go home and sort things out."

THE B&B WAS SILENT when I arrived. I crept to the shed, placing my rucksack under the camp bed, taking three deep breaths as Kurt had said to me to do when I felt overwhelmed. The sound of her snoring carried through to the kitchen and, as I knocked on the parlour door, I imagined Heather's face set in anger, her talon-like nails clenched and waiting. She snuffled. I knocked again.

"Jay?" The noise began high, like a wail, slowly getting louder as she hurried to the door. "Jay!" she said as she pulled me into her arms, weeping into my hair. "Jay."

"I'm sorry," I said.

"Oh, thank God you're all right. When I went to that tattoo place this morning, I couldn't believe it. Asleep in Highgate cemetery. What were you thinking?"

I connected the calls which must have been made about me; Kurt to Dave, Dave to Heather, Heather to…

"I'm just so glad you're safe," she said, pulling me to her once again her bosom enveloping my head. "And I'm sorry I got cross with you. It wasn't your fault."

Uncomfortable in her embrace, I said, "I'm sorry. I said I wouldn't let you down."

Heather took my hand, sat me down on the sofa and poured a tepid cup of tea. "Thing is," she said, "I see so much of myself in you. I assumed you'd want the same."

I sat in silence as her words washed over me and although I should have felt cleaned by them, they seemed to stick in the cracks and crevices of my skin.

"How did Dave find you?"

"It was the blue face man, Kurt; he found me."

"Well, the colour of his face isn't important today."

"He took me to meet a lady with no arms or legs who is having her whole body covered in tattoos because she wants to be beautiful." Heather stared, her mouth falling open so that her bottom dentures slipped.

"But the thing was," I said, "She was beautiful in a kind of way I hadn't seen before. Her body was ugly but she wasn't. Do you know what I mean?"

Heather nodded. "Some people are blessed with beautiful hearts." She hauled herself up out of the chair, turned on the teasmade and reached for a packet of chocolate biscuits. "That Dave isn't so bad. Was worried that I'd be upset with you."

"You should be."

"Well, maybe I should. But I told him, there and then on the phone, that he's been working you too hard and you shouldn't be pushed into things you don't want to do. He said he was sorry."

I doubted it. One of the dolls winked in my direction. Disinterested Highland cattle kept chewing. I still didn't know what to do.

"I was thinking about the room," I said, the words taking on a life of their own on my lips. Heather's hand closed around the biscuits, her shoulders suddenly still.

"Yes?" She tried to sound neutral.

"I was wondering if I could move in after all."

254

"Well, of course you can." She swung around, eyes flashing, feet dancing. "We can decorate," she said, "and you can choose new accessories, a light fitting, a lamp, maybe a new bedside table."

"Maybe just as it is to start with," I said.

"Of course, dear. When do you want to move?"

"I'll do it on Monday," I said.

ON THE MORNING OF MY appointment with Alma, I was sure I wouldn't go. The pork skin occupied my time, pushing the needle into it far enough to spread the colour evenly, not hard enough to damage it. It was cold from the fridge and I laid it on a plastic bag on my lap before beginning Baphomet from memory, his strange goat face peering out from the fat. It was easier than melon, less likely to roll and slip from latexed fingers, the sharp spike scratching the surface to reveal the hideous creature as if it emerged from within.

By lunchtime, I had convinced myself that Alma wasn't the clue to Beano, that my life would be better served concentrating on my artwork and the job at the B&B, forgetting everything that had happened. Moving on. I'd committed, after all. Baphomet's horns reached outwards and upwards towards an impartial sky, ready to be filled with wind and clouds, shading and intricate line work.

By tea time, my heart was racing and my hands shaking, the figure of Baphomet, now complete, shaded and sinister, his phallus huge, pointing towards the clouds I had drawn, no longer apathetic. A moon stared down benignly. I was in two minds.

By six, the B&B had faded and Dave's parlour was the last place I wanted to be. The lump of pork lay on the bench, taunting me with its clues. Washing the day's equipment, I checked the clock for the thousandth time, pinched my cheeks to make them look less pale and put the needles and ink neatly back into their box. My stomach shook as I shut the door, my voice barely audible as I called "goodnight" and scurried down the street for the bus.

Scaramouche was locked, the door bearing a sign which promised better luck tomorrow. I knocked and waited. A minute later I knocked again. Alma opened the door, a vision in pale blue, a dress so tight around her curves that I wondered how she could have zipped it up without help.

"You're early," she said.

"Only ten minutes," I said, following her through the door where a squirrel looked down from under a glass dome.

"Wait in there," Alma pointed to her work room where the black leather couch waited. I sat down, swinging my legs backwards and forwards, my trainer laces flying up and down.

At exactly seven o'clock, Alma entered, crimson lipstick on her perfect lips, the blue dress straining, resembling bondage.

"Take your T-shirt off," she said.

"Can I ask something?" I said.

"Later." She pulled the bottom hem of my top over my head so that my arms flailed and I felt like a child waiting to be washed with spit and a hanky on a grand day out. Throwing my T-shirt into the corner of the room, she touched my spine with freezing fingers, belying the heat in the tiny room which settled on my shoulders. My heart began its familiar percussion beat. She took a pen and began to draw on my back, her strokes hard and firm.

"What are you doing?" I asked.

"Making you beautiful," she said, moving my head forwards so that I couldn't see what she was doing. I succumbed to the strokes of her pen, sometimes caressing, often scratching as it flew across my skin.

"Don't you want my drawing?" I asked, the touch of the pen awakening the tension in my stomach and the longing in my knickers.

"Shut up!" she said and I did, concentrating my attention on the trainer laces which swung with my legs. "And keep still."

The silence enveloped me; Alma's breath came in short bursts. Somewhere, a clock ticked and the squirrel looked down on me from its glass dome. Minutes passed. The pen withdrew from my skin. I could hear Alma panting, her fingers reaffirming the lines she had drawn. I imagined the tree of life twisting up my spine, its leaves heavy with the weight of expectation. And then the light went out.

Alma kissed my neck, her tongue now tracing the lines of the pen. Unable to see, I turned my head to meet her, only to be pushed back so that she could trace her work with her fingers once again. My heart pounded and my breath bursting from pressured lungs. Her tongue traced the curve of my spine, her fingers dipping below the waistband of my jeans. I gasped. In the darkness, she pushed me backwards, laying me on the couch where she let her hair tickle the skin of my breasts before taking one in each hand, squeezing and sucking until I was breathless.

I accepted her advances, moving my body to meet hers, letting my tongue reach far into her mouth, digging short nails into the soft flesh of her arm. She moved me away, gently this time, but definitely, so that I lay on the couch and allowed the sensations in my body to rise and fall with her touch. When I came, her response was guttural. When she came, my heart soared and I squealed with pleasure. The blackness enveloped us both, heaving and sweating in the confined space.

It was over. Alma moved away. She turned on the light and before I had a chance to see it, rubbed the drawing off my back, with swift strokes, greasy yet firm. I asked why.

"It wasn't right," she said. She turned and my body knew she was about to leave me.

"Before you go," I said, braver with the sex serotonin racing around my body, "Can I ask you about the coat of arms on your ankle?"

She stopped, her blue eyes piercing mine. "Let yourself out," she said, disappearing into the one of the rooms beyond.

I couldn't move, didn't want to leave. The squirrel still staring judgementally. Somewhere, a door slammed and distant strains of music slipped under the closed door. I slid off the couch and dressed. It wasn't right. I knew it. My body, still convulsing from the orgasm, lied to me. It's fine, it said. She's just playing hard to get, but you'll get her. I shook the thought out of my head but it lingered in my groin. The T-shirt I pulled on stuck on clammy skin and, as I let myself out into sultry night, I left a note in the diary. "Jay, Thursday at seven ;)"

TUTANKHAMUN WASN'T SURPRISED. "I'm not surprised," he said the next day as I sat against the cool wall, staring into his empty sarcophagus.

"Not surprised about what?"

"Alma."

"That's not what I meant." I said. "I asked about her coat of arms tattoo but she asked me to leave."

"What are you gaining from this?"

"A relationship."

"It isn't a relationship. Relationships are give and take."

"I want her to…."

"What? Love you? Fall for you?"

"No! I'm only seeing Alma because of Beano."

"Lying to yourself is the greatest deceit."

"I'm not!" I shouted the words and several people turned to look.

"Jay, be honest,"

"I'm moving into the house on Monday," I said, changing the subject.

"Well, that's a lot better than the cemetery."

MONDAY MORNING BEGAN WITH a shower of rain which, rather than clearing the air, made it heavier. By the time I had my possessions packed into three large carrier bags, the sun had come out again, large drops of collected rain falling from the dying rhododendrons.

Heather, resplendent in a purple silk sari, the reason for which I didn't ask, directed proceedings from the hallway, ushering me up the narrow staircase into the room at the top. The bed was soft and springy under my bottom as I sat and piled the toiletries on my pillow. The lilac candlewick bedspread had come with me, covering the bedding completely with its scruffy fronds. I took the pictures of Beano and stuck them on the wall above the bed, standing back to show Beano how far I had come because of her. The graphite smile shone out of the paper, her eyes twinkling with delight.

"Are you done?" Heather's voice carried up the stairs. I peered around the corner, nodding as the rest of my body followed it.

"Good. Come in the parlour and we'll sort out the small print."

Down two flights of stairs I plodded, uncertain what Heather meant by small print. She met me by the door, a glass of something sparkling in her hand which she thrust towards me.

"You're not a closet alcoholic, are you?"

I shook my head and she handed me the glass, allowing the bubbles to pop on my tongue before I swallowed.

"It's only ten thirty," I said, raising my glass in her direction.

"But a day worth marking with a bit of bubbly, don't you think?"

"Thanks. I don't normally drink." We sat and sipped our Asti and as the alcohol slipped down, my mouth opened.

"It's a lovely room," I said, "With a great view. I love seeing the rooftops. It feels like flying."

"I started in that room. After the shed. But I was quicker to leave the shed. I like my creature comforts. They don't seem to bother you."

"No, not so much," I said, enjoying the relaxing of my grip on my tongue. "But I like to be dry and I need to sleep. I'm useless without sleep. The camp bed has been very comfortable."

"But it'll get cold out there soon. It's not so much fun when it's cold."

"I didn't think the summer would ever end."

Heather got up from her chair and pulled two accounting books from a shelf. She opened them, leafing through the pages until she found what she was looking for.

"I've been doing some calculations," she said, "And it would appear that revenue is up ten percent on last year, and that's with the disappearing labourers. And the Poles have got an extended contract until next year. They showed me."

"That's good. Were they discombobulated?" I smiled as Heather searched for an answer. "I've been teaching them words," I said. "Or at least, they find words and say them to me and I tell them what they mean and they're supposed to use them during the day. I doubt that they do but the word game is good."

"I wondered why they were shouting frangipani out of the window."

"Almond sponge."

"Exactly. As I was saying, the takings are up and the expenses are down because you do such a good job of the laundry. So, I'm giving you a rise." She waited, her head tilted to one side, a benevolent grin stretching her cerise lipstick.

"I don't need one," I said, the weight of gratitude pulling on my calves.

"You've earned one though. I'm going to give you one hundred pounds a week and your board; breakfast on the mornings you work and cereal on the ones you don't. You're responsible for everything else. I'm not going to charge you rent. But I'd like you to take over the gardening. Cut the lawn once a week and trim back the bits that grow too much. Can you do that?"

"I think so," I said, then, "It's a lot of money."

"Yes, it is, so make sure you earn it." She raised her glass again, her cheeks pink and cheerful.

I lifted my own, leaning across the coffee table to tap hers. "One more thing," she said, pulling at the purple silk, "You're on the night shift from now on. Anything that happens at night, I want noted down and brought to my attention. Any strange patterns of behaviour from any of our residents, anything unusual, you tell me. Okay?"

"Night shift. Do I have to stay awake?"

"No!" she laughed. "Just be aware of what's happening and who's in the house and, if they're new, take extra precautions and keep an ear out."

"Okay," I said. "I think I've committed."

"I think you have." Placing my empty glass on the table, I threw my arms around Heather who, surprised and delighted in equal measure, flung hers around my back.

"I'll do my best, then." I said.

My room was real, a safe haven and, unlike the shed, above everything that happened in the house. I was ready for it, surprised by it. Carpet felt expensive under my feet, the curtains thick and cosy in my hands. I pulled one across the window and the room darkened. There was a radiator, thick with dust, unused for several months, and a mirror. My reflection caught my attention, as long as it was since I'd chosen to look.

Green eyes peered out from under a fringe which had grown too quickly; freckles dotted my nose, proof of a good English summer. My chin was too sharp, my mouth too small for my liking but even I had to admit that I looked well. The hollows under my cheekbones had filled out exposing a heart-shaped face. I pinched my cheeks, cheap blusher. With a hundred pounds a week to spend, I could change myself every week if I wished, learn how to contour and airbrush and eyebrow and eye line like the women who came into Dave's studio. I could start saving up for my own tattoo machine and ink and black latex gloves.

Lying on the lilac candlewick, I wrote a list of all the things I would like to try before the winter came along; things which might make me more

266

attractive to Alma. "You're beautiful," she said. The fear settled in my stomach again. Or was it excitement? I wanted to see her again, to make her notice me and love me. Thursday loomed, a black mark on the horizon.

DAVE DIDN'T RECOGNISE me when I arrived for work the next day. My glamorous transformation at the hands of a sales assistant in the largest Boots I could find, rendered me even more invisible.

"You look pretty," he said when he realised it was me. "You look great, in fact, but you look like everyone else. You've lost a bit of you."

In the bathroom, I wiped away the contouring and the eyebrows leaving a black slick of eyeliner on my top lid. The black and white gingham shirt I had bought and tied at my waist, I undid, allowing the cotton to fall and billow around my slender hips. New jeans encased my legs, designer style rips in the knees above my very first pair of black Converse trainers.

"Love it," said Dave as I wandered past his studio. "That's very you." I smiled, glad to have pleased Dave with the bit of me he recognised and to have wiped off the thick pancake which hid me. Guy winked and ran his fingers along the waxed moustache. I smiled, fetched more pig skin from the fridge and began to draw.

"You need some ink on your skin," Dave called from the back room. "Has Alma started your back piece yet?"

"No," I shouted as his face appeared and his hair moved with the force of my breath.

"Perhaps when you've finished the pig skin, you could do some on your leg?"

"I've been thinking about that," I said.

"It'll need to be on your thigh. Design something. I'll help you place it. I reckon you're ready for the real thing and quite frankly, with the

German about to pop little Cash out, I could do with someone who can manage a few walk-ins."

"Not me, not yet," I said, reddening.

"Yes, you and yes, yet. You can practice forever and never be any good because you can't work on real people. You don't want that, do you?"

I shook my head and wished that people didn't see so much potential, wondering why people's kindness just felt like pressure.

"So, when you're ready, like tomorrow, draw a design for your thigh. Don't worry, I'll be there all the way." I thanked him and busied myself with an order of ink bottles which had just arrived. I rang Scaramouche and asked if Alma was free. She wasn't but she had booked me in. Relief flooded me, reddening the tip of my nose. The ink bottles flew onto shelves in colour order: red, purple, blue and green. I imagined them drifting into each other, held rigid by outlines drawn with real skill on the skin which covered my back.

Kurt opened the door and the moment was gone.

"Morning," he said, a crooked smile on his blue face.

"Morning," I replied.

"Got an offer from Joanie which you might be interested in. She said she'll be your first client."

"Really?" I said, genuinely taken aback.

"Yes. Said she'd like to support an emerging artist and you could design something small and Japanese for her left butt cheek. She hasn't got much room left." He laughed and handed me a piece of paper on which was written a brief and dimensions. "Butts are quite difficult so you need to get the hang of squishy skin before you do it." I nodded and thanked him.

"Don't thank me. It was Joanie's idea. Let me know when you're ready."

"I will," I said, picking up the ink machine and pig skin once again, inspired by a woman who was willing to give part of all she had.

"What have you been doing lately?" said Kurt.

"Drawing and cooking breakfasts mainly," I said. "But I did do this." Opening the fridge door, I took out the pork belly, waving Baphomet in front of Kurt's black eyes.

"Wow," he said. "Thought you were going Japanese."

"I am but this was on Beano."

He moved closer to look at the drawing without touching it. "It's very good," he said, "But I'd expect that from you. Shading's nice and the clouds are wicked. Proper Japanese! Like how you've left space here, for the wind to blow through. Nice work, Jay."

"Thanks."

"Looks like Joanie's arse is safe." He laughed, throaty and deep and the sound of it made my breastbone vibrate the way Alma did. He slipped past me, into Dave's office, leaving a space which Almas face filled, laughing and vibrating my chest as she kissed my neck.

HEATHER REMAINED IN a very good mood. The Polish labourers were delighted for me, giving me a bottle of Polish vodka as a moving in present. I placed it on the window sill of my new room, moving it an inch to the left and then to the right until it was in the perfect position with sunlight forcing through a facsimile onto the window sill. Birds roosted in the tree outside the window and a buddleia forced bloomed branches up into it, the flowers heavy with scent. The small sash windows groaned as I shoved them upwards and a butterfly landed on the sill, drying out its translucent wings before flying off again.

My pictures now covered the floral wallpaper, the tiny gaps becoming patterns in their own right. There were the ones of Beano in pride of place; fairies and butterflies and daggers dripping with blood surrounded them, with old school roses and swallows flying past.

In the en suite, toiletries filled the shower tray, the edge of the basin and the boxing around the pipes. Bottles of 'zingy', 'fresh', 'moisturising' and 'indulgent' soap in different colours reminded me of stained glass. I would worship here, under the clean, hot water that fell from the shower, worship Heather and give her thanks and praise.

That first night, as I tossed and turned on the sprung mattress, I dreamed of Beano. She sat under an arbour, dappled sunlight illuminating her illustrations, ethereal in white cheesecloth. An unfinished glass of Ricard rested in her hand, the cloudy liquid unmoving as she stared into nothing, serenity painted on her face. I tried to reach her, thrusting my hand towards hers but she disappeared as my hand struck the rucksack, nail file and tissue on the night stand. Sweat dripped between my breasts, sliding down my skin as Alma's tongue had done. I touched myself under my pyjamas, remembering, concentrating on every detail until I brought myself to climax.

Disgusted, I went to the shower room and ran cold water until all thoughts of one woman had gone, replaced by Beano, twiddling the dolphin earring in her ear. I felt it in my own ear, turning it once, twice, three times… "I'm sorry," I whispered into a crisp towel. "I get distracted."

"It's okay," her voice drifted with the steam. "You're on your way."

ALMA REMAINED EVERYTHING I thought about as I fried bacon, changed beds, walked to the studio and drew. I drew Alma at home, in private in my room with en suite. I drew her from memory, from life, tracing the parts of her I had only felt in the dark. The pictures found themselves on the walls by the bed, nestling under my pillow and piled on the chest of drawers. The rip on the side of her face revealed muscle and sinew and ligament; deeper, further still into her, I found hardness, biomechanical robotics moving her mouth, swivelling unblinking eyes. Sometimes I focused on her breasts and the octopus which resided there, tentacles reaching over her shoulder to stroke her back. I wanted to stroke her back. I wanted to call her up and tell her I loved her. But she was not available to me, not until seven on Thursday.

Sometimes I concentrated on her eyes, denim blue, the iris ringed with green, trying to see what was behind them as my pencil flew across the paper.

By Wednesday I was shaky with anticipation, my stomach flipping, and pirouetting, my skin clammy from the relentless heat and thoughts of her hands on me again. After work I walked to Camden, standing outside Scaramouche, imagining her hands working a needle into somebody else, someone who didn't need her or want her. Jealousy threatened to choke me. I knocked on the door and when there was no response, I tried the handle. The door opened and, as I stepped over the threshold, strains of jazz music floated from deep within. Closing the door behind me, I stepped towards the reception desk, turning the page until I found myself written in ink. "Jay" was all it said. Other names filled the book, Alice, James, Nicki and Valeria. Did she run her fingers over all of them? Did she blacken the room and feel her way across their bodies too?

The back door opened a crack.

"What are you doing here?" Alma said.

"The door was open."

"So you just decided to let yourself in?" It was less question, more accusation.

"I did. I wanted to see you," I said, voice faltering.

"You have an appointment tomorrow at seven. I've even left that slot open for you for the next few weeks."

"But…"

"But what? Isn't that enough? Why does everyone always want more?"

I didn't think I was everyone, and so I stood my ground, thinking of my drawings of her beauty which I couldn't see. "I'm sorry," I said, "I thought we were…"

"What? What did you think?" Her voice raised; the owl looked down from its glass dome and several mutant creatures shook in their jars.

Alma paced the small floor space, her pink converse trainers slapping against the tiles. She wore jeans and a checked shirt, out of which her breasts heaved.

"The problem with you is that you're needy," she was saying, expressionless from her place of judgement. "A couple of fumbles and you think we're an item, I suppose."

I fiddled with the dolphin earring, trying to remember why I had come here in the first place. "It"s more than that," I screamed. She stopped, her eyes widening as she recognised the passion in my soul.

"Your coat of arms…I've seen it before."

She stopped, hands on hips, a flicker of something I didn't understand dancing across her eyes. "Where?" she demanded.

"On someone else, a girl. I met her in a queue for soup."

"What did she look like?"

"Beautiful," I said. "Thin, blonde, blue eyed and beautiful. She was a beautiful person."

"Was?"

"Yes," I said, unsure how far to go, "Was."

Silence fell on us, a blanket of uneasiness. Alma turned the pages of her book back to where it should have been, moving pens into a pot and paper clips into a bowl. Her red nails were short, cut straight across the top, scraping at something on the desk.

"There's something about you," she said suddenly, "Something intriguing. You're cute too." Order was restored. Now she would take me through to her couch and turn off the light, scraping those red nails down my spine as I screamed in ecstasy. But she didn't. "Where was the girl with the tattoo?"

"On the street, like me. I gave her shelter and we would have been fine together but…" My voice trailed away once more. Alma nodded, a faint smirk on her lips.

Taking a deep breath, I asked, "The tattoo, the coat of arms like yours, why was it there? Does it have some significance?"

"I tattoo people all the time and you expect me to remember one girl."

"Because it's the same tattoo. Because you have the same one."

"Sometimes clients come in and point at my body and say, I want that, and I do it for them because it won't make any difference to my life."

"She had other tattoos, all over her body, weird, nasty, cruel-looking tattoos. They covered her, black and grey and threatening and horrible. Baphomet and demons and scuttling things and daggers and blood. I wanted to know who'd done them and why. I wanted to know all about her and why she was on the street, why she was in that queue for soup on the same day as me when neither of us wanted to be." The words flowed and I did nothing to stop them. "It seemed weird to have those designs all over your body and be ashamed of them. I thought it may be the reason she liked the heroin."

Alma's eyes flickered. I continued, "She was my best friend, we went to Tate Modern and looked at the lobster telephone and The Snail and even the bricks. She loved it. We ate at my favourite Italian and made a home in a railway arch. And then she was gone and I found the tattoos and told someone where she was so that she could be found and then I planted buddleia in different places around the City to remember her."

The check shirt heaved, rivulets of sweat running down between her breasts. "And she died?"

278

"An overdose. She didn't mean it. We had plans, you see. She just got high and didn't come down."

"What a waste of a life," Alma said, sitting on the stool by reception, pulling fluff off the ends of biros which had been huddled in a pot.

"I loved her. I know I hardly knew her. But I did love her. And then I saw your tattoo and I wondered if you could help me find out who she was."

"How can you love someone you don't know?"

I wanted to say, but I love you. My mouth remained still.

"I think it's possible," I whispered, then louder, "Can you remember seeing a tattoo like that?"

"I can't."

Alma's hand slammed the desk. "Thursday at seven," she said, standing and opening the front door.

"But…"

"I can't help with your weird obsession," she said, grabbing my hand as she pulled me towards the door. Her face peered down at mine.

"Thursday at seven," she said, the sound of a key in the lock punctuating the end of her sentence.

"I love you," I said to it before catching a bus back to Holloway.

"GREGARIOUS," THE POLISH LABOURERS said as I brought them their breakfast.

"What does it mean, though?" I asked.

"You," said one. "You're gregarious. You make laughter."

"You're the ones laughing!" I said.

"Gregarious Jay," said another.

"Good word. Say it to your boss today and he'll be very impressed." I blushed and left them to it, sweeping and hoovering the rooms in double time, hurling dirty laundry into the machine, leaving it to do its thing as I flew out of the door.

I bought a dress with a full skirt which swung when I spun, from a shop which specialised in modern vintage, and a pair of Converse trainers, navy with white laces that went with the navy polka dot dress. Scarlet lipstick found its way into my bag, expensive and decadent. In the Soho barber I was trimmed and gelled, smelling luxurious as I left for work at Dave's parlour.

I had decided to work on the design that Joanie would have on her butt cheek, small but beautiful, a butterfly on buddleia, the tiny purple flowers a perfect backdrop to the orange, shimmering wings. I worked because if I let my mind wander further, it was filled with Alma's perfume, her hair, her eyes and her heaving cleavage. The piercings on her face bore holes in my eyelids as I tried to shut them out. I had told her everything and she had not flinched. And it was true that she tattooed a lot of people in the city. Maybe she genuinely didn't know about the coat of arms. Maybe it was a coincidence.

When Guy spoke to me, I ignored him, not because I wanted to but because the vision of Alma filled every orifice, blocking my ears as I toiled on pig skin. The clock ticked. My mind drifted, sure that Alma had, at some point, met Beano and laid her hands on her skin, certain also that she hadn't. I was excited, eager to see the woman who I wanted to spend my life with, sure that together, we would solve the mystery of the girl who had brought me to her.

At six o'clock I slipped into the bathroom, stripped and washed under my arms before pulling on the navy dress. I spun, watching the cotton follow me like a Wurlitzer at a fairground, falling in feminine gathers around my waist. I tied the bright, white laces on the Converses and wiped a slick of red lipstick across my mouth before applying some mascara. Glancing in the mirror I saw a woman staring back, petite and pretty in polka dots. Maybe there had been a time when I had worn a dress before, but I couldn't remember it. It changed me, brought out the slight curves I had; it was a different me.

Guy wolf whistled as I left, shouting after me that he was a lucky man. I thought of Peter in the library and Heather who had said he was sweet on me, and Tutankhamun who had never seen me in a dress either and was bound to be mightily impressed.

I didn't need any of them now, not as I strode out with dainty feet to the person who made me feel like a woman.

The door to Scaramouche was locked when I arrived, perhaps because I had walked in the day before. I knocked, kicking stones on the pavement while I waited. I knocked again, peering through the window, blocking the light with a cupped hand. The lights weren't on and I could hear no music. I knocked, louder this time, so the door shook on its hinges as the bile rose in my throat. No one opened it. Running to the phone box, I rang Dave to see if any messages had been left for me. They hadn't. I sat on the window sill, rummaging in my rucksack for the nail file, scraping it across my fingers in an attempt to look undaunted.

Minutes passed. The door remained shut. I knocked again. Nothing. It was almost eight o'clock, an hour after my appointment time, twenty-four hours since I had seen her.

At nine o'clock I gave up, stomping my new shoes on the pavement up the Holloway Road. Tutankhamun was laughing in his sarcophagus and Peter waved sheets of book paper for me to blow my nose on. I ignored the images, my own tears blurring my eyes as I smeared red lipstick across my face with the snot, running through the gate at the B&B, around the corner, up the path to the shed which was no longer my home. In fury, I kicked the door, watching as the padlock broke and fell on my toe. I don't know who saw me take three stairs at a time up to my bedroom. I didn't care. Throwing myself on the bed I howled, a primal scream which came from the soles of my feet and didn't stop until it had hit the walls and bounced off them.

I don't know how long I cried. Woken by the alarm the next morning, body fluids caked my face, tightening the skin around my mouth. My navy dress was creased from sleep, the trainers still attached to aching feet. I had a bruise from the padlock which had fallen when I kicked the shed door and a pit of despair which filled my stomach, heavy as lead.

The shower cleaned me on the outside, pinking my skin, hot water needles massaging my shoulders. But inside, I stank of something familiar, a smell which crept up from inside and frightened me when I opened my mouth. Filth. I should have known a woman like Alma wouldn't be interested in someone like me.

The bacon caught in the frying pan and the toast burned. Heather nursed a migraine from the safety of her parlour, only popping her head out when the smoke alarm went off and the Polish workers cheered. Their word of the day was monogamy.

At the studio, my needle wouldn't do what I asked it to, jumping and lurching with designs of its own. I worked in silence, hardly acknowledging Guy whose customer was having a full back piece of the four horsemen of the apocalypse. I cried in the market when I went to fetch baguettes for us all. I cried in the bathroom when weeing and in the kitchen when boiling the kettle. I smeared the tears across my face with the back of my hand, clutching my rucksack close. The day struggled on; appointments were made. My hand hovered over the phone, Scaramouche's number indelibly written on my mind but resisted, the sound of her voice too much to bear.

As I locked up that night, the phone began to ring. I dropped the keys, shoved the door and ran in to answer it.

"Jay?"

"Yes?"

"Alma here. So sorry I wasn't there for our appointment. Something came up and I didn't have a number to let you know."

"It's fine," I lied, elated, ecstatic, overwhelmed.

"Well, that's nice of you. I can fit you in today instead. Seven?"

"Thank you, thank you," I said, hearing the desperation in my voice. "I won't be late."

"I'm sure you won't," she said. "The door will be unlocked. Come in and shout for me."

"I will. Thank you, Alma." The phone went click.

I would just have time to wash and iron my dress dry, fix my face and my mind before I went to her, washing away the fears I had as the bubbles swirled around the basin.

AS SHE HAD SAID, the door was open. I pushed it, noticing a sign which said Scaramouche would be closed for the weekend. Was she going away? I nodded to the owl and shimmied past the desk, through the beads.

The room was dark, the light creeping through from the front door casting strange shadows, draping everything in velvety blackness. A faint hum from the fridge where Alma kept her inks, intermittently interrupted the silence. I waited, breath stuck in my throat, listening for signs of her. Tension settled in the tendons which joined my body together, shaking them until the sound of my bones rattling drowned out the fridge. Putting my ear to the closed door at the end of corridor, I felt her presence behind it and knocked.

She opened it, a smile on her red lips revealing her perfect teeth. She wore black, the dress tight around her curves, covering her skin from neck to floor. A waft of musky scent followed her. I stared, words forming in my brain, vanishing by the time they had reached my throat.

"Come in," she said. "I'm all ready."

The door creaked open, gloom draping itself over a leather couch, a table and chair. There were more bottles lining the high shelves, foetuses of strange creatures, an audience for her art. It looked different this evening, sinister in the bluish light. She took my hand, leading me to the couch where she reached for the zip on the back of my dress.

"Why are you trying to look like me?" she asked, folding the blue polka dot cotton neatly before placing it over the back of the chair. I didn't answer.

287

"The problem with trying to be like someone else is that you lose who you are." Goose bumps covered the skin on my arms and back. "This is my look," she said, unlacing the Converse trainers, laying them on the chair next to the dress. "Mine. It goes with who I am, what I do. The pin-ups. My style."

She moved away, leaning against the counter, staring at me with wild eyes. The black fabric rustled, unpin-up like.

"I want to know about the girl you met," she said, moving again to sit on the folded dress and trainers. Her movements were jerky.

"You look beautiful today," my mouth said.

"I always look beautiful. I make sure of it." She picked up my shoe, stroked it and placed it back on the floor. The walls of the room closed in. I shuffled on my bottom, closer to the end of the couch.

"Are we starting my back piece?" I asked.

"Ah, the tree of life! A pretty idea but with no thought behind it. It doesn't say anything about you. What about your life experience?" Her voice was accusing. "The problem with people like you, is that you don't have a self. You have to steal from others. The girl you met, you stole the idea of tattoos from her. You stole her life to make something of your own. Didn't you?" The shrillness stabbed the sultry atmosphere.

"No. It wasn't like that."

"What was it like, then?" she stabbed a finger at me.

"I wanted to help her," I said, the rattling bones dancing once again.

"Help!" She stood again, hurling the trainers in the corner by the door. "She was dead. But you couldn't leave it alone. Poking around in other people's business." Her voice was harsh, tiny beads of spittle flying from it. Any vestige of a smile had disappeared.

"I felt guilty."

"Guilty? Why would a pathetic street urchin feel guilty?"

"Because she died celebrating; celebrating a lie I told her about having a plan to get off the streets." The scream which accompanied the words belonged to me. I bent over, hugging my knees. "She died because I told her we could have a better life. I owed her."

Alma laughed, deep and dangerous.

"Turn the light on," I demanded, the darkness enveloping, changing perceptions until I was in a jar on the shelf watching a two-headed lizard lounge on the black leather couch.

"Light is irrelevant," she said and the silk of her dress swished as she moved backwards and forwards, collecting ink and machines and Vaseline. "I'll do the outline now. Take off your bra."

"No," I said. "I don't want a tattoo. I don't want you to touch me. I want to know why you said I stole the idea of tattoos from her. Did you know her?"

She loomed over me and the perfume was no longer alluring but caught at the back of my throat. I shuddered, my skin prickling with anticipation and dread.

"What was her name?"

Her voice had softened again.

"Beano."

"That's not a name."

"It's what she called herself."

"What was she wearing?"

"Jeans, a T-shirt and a sweatshirt and a parka. She never took the parka off, wrapped it around her like a security blanket, which I suppose it was." A picture Beano flickered in my third eye, as delicate as a butterfly wing, just as fleeting. "She was a beautiful person," I said.

Alma snorted. "What did she tell you about her life?" The tattoo machine started up, droning like so many bees around a hive.

"Nothing. It was the tattoos. If she hadn't had the tattoos I wouldn't have known where to start."

A needle pierced the flesh on my back without warning; I flinched.

"Get off me!" My hand flew backwards making contact with the metal.

"Shut up and do as you're told." She caught my hand, bending it backwards, the muscles tearing as she pulled.

"You want to play like a grown up but you can't do it, can you?" she spat.

"What have I done?" I said, trying to turn and see her face.

She sneered, her lip curling as she held my gaze. "What have you done? What have you done?" Her voice screeched the last 'done'. She pushed my head away and the needle dragged down my spine, vibrating through to internal organs which shook like jelly. I screamed but her free hand gagged my mouth with latex-covered fingers.

The machine stopped. She let me go, walking to the door which she closed, placing the key down the top of her dress. She stood facing me. "Do you know what happens to the snivelling, whining, and pathetic? Girls who hang their heads because someone's been nasty. Beautiful, young, pathetic victims of life?" Her top lip curled. "Do you?" I felt her breath on my face. I couldn't answer.

"They get punished," she said, placing her hands on her hips as she spoke. "The checkerboard dick, the bees, Baphomet, death skulls and daggers. They're mine."

I swallowed.

"I made Kurt what he is today. I gave him everything he has. It started with his dick which he couldn't control. He said getting a woman was like playing chess so I gave him a chessboard dick. And Kurt took my gift. He took it and made something of himself because of it." She strutted, proud of her achievement. "Before that he was nothing. Nothing!"

I wanted to run, back to the railway arch and the brave buddleia, nestling into a rat-infested dungeon of my own. "You did Beano," I whispered.

"Did I?" The machine jolted into life. I flew from the couch, twisting the handle of the door I knew was locked.

"Want to know about her?" Alma lurched into the corner with me, her breath blasting the

291

back of my neck. "Want to know about Ivy the Terrible, do you?"

"Who?" I said, searching the walls for another means of escape.

"Ivy the Terrible. That's what I called her. The nurse in the hospital where she was born said she was so beautiful she should be called Helen, Helen of Troy. Call her Helen, they said, and took her off round the maternity ward to show her off, leaving me deflated and bleeding on the delivery table, the fat wobbly stomach where she had been, rippling. Didn't even ask how I was!" Alma's eyes rolled almost into the back of her head; spittle formed in the corners of her mouth. "Helen of fucking Troy! So, I called her Ivy the Terrible, from the Beano, but you'd have worked that out by now, wouldn't you? And I put a Hannya mask on her as soon as I could, the evil eye watching over her, I said, watching to make sure she didn't step out of line."

"You're a real bitch, aren't you?" I said, my teeth grinding.

"Oh, a bit of life left in you, is there?"

She grabbed my arms, twisting them behind my back. A cable tie secured them and my ankles. She threw me, face down on the couch, straddling me, slapping my back repeatedly with the palms of her gloved hands.

"Let me go," I whispered. "Dave knows I'm here."

"Actually, I rang Dave, asked him if he had a mobile for you. Said I had to cancel our appointment."

I couldn't move, my body weighted down by hers, my head searching pointlessly for an escape route. My rucksack was on the floor, the nail file nestled in its folds. With enormous effort, I jerked my body upwards hoping to knock her off and reach it. But as she pitched upwards, the cable ties wrenched into my ankles and she thumped back down on my spine so I screamed in pain.

"You are a feisty one," she said. "More fun, but…" She pushed my face onto the couch, turning it to one side, took a belt from a drawer and strapped my neck to it. My hands behind my back, I was prey. I watched as she took two olive green pills from a tin on the side, crushing it with the end of a wooden spoon, stirring it into water before holding it to my lips. I clamped my mouth shut.

"You can drink it or I'll inject it. It makes no difference to me."

"What is it?"

"Something to help."

"Help what?" I struggled against the plastic ties, heart racing, stomach lurching.

"Me," she whispered leaning in to the side of my face.

"What are you going to do?" I asked, not wanting the answer.

Filling a plunger with the olive-green liquid, she forced it into my mouth, finding the one gap where a tooth should have been. The bitterness hit the back of my throat; I tried to spit but swallowed instead.

"What is it?" I spluttered.

"Roofies. You'll feel drunk soon and you won't care. It's kinder for you this way." She stroked a wisp of hair from my eye, the tenderness striking me like a burning poker. "They call it the date rape drug because you won't remember a thing."

Finding the gap in my mouth once again, Alma squeezed the remainder of the liquid down the back of my throat. I coughed but it didn't come back. I couldn't get out. I couldn't run away. The weight of resignation crushed my chest.

"Are you going to rape me?"

She laughed. "Why would I want to do that when you give yourself so easily? I can take what I want *with* your consent. I could probably tattoo you with your consent but then it wouldn't be as much fun, would it? I want you to know what I'm doing. I want to tell you how it makes me feel to mark your body for life without your consent, how the orgasm is like nothing you could ever make me achieve. I want you to know how it gives me power, strength and gratification. I want you to know. It's not the ugly images that will cover your body that's your torture, Jay; it's knowing that I could never love you, that I don't care what happens to you after this. You won't remember, but you'll know while it's happening."

She moaned, touching her breasts with black latex covered hands before continuing. "And what you choose to do with what I've done to you is up to you. Live or die, take drugs and go back on the streets or turn yourself into Boadicea. It's your choice."

"I'll go to the police."

"And say what? You won't remember what happened. And do you really think the police are interested in people like you? You're nothing, like Ivy."

Alma relaxed, kicking off her heels, rubbing her toes. "It'll take twenty minutes or so. Would you like a drink?"

I shook my head, watching as her shoulders lowered and she caught a strand of red hair, placing it behind her ear. I had frozen, unable to fight or run.

"It's just my body," my mind reassured me. "I can buy a parka."

SMALL TALK FILLED the silence. Alma told me about the girl who made her dresses, a girl who had two degrees from top art colleges and who came to her for a pin up on her thigh. With Alma's help she had started a business and was doing well but never made in bulk the dresses she made for Alma. "I'm unique," she said, straightening the black silk over her round stomach. "Beautiful, one of a kind."

The room began to swim, pictures of dresses flickering before my eyes. I imagined Alma in skinny jeans and a hoodie, walking to a supermarket to do the weekly shop, Beano in tow, hanging on to a trolley. At the sliding door entry to the superstore, Tutankhamun stood handing out baskets, his golden death mask glinting in the last of the day's sun.

Alma released the cable ties just enough to turn me over on the couch; the bottles and jars danced, synchronised in slow motion, mutant disco. With no control over my limbs my hearing expanded; a clock ticked in the hall; a rat scurried in the rafters. Alma breathed, touching me as she pulled my knickers over my knees, shaving my pubic hair deftly and smoothly.

"Are you ready?" she asked. I couldn't reply. She turned me again, face down, twisting my neck so that I could breathe. The machine started up, whining as she tested the ink flow, her black dress and gloves witch-like in the half light from several thick, red candles she had lit.

I felt the needle pierce my skin at the nape of my neck, the sensation muffled by the drug now pulsing around my blood stream. Somewhere, a phone rang twice before the click of the answerphone halted it. She leaned over me, stretching my skin as the needle pressed into it. I followed its course in my mind, attempting to join the dots into something I could recognise, something beautiful, exquisitely drawn. The room spun, my dizziness and nausea taking precedence over the needle as it faded into background noise.

Alma stopped. Silence enveloped me, wrapping me in its peace. Before long, a smell I recognised but couldn't place, permeated the room. And I was in the railway arch, lying next to Beano, silver foil littered around the mattress. Heroin. She moaned, taking several deep breaths, speaking softly to the mutants as she returned to my spine, slower and more definite now, the black latex pulling at the surface of my body as she worked.

Time passed. A clock ticked. My rucksack on the floor by the door called out to me, the nail file a weapon of release. But I couldn't lift an arm to reach it and it backed off into the shadows.

"How did she get back to London?" Alma asked me, slapping my face to make me listen. I spoke words which slurred and ran into each other rendering them useless. Beano had taken heroin and drifted high above the railway arch; Alma took it and asked questions. They came quickly; "What was she doing? Why was she here, so close to me again? Why did she cover her art and not celebrate it?" I had no answers. My eyes closed. And before long, I was floating on clouds with Beano at my side, Tutankhamun holding a huge arrow-shaped neon sign which said, "THIS WAY."

BREAKFAST ARRIVED, TWO BOWLS of gloopy porridge with raisins. I could sit now, the pain from the illustrations on my back which I couldn't see, raw and sharp. I took the bowl which was handed to me but, without the benefit of motor skills, eating it was impossible. My head throbbed, dry mouth gasping for water. Alma handed me a glass which I spilled down my breasts, managing to pour a quarter of the glass down my throat which spasmed in gratitude.

"Take this," Alma said. I recognised the olive-green liquid, pushing it away with flailing arms. She persisted, tipping back my head until she could pour it into my mouth. I coughed, choking on the sludge which coated my teeth. The mutant audience looked down on me, uncaring. More porridge was shovelled into my gaping mouth, the grey gloop tightening on my lips. It must have been hours. What had happened? Beano's Mother, the witch with the needle.

Alma laid a hand on my chest, pushing me backwards onto the couch. My back burned, sticking on the leather as she pushed me further up. Smudged lipstick distorted her face, the red hair pulled back into a tight pony tail. I could see inside her face, past sinew and ligament into the hard metal beyond. She had taken off the black dress, now wearing a black shirt and jeans which were too tight, forcing her belly over the top, a fountain of flesh.

Devoid of emotion, her eyes took in every inch of my body, a pen marking the places where her design would come together. I noticed fillings

299

in her teeth, dark and sinister in the back of her mouth; nostril hair escaping from their cavernous home; bloodshot eyes, the intensity of their gaze muted by heroin which I could smell again.

She bit my nipple, taking it in her fingers as she twiddled, opening the zip on her jeans. Straddling me, she thrust her hand down into the black denim, moving fingers and body in rhythmic motions across my pubic bone. She came suddenly and violently, throwing her head back as she moaned. As the room disappeared and the dizziness took over, Alma dismounted as if from a horse, pulling up her zip, arranging her escaping flesh over the top of the waistband.

The whine of the machine started up again. The pain from my back, burned. I closed my eyes, a rabbit no longer frozen in the headlights, complicit in my torture.

Searing pain from my left breast stirred me. I moved my eyes to see what had happened but they couldn't follow the pain, taking their own route to Alma's face, contorted in an angry frenzy of shading across my nipple. My arm twitched; she stopped, staring into my eyes, my pain her drug of choice. Laughing, she swigged beer from a bottle, pouring a little into my mouth. I choked, throat pulsing before losing myself in the great beyond once more.

Buddleia pushed through the roof, opening it to the heavens where Beano held out her hand for me to grab. A pink and blue neon sign lay on the floor beneath her feet, broken and unwanted. I watched as she shook a pillow case releasing a thousand feathers into the air. They landed on my head, my shoulders and breasts, coating my agonizing skin with softness. Alma cackled. Beano disappeared. Darkness enclosed me again. Time passed. A clock ticked. The pain moved down from my breasts to my stomach, down, down until she was parting the lips of my vagina and the needle stabbed me back into consciousness.

I made a noise in my throat. Alma stopped, reached up and slapped my face before resuming her position between my legs.

"Like me down here, don't you?" she said.

The needle scratched; Alma taunted; I prayed for death, swift and kind, to join my Tutankhamun in the space between worlds.

ALMA WAS SINGING. I heard her voice, gruff and coarse, attempting to follow a tune I had heard before. A light in the corner of the room indicated an iPod. Ella Fitzgerald held the notes perfectly, sliding them up and down with ease. I blinked and groaned. She stopped singing. The skin on my body sizzled and screamed, blood dripping from my chest down, down towards the black leather.

"Little bitch," Alma said. "Pretty little bitch. Poking about where you're not wanted." She stood, looming over my face, the black lace of her bra stretching as her breasts fell forwards. "She was *my* daughter, mine. And you killed her." She slapped my face and the sharpness of it focused my mind.

What had she said?

In and out of consciousness I fell, each bout of awareness allowing me to concentrate on her words, storing them somewhere for later. She said I wouldn't remember. I would make sure that I did. Like Hansel and Gretel, I would leave breadcrumbs for my mind to follow. Beano's face and Alma's merged, their features similar, Alma's hard, Beano's soft with sweetness and suffering. Their eyes, noses, chins and cheeks transposed until they became one. Beano's Mother and torturer.

"Ruined my figure," she was ranting, "Possessed not one iota of gratitude. Trouble from the day she was born. Helen of fucking Troy! A whining, snivelling child, not the child I should have had."

I filed the words somewhere in a chest in my head. I could see the chest, full of drawers, each one containing something I could open later.

The needle touched my thigh; her head bent over my skin and the droning and scratching and stinging took me with them, higher and higher into the nothing beyond.

TUTANKHAMUN WAS WAITING FOR me. He held out a manicured hand, pulling me into an embrace. "Don't give up," he whispered. I stayed with him for a moment, the whiteness a warm blanket around me, caressing where the burning needles had torn my flesh. I heard bird song and a tiny white feather fluttered before me, followed by an iridescent butterfly, its antennae bejewelled with sparkling blue eyes. And then I was falling, through the earth to a black cavern deep beneath, fighting for breath in the cloying heat.

SOMEWHERE IN THE CITY, a siren whined. My body was being moved, shoved and manipulated out of the blackened room. Light from a waning moon illuminated a yard, high walls and large bins decorating the area. A car seat rose to meet my face, my legs bent and pushed until I fit in the confined space. An engine started, the radio declaring the latest number one in the charts. Air rushed past my ears, the sounds of an awakening city flooding through the opened windows. My hands and feet still tied, I wriggled into a position where I didn't feel the thump of pot-holes in the road, taking in as many sounds as I could, storing them in the chest of drawers.

We drove for hours, the lull of the engine soothing and ordinary after the black cell. City smells were replaced by fresh grass, dampened by the relentless rain which accompanied us on our journey. I detected a motorway, straight lines of endless acceleration, speeding towards a destination I couldn't imagine. Tutankhamun tutted and tears streaked Beano's face. A butterfly hit the window, splattering itself across the glass.

"Gregarious," I said, testing my mouth. It didn't sound right. Lifting my head very slightly, I could see Alma in silhouette, her red hair flowing in the blast from her open window. Pushing a button on the dashboard, she changed the radio channel and the serious tones of a newsreader reminded me of the world from which I came.

It was Monday morning, the news at four o'clock telling of possible attacks by insurgents during the summer of sport. The sun rose, shining through the car windows, drying the road, silencing the splashes.

Abruptly, the car pulled off tarmac, the bumps and craters in the road shaking my naked body as I lay on the back seat. I hung on to the edge of the seat as we jolted over uneven ground. Birdsong punctuated the silence, a call to feed their young. From my position on the back seat, I saw only sky.

Finally, the engine stopped and Alma got out of the car. Her door slammed and all was quiet. I tried to pull myself up, to become human again and walk, talk, think, but these skills were still beyond me. Flopping back on the seat, I waited, noticing congealed blood and the beginning of scabs on my arms, legs, stomach and chest.

A moment later, the back door of the car opened and Alma grabbed my arm, pulling me out onto dew covered grass. She hauled me away from the car, puffing and panting as my skin grazed the ground beneath me, not stopping until she had pulled me down a slope, hidden from the car. Fumbling in a bag, she pulled out a syringe and some of the brown powder, mixing it with water and something else, holding a spoon over her clipper lighter to complete the task. Once cooked, she drew the liquid up into a syringe, took a cable tie from her pocket and placed it on my right arm, pulling it tightly until it throbbed. Taking my hand, she manipulated my fingers around the syringe, holding them tightly within her own. As the needle punctured my skin, she squeezed my hand and in that movement, I administered my own fate.

"I hope you die," she said, dropping my arm. "If not from shock, from heroin." Alma leaned over me, spit dripping off her chin egging me on. "Die and it'll all be over."

She walked away and I thought I heard the car engine start and a door slam and birds somewhere above. And then I was floating, higher than the clouds, higher than Tutankhamun and Beano, waving to them as I went, a feeling of peace and contentment flooding everything I was. Onwards and upwards I went, leaving the earth behind, riding a white wave of knowing, understanding everything and nothing at the same time. Simple happiness engulfed me. I was happy that I had met Alma and could see the beauty in the smile lines around her eyes. I was happy that Beano had died this way, leaving the grot behind. I was happy to be lying on dew-covered grass somewhere out in the beautiful world where trees and grass and heather didn't judge you and birds landed on your arm to sing a song, happy that the breath moving round my body was mine to control. I could stop it at any time.

A sandaled toe touched the side of my face, a fine dusting of sand covering my skin. "The thing is," he said. "You'll always have an opportunity to give up. You can breathe or not." Tutankhamun sat down next to me, drawing symbols in the sand between us.

"What if I don't want to make that decision today?" I thought and he heard me.

"It's up to you, as always." He scratched his smooth chin with a long, slender finger, turning his face away from me.

The warmth of the sun touched my body as Tutankhamun stroked the back of my neck and goose bumps travelled from that place down my spine and along my limbs until I tingled. The sand was soft and fine, slipping through my fingers, "Am I in an hour glass?"

"You could explain it that way. Or you could say that you're "in between". Time has stopped." He stared past my face to something I couldn't see. "We're waiting for your decision."

"What decision is that?"

"To breathe or not to breathe."

I turned and followed his gaze. In the distance, Heather waved a green clad arm, her blue, iridescent nails catching the sun. Dave stood next to her, a slab of pig skin in his hand; Kurt and Joanie were there too, and Beano. She stepped forward, her blonde hair billowing around her face. She was dressed in her parka, wrapped, as usual, tight around her body. Stopping for a moment, she looked at me and walked forward, unzipping the khaki coat as she did so.

"I forgive you," she said.

I blinked and they had gone, Tutankhamun filling the space where they had been, white robes rustling in the breeze. He held out his hand becoming a silhouette against the white light.

"Breathe or don't breathe," he said. "It's up to you."

THE BOOT MADE A sound like squelching as it crushed the mossy ground next to my face. I moved my hand an inch.

"She's alive."

The boot was joined by another and another and then a knee as someone crouched down and looked into my eyes. "Call 999." A hand reached my hair, stroking the top of my head in gentle, short movements. "You're going to be okay," a voice said. Someone threw a coat over me and the weight of it pushed me down into the earth.

A crack of thunder pierced the atmosphere and rain drops fell.

"What's your name?"

"Jay,"

"Have you fallen? Could anything be broken?"

"No."

"Can you remember what happened?"

I searched my mind for something which I knew but couldn't find. "No," I said, closing my eyes.

"Stay with us," a woman's voice said. She sat down next to me, touching my face with a slender finger. I noticed her hair, auburn and bouncy, as she took my hand and massaged my fingers.

"How did you get all the way out here?" she said.

I didn't know. "Where am I?"

"Ilkley Moor."

"Where's that?" I mumbled but the words didn't sound as I had intended them to.

"Don't try and speak. We've called an ambulance. They should be here soon. I'm not going to leave you. Are you cold?"

I shivered. The bouncy-haired woman placed another coat over me and the weight of it pushed me further into the mossy earth. Words, sounds and images flickered in front of my eyes, in and out of shadows. Sometimes I was aware of several people in boots, carrying plastic covered maps, talking about me as the rain fell on my aching body. Sometimes, it was the rain itself, engulfing me in its soothing coolness.

And then people in green, reassuring me as they moved my body onto something hard and shiny. A woman removed the coats which had pushed me into the earth, replacing them with a blue blanket which caught on my scabbing skin. I was moving, picked up by able hands, carried to a waiting ambulance, and as the doors closed, so did my eyes.

"A good choice," Tutankhamun whispered into my ear. He hadn't left, but hovered in a corner of the ambulance as the engine turned over and the bumpy, mossy earth flattened under the wheels. Motionless he smiled at me.

Minutes later, the engine stopped and the doors opened. Faces loomed towards me, pulling the stretcher bed out of the vehicle, running down corridors towards plastic doors which warped as we pushed through.

"Possible overdose," I heard. "And multiple abrasions and trauma to the skin caused by tattooing. I've never seen anything like it." Something beeped and lights flashed overhead.

Someone put an IV in my hand, wheeling me away to a room where the only sound was the continuous beep of machinery. I closed my eyes, uninterested in the efforts they were taking to keep me from falling into unconsciousness again.

Something hit my blood stream, a wakening wave of energy forcing its way down veins and along arteries, forcing my eyelids open. Two nurses smiled benignly.

"Hello," one of them said. "How are you feeling?"

"I...don't...know," I said.

"The police are waiting to talk to you. Are you up to it?"

"No," I said.

"You can have a bit more time. We've given you Naloxone which has reversed the heroin overdose you took. Are you a regular user? We couldn't find tracks."

"No. I don't do drugs," I said, fumbling for some kind of recollection to explain my situation.

"They're waiting outside. I'll tell them you need another hour. It's up to them if they wait or come back."

They waited. A slow crime day on the Yorkshire moors allowed it. When the nurse let them in, even their booted footsteps couldn't drown out the pounding of my heart. A female PC stood by the bed, a notebook in her hand.

"Can you remember what led up to you being found naked on the moor with a syringe containing heroin in your arm?"

"No. I don't remember."

"We're waiting for the results of your blood tests to tell us what else may have been in your system. Can you help us with that at all?"

"No. I don't drink or do drugs."

"You did today."

I swallowed, the spasm sticking in my dry throat. The policewoman passed me a glass of water.

"Did you arrange to have these tattoos done all in one go?"

"What tattoos?" Her eyes raised towards her partner, a man staring down at my shoulders and arms which were outside the sheets and blankets piled up on the sweaty, plastic-covered mattress.

I looked down. A huge spider crawled up from my left elbow, its hairy legs poised in the direction of my throat. I screamed, frantically trying to brush it away. It didn't move. My eyes travelled further, down my arms which were covered in bugs; beetles, more spiders, ants and slugs crawled across my skin. Carefully, I lifted the blanket. From neck to ankle my body had disappeared, replaced by a menagerie of creatures, all crawling up towards my face. On my chest, a huge goat's head with horns and red eyes, straddled my breasts, a raven balancing on one horn, an anatomical heart drawn over mine, a dagger piercing its centre. Blood dripped down, red and vivid, down onto my hip where it settled in a puddle and something hideous was born from it, reaching out a clawed hand.

"Where are you from?"

"London."

"What's your name?"

"Jay."

"Jay what?"

"I don't remember."

"How did you get onto the moor?"

"I don't know."

"Did someone drive you?"

"Maybe. I can't remember."

"Did you want these tattoos?"

"No!" I forced the images back under the blanket, choosing not to believe they were there.

A curtain twitched; a nurse entered and shushed. The police moved away and whispered, turning to look at me several times so that I knew they were talking about me. I hauled myself up into a sitting position, the drug working its magic as I regained control over myself.

"Heroin and rohypnol. That's all." The nurse said. "No sign of habitual heroin use or any other kind of drug."

"Could this have been done to her rather than her doing it?"

"It's possible. I can't imagine anyone choosing to have their whole body tattooed in one go."

"People are weird. We get to see a lot in this line of work."

"So do we," said the nurse, "But I've never seen this before. We're mainly concerned about sepsis. The trauma covers her body and she's swollen and showing early signs of a fever. Over eighty per cent of her body is tattooed. No one would ask for that, would they?" She shook her head and glanced over her shoulder. "You can have another few minutes. Then we need to have a look at what's happening because of the tattoos."

They turned and approached the bed again, their words fading into the percussion of beeping.

"Can you remember if someone gave you a drink? Were you out? In a club? In a pub?"

My mind fought the chaos which filled it. "I don't remember," I said. "But I know something happened. It's in my head but I can't get it out."

"Don't worry," the policewoman said. "We'll come back in a day or two and see how you're getting on." I watched as they wrote in their notebooks and put on their hats, leaving as they had arrived, noisily with heavy footsteps.

THE DICTIONARY SAYS - "Sepsis - the presence in tissues of harmful bacteria and their toxins, typically through infection of a wound."

Wikipedia says - "Sepsis is a life-threatening condition that arises when the body's response to infection injures its own tissues and organs. [1] Common signs and symptoms include fever, increased heart rate, increased breathing rate, and confusion.

I say – Sepsis makes you mad. Sepsis makes you wish you were dead. Sepsis is cruel; it gets into your head, wrecking your powers of rational thinking. It makes you stupid and weak and crazy and very, very sick.

I started seeing the images as soon as they moved me into intensive care. Tubes reached from my body to bags with liquids to keep me alive. My entire body swelled and reddened, stretching the skin on the backs of my hands until I couldn't recognise myself. My eyes closed, unresponsive to the outside world. A branch of buddleia reached in through the fourth-floor window, stretching towards my neck where it curled and wrapped around my wind pipe until it snapped. I gasped for air. A nurse approached, a fire extinguisher in her hand, beating back the rampaging plant and my own head which was in the way. I watched my brain splatter against the wall. The nurse laughed, calling a porter who arrived in tap shoes, tap, tap, tapping across the shiny floor. He twirled an umbrella and turned a cartwheel. And then he was gone and I was left scraping bits of myself off walls, collecting them in a crash helmet before stirring them into some semblance of order in my head.

The spiders and insects crawled up my legs, entering my body through a slack-jawed mouth, panting for breath as they filled my throat, down into my stomach, scratching and scrabbling at my internal organs which whined and strained under their burgeoning weight. I screamed and three nurses ran into the room, restraining my body which spasmed as the intruders marched their way through veins which stretched the length and breadth of my body.

Giant scorpions in Roman centurion order, marched towards me waving their pincers, tails bobbing up and down as they came. I hid under the blanket, one eye keeping guard as the scorpions surrounded the bed, backed up by ants who crawled over each other's backs to get a better view. The fear sent me back under the covers, my hands covering my ears from their incessant clicking. Machinery beeped and nurses clucked. A doctor in a white coat, stripped down to his underwear and danced the cha-cha with my notes, swinging his hips suggestively. Alma laughed in the corner, swathed in black chiffon which billowed out with each breath. Beano pointed an accusing finger, growing and growing until her head hit the ceiling and she burst into a thousand iridescent butterflies. I fought the demons in my veins. The swelling went down a bit. The pressure in my head eased too. The monkey who had sat on the curtain rail for several days, waved before jumping off the window sill into the great beyond. Alma shrank into the chiffon until there was nothing but a pile of ash on the floor, swept under the Axminster carpet by a woman with curlers in her hair. The creatures retreated to their positions on my body, twitching and stretching until they were comfortable in their resting place. A strange peace settled over me. I slept.

I WAS LUCKY, THEY said, very lucky. White coated men and women with clip boards and equipment to measure my heart beats and rhythms, all said it. The nurses who fed me and gave me water said so. Even the Nigerian cleaner who came in the dead of night, said so.

The psych nurse agreed.

"You've been very lucky," she said. "How did you come to be there, out alone on the moor?"

I recalled nothing. I told her.

"Did someone bring you here?"

"I don't know," I said, a picture of Alma's straining breasts as she hauled me out of the car flashing through my mind. Her pierced bottom lip studded the muddled picture.

"Rohypnol can make it hard to remember but the memories are there, still inside your mind. You just may never get them back."

"Breadcrumbs," I said.

"Excuse me?" the nurse asked.

I closed my eyes. "I don't remember," I said, mentally fighting back Alma's hands as she drew her nightmare on my skin.

"I'd like to help with your heroin addiction."

"I don't have one."

"You had heroin in your body."

"I didn't put it there."

"You know that the police want to interview you now you're out of IC?"

"They came before…"

"They did. They want to know who did this to you. They think you know something and you're not telling them."

"I don't remember anything."

"I know. I have told them the effects of Rohypnol. I'll be back tomorrow. If you can remember anything at all, no matter how insignificant it may feel, tell us. It might help them to find out who did this to you."

I looked away as she stood to leave, down on my arms which dripped with tattooed blood from drawn gashes, maggots and flies fleeing the carnage.

Looking for my rucksack, I remembered seeing it by the door in the studio and cried for my loss; the mother-of-pearl handle nail file, my only treasure. And the polka dot dress, worn once, folded neatly on the back of the chair. Breadcrumbs.

When the psych nurse arrived the next morning, she found me broken, rocking as I held my knees. She wanted to help, she said, but I had nothing left to give her. She brought the police with her, their notebooks poised, but I told them nothing.

"Who did this to you?" they said. "It's abuse of a most serious kind, ABH, attempted murder; you could have died. Don't you want whoever did this to be brought to justice?"

I said I did but I couldn't help them, that I would call them if I remembered anything, that I wanted, more than anything, for this not to happen to anyone else and that I would be a witness if I ever remembered what happened.

They asked me where I lived and I told them I stayed in a railway arch somewhere in East London. They nodded, eyebrows twitching as they passed knowing looks.

"Were you working on the streets; a prostitute perhaps?"

"No."

"You might have been randomly picked up off the street by someone who didn't think you'd be missed. Is that possible?"

I nodded and they seemed pleased. "If you remember anything else…" they said, handing me a business card with a selection of numbers printed on it.

The psych nurse saw them out. I sat in bed, waiting for the catheter to be removed so that I could wee on my own, testing my legs after their unwanted rest. They wobbled, unused to weight, but bore me valiantly to the ladies where I sat and stared at the pale grey tiles.

Dinner was minced beef and mashed potatoes followed by cake and custard. I left the meat and potatoes and wolfed down the cake and custard, asking to be able to finish any left on the ward. I ate three and the sugar coursed through my veins, offering energy I didn't remember.

The next day, a doctor told me that I was making good progress and that in a few days I would be able to leave as long as I had somewhere to go. I nodded, planning the lie I would tell as soon as I was ready. Next morning, I had a visit from social services. They offered me a room in a hostel near York, a room of my own where I could begin again. They brought a bag of clothes which didn't fit me and left, embarrassed by their inability to guess my size.

That afternoon I had another social visit from the same service. A woman with a huge afro and colourful dress sense which reminded me of Heather, sat on the chair next to the bed and touched my hand.

"You've been through it," she said, running a finger over a particularly nasty looking stag beetle rearing up on my wrist. I pulled it away.

"We run a place for abused women. We think you should have a room there until you're back on your feet. Until we can find you something more appropriate." She grinned, her line-less face, kind.

I nodded, smiling with my eyes. She was gentle and firm; Heather with psychological training. "We've got some paperwork for you to sign and we can get on with organising everything. What size are you? We have a budget of fifty pounds we can spend on clothes for you. What would you like? Jeans, T-shirts, trainers?"

"Thank you," I said, more quietly than I had intended. "And a hoodie." I could hide in a hoodie.

"I'll sort that out for you. I'll nip into Primark, get some knickers and a couple of bras too. Did you have clothes before..." She waved a hand across my skin.

"Only what I could put on," I lied, missing my fluffy red jumper more than I thought possible.

"Okay, I'll get you going. I've got paperwork for claiming benefits here; let's see if we can get this done so you've got something to live on when you come out of here."

THEY MOVED ME TO a different ward the next day, a holding pen for those of us who were almost ready to go back out there. The crowd here was livelier, a little stir crazy and ready to call a nurse at any opportunity. I found their antics annoying, wanting the peace of the ICU and the beep, beep, beep of the monitor to propel me through the day ahead.

Afro lady returned with a carrier bag full of clothes for which I was truly grateful. I knew I would disappoint her, leave in the dead of night when she had worked so hard to set me up with a fresh start. It wasn't fair but it was necessary.

"What were you doing in London?" she asked for the hundredth time.

"I was homeless. I nicked food and money to live in a stinking railway arch with rats."

Her nostrils flared as she grimaced. "You poor soul," she said, stroking my hand. "And you have no idea why this happened to you?" She waved a bangled arm in the direction of my tattoos.

"No."

"You're lucky they didn't do your face. Now, that would be difficult to cover."

"I don't think I'm lucky."

"I'm sorry, of course you don't. It just seems like such a specific crime; you know, to target someone and tattoo them which takes time and effort and resources."

"There are some weird people out there. You should know that."

"If you don't mind me asking, why were you on the streets in the first place?"

"I do mind." My eyes met hers, the conversation terminated.

A doctor approached, pulling the blue curtain around him as he entered my space. The woman gave hand signals to say she would wait somewhere and the doctor smiled.

"Jay," he said. "We've had a chat with your social worker and decided you can leave in a couple of days She's organised somewhere for you to stay. You need to be quiet for a while, gain your strength back. Accept the help, please, so you're not tempted back onto the street." Concern crept into the crow's feet around his eyes while his mouth kept up the smiling charade.

"I will," I said.

"Please do, Jay. It's not safe."

I nodded.

"I'm off tomorrow, so you'll be seeing Dr Patel. Remember her?"

"Yes, thank you." I joined in the pretence, smiling widely.

"Well done," he said. "You've done very well so far. I have every faith in you."

He turned and tugged at the curtain revealing my social worker, folders clutched in her arms.

"Where are we?" I asked.

"Beautiful York," she said. "The refuge isn't far from here."

"And you're my social worker, assigned to me, I mean?"

"I have that privilege. I was called when they brought you in. Many people have been working on your behalf behind the scenes. I'm Cynthia."

"I'm grateful," I said, watching as nurses came and went, taking blood pressure readings and temperatures, chatting about what they were going to do at the weekend. I had to take it all in, remember this time so that I could look back on it one day. Cynthia left my bedside, reassuring me that she would return in a couple of days to accompany to my new home, my new life in Yorkshire, God's own county, where I would be safe from harm.

I WAITED FOR THE shifts to change before slipping into the bathroom and locking the door behind me. I would leave tonight, head back to the city which had tried to shame me and failed. The breadcrumb trail had led me to Scaramouche, my rucksack on the floor in the corner of the blackened cavern. Alma, her haughty beauty holding court, another victim lying on leather. The antibiotics coursing through my bloodstream had brought clarity with them. I knew who I was. And Alma would not get away with her games twice. I had no plan but that had never stopped me before. No plan had brought me here. No plan was the best plan I had.

It took a few moments to acknowledge that the woman in the reflection was me. Skinny in bra and knickers, the extent of my artwork assaulted me, forcing me backwards until I was sitting on the toilet, eyes burning into the glass in front of me. If Beano's art had been ugly but beautifully made, mine was just ugly. Alma hadn't bothered with her best work on my skin. The vile creatures which appeared to be marching up my body in formation had been born of a sick imagination. Hornets, wasps, scorpions, locusts and beetles jostled for space on my limbs; on my thigh, a black widow munched on her mate, half its body protruding from her jaw. Flies swarmed up my calves and torso, locusts joining them over my stomach. They flew towards my heart, the bleeding mess with a dagger through it, biologically correct and beating with the movement of my own. On my shoulders, webs and more spiders, a scorpion arching its tail in readiness to strike and three huge stag beetles, rearing up to each other, angry and combative.

Turning my body so that I could see as much of my back as possible, the head of Baphomet stared back, large horns reaching across my shoulder blades, a phallus in his mouth, red eyes leering. There was no body, but a hole in his neck from where the creatures crawled and scuttled, flies, spiders, ants and hornets, angry and uncomfortable on my skin.

I stared, seeing myself for the first time, disgust rising in my stomach, rushing to the basin, where I threw up, my mind rejecting the person I had become, yearning for the pale-skinned girl I had been. Smashing my fist into the mirror, I sank to the floor, becoming as small as possible as the images were folded away, skin on skin. Someone knocked on the door, asking me if I was going to be long.

"Yes," I shouted. The handle rattled and the sound of feet slipped away.

Forcing myself upwards and away from the disgusting truth, I turned on the shower, the water scalding and steaming as I stepped in. For a moment, redness blurred the images as they ran in to each other but as my skin grew accustomed to the heat, I saw them again in the reflection from the mirror. It began in my stomach, churning and heaving, bursting into my veins, tingling through my limbs. The rage of what could have been a thousand years burning my flesh. The rage of the invisible, unlovable, lonely people who wander the earth looking for something they've lost. The rage of the downtrodden, the weary and the thoroughly pissed off. My rage.

Rushing from the shower, I scrubbed my skin with the hard towel but the images didn't disappear, taunting from the skin which belonged to me. I pulled the new clothes on, bought by Cynthia, chosen by her as my flesh was now chosen by someone else. The hoodie hid all but the tattoos which crawled up my neck, ants and a viper, curling around my throat, its head behind my ear. I ripped a spare T-shirt into strips, tying them together before looping it around my neck. The creatures disappeared. I recognised myself again. I could breathe.

The ward was quiet, a group of nurses discussing a tricky patient at the desk in the main corridor. No one noticed me as I packed the paper carrier bag with spare knickers and socks, a bottle of water, a tuna sandwich and three yoghurts from the fridge. No one watched me as I padded towards the swing doors, out into the corridor which led back to the outside world. A porter smiled and held open the heavy door through which he was pushing an empty bed.

The air was fresh and clean after the heavily heated hospital. It was very late, the darkness making it impossible to get my bearings. A bench near the children's wing caught my eye and I sat down on it, watching the sky for signs of the impending dawn. Time stood still as my mind raced. I had to get back to London. My jaw set. My teeth ground together. The remaining scabs on my body itched, reminding me of the horror underneath grey cotton. Somewhere high up in the trees, a bird began its morning song, shrill in the silence. Slowly but surely, light hinted at morning and with it, the light of resolute determination to get somewhere other than where I was. Somewhere familiar, where people didn't call you 'love' and didn't care if you had a nice day. The place where Alma resided in her black web, waiting for unsuspecting flies to get caught in her sticky chains so that she could suck out their insides.

I had never been to York. It could have been New York or Johannesburg or Delhi. With no money to get a cab, I had to rely on my old skills, walking until I found a street sign to help me gain non-existent bearings. The roads were quiet, the silence punctuated only by bird song and the occasional siren.

Only minutes later, I stood in Museum Street, the sign for the York Library before my eyes, a sign told me it opened at nine. The clock tower said it was five thirty. I had expected it to be further and now I had time to kill. Market traders were setting up near The Lanes, a warren of tiny shops selling expensive gifts, souvenirs from a weekend away. I skulked on the edge of the market, hood pulled over my head, watching the traders as I had done a thousand times in Camden. They were friendlier here, chatting, laughing and slapping each other on the back as they downed copious amounts of tea from thermos flasks.

"Is that Billy?" someone asked, pointing at me.

"No, that's a lass," said another. I clutched my paper bag, backing into an alley where an old fashioned sweet shop offered penny sweets for five pence each. I sat on the window sill, peering round the corner at the traders, piling fruit and veg and scarves and handbags and floppy dresses onto stalls with brightly coloured awnings. After the sterile hospital it was exciting. Fresh bread arrived in a white van, the smell bringing saliva to my mouth. I swallowed and, as the baker's back was turned, slipped towards his stall, placing a tomato loaf in my bag. I almost ran away, ashamed and delighted in equal measure. I hadn't lost my knack. Turning left then right, then left again, I stumbled across York Minster, sitting on the steps, tearing chunks off the bread, stuffing them into my mouth until it wouldn't close.

People were emerging from every corner, smart suits and day dresses, perfectly turned out, heading for a day of normality in air-conditioned offices and shops. They were just like Londoners and yet not at the same time. More people smiled. Someone tossed a pound coin in my direction. I caught it, nodded and stuffed it in my pocket. I could stay here, if I didn't have business somewhere else.

The bread eaten, I walked for a while, noting the gates and the high walkways which would be filled with tourists later. The river stretched away from me, a sign proclaiming that otters had been spotted on its banks. I peered over the bridge as a heron took off, its huge wingspan moving the air with a rumble. The smell of wet earth came to meet my nostrils, inviting and calming. Taking the steps down to the river, I squatted in the place the heron had been, noting lazy bees starting their hectic search for food, the low hum like music. I promised to return one day, to enjoy this place.

Shops were opening. I stood, shook my limbs and headed for the library. I entered, walking towards the desk and the librarian who sheltered there.

"I need to find out about tattoo meanings," I said, breathless and urgent.

"You can use a computer over there," the woman said, vaguely pointing in the direction of a bank of computers. "Number two," she said. "It's a pound for an hour."

I searched in my pocket for the pound I had been given, handing it over to her triumphantly.

The screen lurched into life as I searched for the possible reasons Alma had tattooed the menagerie on me; what had driven her to these symbols?

"Flies: weakness and sinfulness. Hornets: divine retribution in the form of a swarm. The same with locusts. The black widow was obvious, a woman who eats her mate and spits her out again, control, possession. Spiders: fear and loathing, perhaps representing control over fear or, more likely, fear of the beast itself. Again, by controlling the image, we hope to control our fear, it said. The corner of my mouth turned. Fear was controlled. Rage had replaced it.

Baphomet with phallus: an idol, falsely worshipped by the Knights Templar. Baphomet, the benign one, leader of the Pagan tradition, Lord of everything. My Baphomet sneered from between my shoulder blades, the moon peeping from behind his enormous horns as he performed a sex act on an

334

unattached phallus. This wasn't on the internet. This was from Alma's mind. What was she trying to tell me? That I worshipped her as a false idol? She was right of course, right about almost everything about me. I was weak and sinful and stupid, swept along on a wave of desire for a woman who could offer me nothing. My mind contained a blank space where the answer might be. I searched for more breadcrumbs but found none. For Beano's sake, I had sought her out. And for Beano's sake I now wore her image of me, her interpretation of who I was. But it wasn't for Beano's sake that I had lusted after the octopus breasts, the vermillion hair. No, that had nothing to do with Beano at all.

"Can sepsis leave you angry?" I typed into Google. One hundred and forty-five thousand results came up. I read the first seven. It could, but it was more likely that someone had done something really cruel to me. I dismissed sepsis and concentrated on Alma. Her head bent over me, the red hair scraped from her head revealing roots as black as her soul. Had I loved her? I couldn't remember as the rage churned in my gut and the adrenalin surged through my body.

I left the library with fifteen minutes of computer time to spare, running outside to breathe in cool, fresh air, lightened by the rain which had begun to fall. Slowly, I reclaimed my mind, the images fading with each breath. Breathe in "let". Breathe out "go". The rain touched the only visible skin, my face. I turned it towards the sky, enjoying the sensation, opening my mouth that it might wash me from the inside out. My mind calmed, I could

335

breathe normally and took in my surroundings to ground myself. In the same street, a sign for a museum drew me towards it like a magnet.

In the archaeology section, Roman, Greek and Viking remains filled cabinets, helmets, masks, weapons and fertility symbols nestled together under glass. Scanning the exhibits, I moved through rooms, finally stopping by a tiny, soapstone scarab beetle, definitely Egyptian, the like of which would have filled Tutankhamun's tomb. Sitting on the bench provided, my eyes bored holes in the glass between the me and the scarab until Tutankhamun's face appeared and I had never been so pleased to see him.

"Feeling better?" he said.

"It's not been a great few weeks."

"No, it hasn't."

"What next?"

I hugged my knees, pulling my feet up as far as I could, burying my face in the space between my thighs. Tutankhamun tutted, his doleful eyes dark and shining.

"Come on," he said eventually. "You can do better than this."

"What if I don't want to?"

"Feel free to sulk with me. But there's a reason you came."

"Oh, shut up! Next you'll be telling me there's a reason for these!" I pulled up my sleeve, thrusting my arm under his delicate nose. "What possible reason could there be for doing this to me? Sexual gratification? Control? Power? Evil? I've been through it all. And it could all be true. Or it could just be that she enjoys it. She actually enjoys the process of ruining someone's life."

"Has she ruined yours?"

"I've lost my home, my job, friends, my nail file. My fucking nail file! Do you know what it's like being without the thing that's got you through everything that's ever happened?"

"I do," he said. "I feel your pain."

"Don't fucking patronise me, you bastard!" Several tourists turned to see who I was shouting at and, seeing no one, passed me off as a nutter hurrying through to the next room.

"I feel your pain, Jay, whether you want me to or not. I know where you are now and what it's going to take to get you out of it. Anger is new to you, isn't it?"

The question was rhetorical. I hated him. I told him so. I beat my leg with my fist, somehow controlling the urge to kick the glass cabinets into the street. A low rumble built in my throat. Would I scream? It had a life of its own. It rose from my stomach, gathering in my chest, blocking the air in my throat. There was no controlling it. The noise which followed was primeval, drawing the attention of a security guard who guided me towards the café and made the staff get me a cup of tea. I tried to thank him. I sipped the tea. Tutankhamun was sitting opposite.

"The thing is," he said, "It's like she said. She's done this to you but it's up to you to decide what you do. Let it break you."

"Don't be cruel."

"What have I said?" Tut leant forwards, resting his elbows on the table, rattling the tea cup.

"I loved my life."

"Did you?"

"Yes! You know I did."

"Do I? Did you tell me that or were you too busy looking for something else?"

"I had to do this for Beano?"

He tutted.

I pulled the hoodie around my neck to hide the snake's head spitting venom in my ear. "I don't know what you're talking about. You're harsh," I said, fiddling with the teaspoon.

"You can be difficult. You can be obtuse and ignorant. You can be all those things whenever you like, but not with me." He pushed his golden headdress back towards his hairline which was thinning despite his youth. "There is no answer. You need to decide about your future. Stop looking for answers and make a decision about your life."

Downing the tea in my cup, I shovelled spoonfuls of sugar into the cup, pouring the remainder of the tea on top, watching the tiny crystals dissolve before tipping the syrup down my throat. It soothed me, lifting my mood from the basement café up into the halls above.

"Walk," I repeated several times, standing and pushing the chair back into position. Somewhere, a child cried as its mother chastised it. I felt the sharpness of her rebuke, pulling my shoulders back in defiance. "I could walk. Some of the way at least. Maybe hitch a ride. I'm going back to London, I know that. That bitch isn't going to get away with it twice. I just don't know what I'm going to do when I get there." I paused.

"You don't need to know."

338

"Heather and Dave might not be forgiving."

"No, they might not." Tutankhamun hovered by the exit. "But they might," he said receding into the architrave, disappearing as quickly as he had arrived.

"I must see Alma," I said to the space where he had been.

A CLEAR BLUE SKY introduced itself later that day, the day of my departure. I had printed off a walking route from York to London, a route which would take me about ten days to complete if I didn't get a lift.

The streets of York were packed with tourists, jostling in The Lanes, the overhanging Tudor buildings providing welcome shade. I dipped a wallet belonging to a Spanish tourist, hiding in an alley to count my winnings. Fifty pounds. I left it and the credit cards in a place where it might be found and bought a bag of rhubarb and custard sweets, some apples from the market and another loaf of bread from the trader I had stolen from earlier. I added a block of cheddar, the most mature I could get, and several bottles of water. The carrier bag was splitting. In a luggage shop, a blue rucksack caught my attention, brown leather buckles securing pockets for the treasures I was sure I would find along the way. I bought it without considering the cost: easy come, easy go. The cornflower blue canvas lifted my heart. Packing my food and money in the different pockets, I swung it over my shoulders. It rested perfectly in the small of my back, releasing the pressure in my shoulders, making the journey possible.

I left York an hour later, waving sightlessly and gratefully to Cynthia and the nurses who had looked after me, sorry to have let Cynthia down, another casualty of a hopeless case.

A flock of starlings looped and swirled in the sky above my head, a murmuration filling the sky with fluttering wings. I continued walking, down suburban streets and out into the farmland beyond.

The air was sweet here, filling my lungs with something other than vehicle fumes and overseas perfume.

I pulled a chunk of bread from my loaf, biting the cheese and swigging from one of the water bottles in turn. I weed at the side of the field, uncaring in the emptiness. I joined the road again, feeling the bounce of new trainers on the asphalt. Inside, my feet throbbed and I sat for a moment, removing them to see what was happening underneath. My toes and heels were bleeding but the worn skin had eradicated the flies placed there by Alma, a small victory.

The ground was cool under my feet, the tiny stones reminding me that I had grown soft. A gentle breeze stroked my skin; the hoodie found its way into my bag now, and I walked with arms shown to the world as the menagerie of insects felt sun for the first time. Sweat trickled down the viper's body, pooling in the gap between my breasts. I wiped it away with my hand, flicking beads of salty water into the road next to me. A bee flew into my bag of sweets, buzzed and flew out again and a butterfly fluttered before my eyes to land on one of the yellow flowers that littered the hedgerow. I let the sound of vehicles recede and life burst into song. Returning to my feet, I put two pairs of new socks and the trainers back on my sore feet, better padding for the miles which I might have to cover.

Plodding on, I stuck my thumb out into the traffic, empty-headed, the rhythm of my feet punching out a beat to which I wrote poetry. No one stopped.

Tutankhamun joined me.

"I'll walk with you a while," he said, slipping his long fingers through mine, swinging my arm, putting rhythm in our movement.

"It never occurred to me that you could leave the museum," I said.

"Why would it?" he said.

And so we walked towards the clouds which gathered and churned and blackened ahead, sidestepping off the pavement to walk by the side of a barley field. The fronds waved at me, swaying from side to side making a hissing sound as a distant combine harvester rumbled.

I turned to embrace him but he'd gone, and I remembered what it felt to be alone. The pain rose from my toes, up the bones which stopped me from becoming a ball of jelly in the dust. It settled in my stomach, a fist of anger which burned as it journeyed up my chest, locking my throat. It spread, tentacle like up my neck until a huge claw gripped my skull. I roared it out, coughing and spluttering as I fell to my knees, vomiting breakfast onto the soil. It passed; I stood slowly, aware of the rush of blood downwards where I didn't need it.

Tutankhamun did not pick me up, nor did he offer to walk with me again. I put one foot in front of the other, scanning the horizon for a farm building and the clouds which would push me back off the road again.

A feather fell, landing on my nose before sliding down to settle on my T-shirt.

"Beano?" I called.

A butterfly hung in the air before me, floating on an unseen thermal, fluttering her long eyelashes under long wisps of blonde hair.

"I didn't think I'd see you again," I said.

"I never left," she said, winking as her wings beat, holding her close to my face.
I watched her fly, the wind under her wings lifting her higher into the atmosphere until she was out of sight and the clouds were parting to let her through.

A shaft of sunlight hit my face, burning my cheek with its intensity. Steam rose from the shoulders of my T-shirt and from my thighs and the laces on my trainers. I rushed forward, hoping to catch another glimpse of the butterfly but it was gone and the path in front of me devoid of human company.

I walked, keeping an eye on signs which might direct me to a short cut or a place to stay but there were no short cuts. The road to London was long and lonely, mine alone to navigate.

"What are you most afraid of?" Alma had asked and I had told her. "What are you most afraid of?" she had asked and I had given her the answer. And as clearly as I could see the tattooed menagerie, I could see her asking what she could torture me with. Cockroaches, spiders, beetles and flies adorned my skin. My Room 101. The weight of knowledge pressed on my shoulders, bending my head until my chin rested on the zoo beneath. I thanked God that I hadn't told her the truth. Alma scratched into my skin would have been too much to bear.

I went forward, not looking back until the sun had burned off the hazy clouds and begun prickling the back of my neck. I stopped in a layby, ate some bread and noticed a burger van.

"Fancy a cup of tea?" The man called from his kitchen. "It's quiet today for some reason."

"I do," I said back.

"Where are you going?" he asked.

"London," I said, approaching the van, reaching out for the steaming polystyrene cup. "Thank you." I handed him some change.

"That's a long way."

"I've come from York."

"You raising money for charity or something?"

"No, I'm going home."

"Well, you picked a good day for it." He laughed, pointing at the black clouds darkening a few miles away.

"I'm looking for a ride," I said, sipping the sweet nectar.

"There's a truck stop." He pointed vaguely south. "You might get lucky there."

"I'll give it a try," I said, thanking him.

"Been a corker of a summer," he said.

"It has. Never known it so hot for so long." The ordinariness of small talk was a welcome relief.

"Good for business." He waved a hand towards his fridge. "People stop for a bottle of water and end up having a full English bap. Fancy one?"

"Just eaten," I said.

"Oh, go on." He stuck two rashers of bacon on the grill. "You look like you could do with a good feed. Egg?" I handed him more coins but he waved them away. "Just become a Granddad. If you stay and eat this I can show you the

345

photographs and, to be honest, I don't think I'm going to sell many more today. I'll have one too if it makes you feel better." He winked. I thanked him again.

"What did you have?"

"Bacon, sausage…"

I laughed. "No, the baby."

"Oh, of course." He patted his oversized stomach winking repeatedly. "A boy. Isaac James Brian. James after me and Brian after his other granddad."

"Nice name."

"Isaac, eight pounds ten ounces. Born yesterday morning." He fished in his pocket and pulled out a phone, showing me a picture of Winston Churchill in baby form.

"He's beautiful," I said. He handed me the bap, egg yolk oozing from the side. I ate, savouring the saltiness, remembering all the times I had cooked for the Polish labourers.

"I used to work in a B&B," I said, "Cooking breakfast for migrant workers."

"Oh. Migrant workers, eh? Did you enjoy it?"

"Yes," I said without hesitation. "I did enjoy it but I had other things on my mind at the time."

"Shame."

"Sorry. I didn't mean…"

"Don't worry, love. You meet all sorts at a roadside van. So where are you going to in London?"

"I'm going home to see if I can salvage whatever's left of my life there."

"Good for you. I wish you all the luck in the world." He raised his hand up to his eyes in a mock salute.

"Thanks, Granddad!" I said. He continued to tell me about the extended labour which produced Isaac, his blue eyes just like his mother's and the enormous array of equipment which he had bought to make life easier for them all. I nodded, chewing bacon with crispy fat, glad for the punctuation in an otherwise unknown journey.

"How far is the truck stop?" I asked when he stopped talking for a minute.

"Not far, about a mile. They often pull up here and get a bap. Say my food is much better than the overpriced stuff at the stop." I reassured him that it was the best bap I'd ever had.

"I'm sure you'll get a lift there. Straight down the A1 to London."

"The Holloway Road," I muttered.

"Only been to London once. Bloody busy it was but then I s'pose it would be. You'd better be off, lass, before the big 'uns have all gone. Nice to have met you."

I nodded, thanked him and wished Isaac all the good things life has to offer. A few minutes later I saw the trucks lined up, four of them, laden with produce ready for London stores. Steam and smoke belched from an extractor hose which clung to the side of a building. The smell of frying and diesel filled the air, the trucks lined up in rows on the tarmac, cavalry preparing for an advance on enemy lines. I sat down, crossing my legs, watching from a safe distance before taking my chance.

Approaching the first truck, I knocked on the window, jumping up so I could reach the glass. The man inside was drinking tea, watching a movie on a DVD player. He wound down his window an inch.

"What you want?" he said in a thick accent which I recognised as Polish.

"A lift to London. Any chance?"

He looked at me, winding the window down a little lower so he could stick his head out. "Where you come from?" he asked.

I pulled the hoodie up around my neck. "York, was seeing friends but couldn't get a lift back. Ran out of money in the clubs, like you do." I feigned a smile.

"Humph," he said. "I go Acton."

"That's west London. Anyone else going into the City?"

"No. I only one going London." I looked around.

"I'll check and get back to you," I said. He was right, none of the other lorries were heading for central London; two stopping in Birmingham, another in Southend. Acton was my best bet.

I returned to the first truck, my rucksack in my hands. "You were right," I shouted up to the now closed window. "Could I have a ride, please?" He looked skywards, then nodded.

"Go round," he said pointing. I ran around the front of the truck and climbed up the steps, opening the door, leaping onto the black leather seat. "I not tell boss I give you lift."

"I've told the other drivers," I said, "And the woman in the truck stop. She said I shouldn't be hitching. I said I've told you so if I'm on the news you'll know who did it. Is that clear? You won't get away with anything. They all know I'm here."

"What?" the man said, turning off his DVD player. "Speak slow."

"It doesn't matter," I said, looking at the dashboard with flashing lights and a tachograph, a mobile phone stand, the DVD player and a sat nav. "Nice truck."

"No funny thing," he said, shaking a finger at me. "No hand on this." He pointed to the dashboard.

"I won't," I said. The engine sparked into life, deep and thundering beneath my body. We pulled out of the truck stop. From the height of the cab I could see across the hedges onto fields and farm buildings beyond.

"I'm Jay," I said. "Thank you."

"Pavel," he said, his eyes not leaving the road.

"I teach Polish men new words," I said. "Like discombobulated." He didn't reply but fiddled with the radio until the sound of Radio 2 filled the cab, silencing me.

The rain began five minutes into our journey, beating against the windshield as the wipers tried their hardest to clear it, squeaking with each swipe of the blades. Adjusting the torn T-shirt scarf to be sure that he couldn't see my tattoos, I settled back into the seat, my head swaying with the wiper blades. The miles vanished underneath the enormous truck wheels, the radio news, on the hour, every hour, the only indication of time passing. Soon, the landscape changed, vast open stretches of farmland eaten up with housing estates and industrial parks. Pavel did not speak, his eyes fixed on the road as we sped along the tarmac. Sometimes his fingers tapped the rhythm of the music on the steering wheel; other times he gripped it and I could see white knuckles as a sign of concentration. I clutched my rucksack and stared ahead too.

No plan had formed for what I would do when I got to London. My only desire was to stand in front of Alma. What I would do or say when I got there remained a mystery. Whether Dave or Heather would want me back remained a mystery too, one I had no control over and, therefore, filed in the chest of drawers in my head next to the breadcrumbs, Baphomet, coats of arms, Peter and a future. There was only the moment when I would see Alma again, only the shock it would give her. I longed to see her eyes widen, her mouth set in fear. The octopus on her chest might strangle her. She might fall into the drawn hole on the side of her face. I hoped that she would, imploding until nothing was left but dust.

The lorry drew up in a layby. "You leave here," Pavel said.

"Where are we?" He pointed at the satnav. Ealing. The shock of London startled me. Outside the window of the cab the landscape had transformed, the roads narrowed and a thousand buildings now jostled for space a few feet away. I thanked Pavel, opening the door of the truck and climbing down. I waved but he didn't look as the truck thundered out of the layby, belching out diesel fumes as it went.

Ealing. London. I had arrived. I turned around three times in the hope of enlightenment from above but nothing happened. I walked backwards and forwards, up and down the pavement before heading for the tube as a place of refuge. Just outside, I noticed a board with advertisements badly stuck to it. One caught my attention, a tattoo convention in Tobacco Dock, East London. Stopping a passing Londoner, I asked, "What's the date today?"

"The seventh," she said, not breaking her stride.

The seventh and eighth, the poster declared. It wasn't a plan but it was a place to start, a place where I might disappear in the illustrated crowd. It would be familiar, overwhelmed as I was, by the smells and sights of London.

Down the stairs to the tube I went, pulling the hoodie down over my face, anonymous in the crowd of faceless people, stepping onto the first available carriage towards east London, finding a seat in the corner.

MOTHER SAID I WOULD never amount to anything. I shivered in the heat of the underground as her face filled my vision. It wouldn't swipe away this time, wouldn't budge as the world went on around me.

She said I was an accident, a thing she had neither wanted nor tried for. She said I was a waste of space, taking but never contributing. Her eyes widened with disgust as she loomed in my vision, hard lines set around her pink lipstick. With each "uncle" that arrived at the two-bedroom terrace I shared with her, she loved me a little less.

"I chose him," she would say. "He has to come first." I had hidden in the airing cupboard, squeezed up against the unlagged tank.

"We only ever argue about you," she screamed from the kitchen, smashing a bottle of gin on the counter with venom. I had gone out to the park, swinging mindlessly for hours until the bigger kids tormented me and I ran home to hide again under the blankets which had been thrown on my bed.

The carriage lurched in and out of stations, people entering and exiting, bumping into and avoiding each other. No one looked at me.

I had chosen never to think about Mother. Now, she arrived without warning, a jealous, unkind woman who hated me every bit as much as Alma hated Beano. Expensive dresses and regular hairdresser appointments were prioritised, money that could have been spent on food for me. She said I ate at school and didn't need her to cater for me. I scavenged out of the neighbours' bins. Once, the mousy woman next door caught me doing it and invited me in for tea. I ate the shepherd's pie and tinned peaches and heard her offer to feed me once a week. I never returned, terrified that Mother would find out and withdraw the school meals as well.

I felt the broom handle land on the small of my back when she discovered pennies missing from her purse. The red stripes it left were there for two weeks. The shame of second hand uniform reddened my cheeks under the grey hood. Shoes too big, dresses too small. She knew the other children would laugh at me and sometimes she would even ask if I were having fun at school or if the other children bullied me.

"You never bring anyone home," she said, smirking. "And you never ask my advice to make yourself look a bit better."

The train jolted, pulling into a station, doors opening and closing over announcements to look out for unattended baggage. I had been unattended baggage, the route from Mother to streets simple and unencumbered. London was like my Mother, disinterested with pockets of cruelty. I could take my chances there; there were numerous places to hide, so many people to steal from. I could survive just as well; I was accustomed to it.

Mother loved good clothes and wealthy men, piano bars and seedy parties where she and her friends snorted cocaine and drank gin until they fell. She said I'd ruined her figure because I had been a fat baby and that's why she hadn't been able to get anyone to marry her. She said my hair was dull, unlike her own blonde locks. She said my eyes were squinty and ugly. She said it was impossible to love me when I did nothing to make myself loveable. Had Beano heard the same?

With each opening and closing of the train doors, the memories crept from their hiding places, each one a parallel with Beano's imagined life. Alma's haughty expression was my own mother's. Alma's cruel words, Mother's too. I laughed under the hoodie, seeing with absolute clarity what had drawn me to the woman I wanted to make love me, knowing for certain in that moment that she was incapable.

The day I left home, Mother had broken up with my latest uncle, a man with a huge gut and a wife in Ruislip. Mother had wanted him to leave her. Her shrieking drifted through the floorboards and into the airing cupboard. He slammed the door when he left. Mother pulled me out of my hiding place by my hair, slapping my face as she spat that my presence in the house was enough to put anyone off. When she let go, I grabbed my school bag and ran downstairs.

"I'm leaving," I said.

"Go on, then," she had screamed, lunging at my face, slapping it hard with her outstretched hand. I pulled the nail file out of my pocket, the one with the mother-of-pearl handle. I held it up.

"Hit me again," I said, my voice calm, "And I will stick this in your eye." She lunged for it but I had been too quick for her, parachute-rolling across the shag pile carpet towards the front door, in and out before she had reached the hall. I ran along the suburban road past houses which all looked the same, running and running and running until there was no breath left in my body, collapsing in a park some distance away, rocking as I clutched my knees and the nail file. I was fifteen.

The following four years were not desperate. They had brought me to this point, on a tube train, travelling to East London to face not just Beano's mother but my own. A serene smile settled on my lips as all the little breadcrumbs from years past were gobbled up, transformed into a path to the truth.

"Knowledge is power," I mumbled but nobody noticed. I understood the phrase for the first time. The train pulled up in another station and people got on and off, unaware that under a grey hoodie, an epiphany of enormous consequence was occurring.

I changed trains somewhere, autopilot clicking in as my mind raced with past images. I wondered what Mother was doing now, if she missed me, but my soul knew that nothing would have changed and that the space I had occupied would have been filled with gin and more cocaine and more uncles who would no longer have to be called uncles. It didn't upset me, nor was I numbed to it. It was what it was, something I had known all my life, grown up with and assimilated into my psyche. I knew it from the inside out. But it wasn't alright.

On the next tube, I stood by the door, holding on to the post as the train strained and lurched towards something new, the hoodie pulled right down over my face, the rucksack clutched to my breast. The nail file had gone. Alma had stolen it.

As the escalator propelled me towards the light, I breathed in "let" and breathed out "go". The people surrounding me all had lives too. Their mothers lived and loved and swore and argued. Their mothers blamed them for things which weren't their fault and they bore the scars, hidden by work suits and laptop bags. They kept their shame hidden as I did, the only difference the price of the clothes they wore. A poster bore the image of a young, blonde, nubile woman, my mother many years ago, the woman she wanted to be before bitterness and hatred contorted her face.

Tutankhamun's golden mask slipped behind a street lamp, catching my attention, diverting me. I stepped sideways, ready to catch him as he jumped out, but a woman in a track suit with a pushchair barred my way and he was gone in a flash.

"Did you see him?" I asked a woman with her world in a shopping trolley, trawling through a bin at the side of a bus stop.

"Fuck off!" she screamed.

"I will," I said, grinning so widely that I felt the skin crack on my cheeks as I dropped two pounds in her pocket.

Someone said that as soon as you stop running from yourself, you've reached your destination. Who was it? I searched the corners of my mind for a song, a book...

By a fast food restaurant, I stopped, tempted not by the food but by running water and a flushing toilet. Invisibly, I joined the crowd milling outside then slipped in and up the stairs.

The water was hot as I scrubbed my face and dampened my hair into some semblance of order. In a cubicle, I changed my knickers and wiped damp toilet paper under my arms as I had done many times before. So many days had started this way. So many days spent lying to wash or eat or sleep. Tricks learned to make life on the streets easier. In the mirror, I saw a woman, lined and with hollow cheeks, her hair flopping over one eye, her jeans slipping down over her skeletal frame.

Two young girls entered the room and the moment flew up through the air vent. I smiled at them before drying my hands under warm air. Outside, men had taken off their suit jackets as the sun beat down on crisp, ironed shirts. A child wailed as her ice cream hit the tarmac and my feet found a pace which was manageable in the late summer heat.

I HEARD THE CONVENTION before I saw it. Bass guitars throbbed, the pavement outside vibrating with the sound. A woman on the door was selling tickets but I had given the homeless woman my last coins. As a group of bearded men approached her, I took my opportunity and slipped past them, finding myself in a hall filled to bursting with colourful, patterned people. Several men strutted, bare-chested, showing off designs which covered their skin from neck to waist. I noticed Japanese work, similar to Kurt's but not quite as beautiful, the outlines a little too strong for my liking, the wind not ethereal enough. Finding a corner, I backed into it, my eyes searching the multi-coloured bodies for something familiar.

She was easy to spot, her vermillion hair piled up in a beehive, inches above most of the people who bustled in the space. She was talking to someone, waving her hands around. I couldn't see her expression. My breathing shallow, I inched around the edge of the room until I was opposite her, the mobile tattoo parlour set up exactly as it had been the first time I'd seen her. Slipping behind a point of sale stand, I peered around. She wore green, shiny fabric, stretched across her torso, plunging down so that her breasts heaved and wobbled as she spoke. The skirt stuck out, stuffed with petticoats and a hoop which swung as her hips moved. Leaning further left, I strained to see who was making her so animated. Kurt's blue head appeared, his finger wagging as he snapped, his mouth opening and closing in anger. Their words were lost in the cacophony, blues pumping out from the bass guitars, a stringy young man bemoaning his lot on the stage. Further I leaned and peered through the crowd. Someone was lying on Alma's couch, an outlined pin-up on his chest. He was wearing earphones and his feet tapped to a rhythm which didn't match the band. I watched the three of them for a minute, until Kurt threw his hands up and stormed away from her, knocking a bell jar off the side as he went. Alma bent down to pick up the glass, her huge, frilly behind reminiscent of one of Heather's dolls.

Darting back behind the point of sale stand, I hid from Kurt as he walked past, unready for what a meeting would begin. His brow furrowed, his hands thrust deep into ripped pockets, he brushed aside the men who stuck out their hands for him to shake, heading for the door, his stride wide, his boots smacking the concrete floor. He was gone. Breaths came, shallow and short, not filling my lungs. Alma had gone back to her model, bent over his chest, concentrating on the outline she had started.

Pulling my hood tightly around my face, I stepped out into the crowd, following the flow as it went clockwise around the convention. As I reached her stand, I stepped out, so close I could smell her perfume, musky and sweet in the mote-filled air. She didn't notice me, bent as she was, working on the taut flesh of the young man. Closer I went until my hoodie nudged the table next to her, then, stepping back to the other side of the walkway, through the crowd. She looked up. I dropped the hood, meeting her gaze. I saw her eyes flash, her eyebrows crinkling for a split second before I slipped into the crowd again, unnoticed.

She stood, scanning the room, then shrugged and sat down. I carried on walking round the convention until I approached her station from the other side, hiding amongst people until the time was right to step out again. This time I pulled up my sleeves before dropping the hood once again. It took a second for her to see me; confused, she looked back to where I had been before. As she did, I vanished from her sight, watching as panic flew across her features and she searched the room once again.

I began to enjoy the game. Bolder this time, and from another angle once again, I popped up in her eye-line, pushed back the hood and smiled. Alma flew off her stool, dropping the machine on the floor. I heard the model shout "Hey!", saw her rummage on the floor for the missing equipment and best of all, saw her search the crowd once again. Retreating to my original corner, I settled my thumping heart, breathing in and out purposely and rhythmically. I could still see her, working as before but rattled, her head jerking upwards every now and then to look for the ghost she may or may not have seen. When she appeared to have gained control again, I made my move, slipping in and out of the crowd until I was parallel with her station once more. This time she looked up just as I pushed back my hood. An arm lunged forward but I was too quick and, sensing the end of the game, darted out of the door, leaving her stewing in the sweaty room beyond, unable to leave her client or her belief that she had won.

Back on the street, something new filled my body. Muscles twitched with power. I threw back my hood and the sun prickled my forehead. Mother retreated. A woman, myself, stood before her, squaring up.

"Bitch!" I said. Her eyes flashed fear as she ran, escaping through my ear, falling onto the pavement. I stamped on her.

I had to have a plan now, had to make those first steps count. An open back pack called to me; I lifted the purse inside, took out the cash and left the purse on a window sill nearby. "Needs must," I said, repeating words I had heard at home when a new face cream replaced bread and milk.

Looking around, I noticed a church set back from the street, its graveyard cool and peaceful, a refuge. Sitting on a pew at the back of the church, I counted the cash: forty-five pounds. A good haul. I could eat pizza and plan my next move. Alma was rattled. She would be on her guard but couldn't tell anyone nor ask for help. I was in control. The words tickled my abdomen, their effects spreading until they reached my fingers, like pins and needles but without the pain, laughing fingers. I liked them.

I WANTED TO BE clean, to scrub away the grime of the past again, to see blood ooze from the pores which held so much black ink. I wanted to scrape filth from my organs and dump it on the doorsteps of those who should carry the guilt. I wanted to stand under a shower for hours as the water hit my skin like needles, washing away the impurities from another's hand, leaving nothing but illustration behind. I wanted to free myself.

I asked God if he minded me being in his house when my intentions were not Christian in the slightest. He didn't reply. Checking the door for closing times, I skipped down the road. The smell guided me to a public toilet, ammonia filling my nose, sharp and rancid. But there was hot water. Hanging my hoodie on a cubicle door, I washed in the clean water, scrubbing my ear where my mother had left, challenging the creatures which lay dormant on my skin. I dropped my jeans, using the soap from the dispenser to clean the space between my legs. A pile of scratchy, blue paper towels left bits on my arms which I flicked off like the ants underneath. Avoiding a puddle of urine in the cubicle, I emptied my bowels, the rush of waste cleansing my insides. Lightness replaced the dark, my body responding positively, energy seeping through my veins where only dirt had been.

I dressed then, slowly and methodically, noting the spiders' fear of me as I covered them in cotton. Rubbing a finger over my teeth I grinned at the mirror. I looked normal, the tattoos covered but not hidden, a choice.

With a pizza box in my hands, I headed back to the church before it was locked up for the night. I knew the drill; a pleasant Vicar would come and check the pews for vagrants before locking the doors. The altar cloth hung low over a wooden table. I crawled underneath just as a small man with wire-rimmed glasses came through the vestry door. I heard him sniff and shifted the pizza box under my chest. His footsteps echoed around the building, down past the pews, looking left and right; checks made, he went back through the vestry, the sound of the key turning in the ancient lock. I waited a minute before crawling out, picking a pew in the middle, arranging knee pads on the seat for some padding. I lay down, the pizza box on my chest, chomping on the meat feast, fragments of ideas flitting through my butterfly mind.

When I woke, light was already flooding through the curtains. I rushed back to the altar, crawling under the cloth to wait for the Vicar who would open up again. I dozed, pictures of Alma in too-tight dresses floating seamlessly through my mind, wondering at the undergarments which held her in place. He came eventually, through the vestry again, clicking heels across the stone floor. I waited until they faded back, sure that he wouldn't be leaving but setting up for the day ahead, and dashed to the door, letting myself out into the graveyard, under the lichgate, back out onto the street.

Camden teemed with tourists in bright colours and fantastic hats. I disappeared into the crowd, picking out Scaramouche from across the road, the door open, inviting "walk ins" from a hand-written note on the window. My heart threatened to leave my chest, so hard was it pounding and, as I stepped out into the road, a black cab hooted, slamming on his brakes to miss me. Waving my arm in apology, I stumbled across the road, balancing myself against the window before stepping inside.

The studio was dark and claustrophobic, a fan trying its best to move the stale air from corner to corner. The receptionist was nowhere to be seen; the sweet smell from a sandalwood wax melt caught in my throat. I went to blow it out but left it, disturbing nothing. Creeping forwards, I leaned against the door frame, moving the beaded curtain slightly to peer inside.

"And I'll keep telling you the same thing. She never turned up!" A telephone slammed back on its base. A strangled scream followed, and banging, crashing sounds. I hid behind the desk. The air quietened, a CD player burst into life, strains of soothing jazz funk drifting from between the beads. I parted them carefully, stepping through on tip toe, soundlessly inching forward.

Alma stood, hands on hips, the octopus heaving from a purple corset, her red hair scraped back into a pony tail with an Alice band to keep it in place. Her hands fiddled with bottles of ink, lining them up then re-arranging them again, shifting foil an inch to the left then back again.

Pushing the door open, I stepped in to the black room, the mutants in their jars turning to face me. It took Alma a moment. She swung round, tattoo machine in her hand, her jaw set, eyes boring into me.

"I knew it was you." She said, her shoulders shaking.

I peeled the T-shirt from my clammy body, tossing it on the floor at her feet before doing the same with my jeans. "You've got a dress of mine," I said. "And shoes. And a bag with a nail file in it."

"They've gone," she smirked. "Landfill." Beads of sweat gathered on her forehead and dripped down her nose and her neck, pooling where her breasts met and heaved, the cheap polyester fabric darkening. I saw a drawing of a Hannya mask lying on the desk – the jealous woman.

"What's your Room 101, Alma?" I asked.

"I told you, I fear nothing."

"You're sweating though." Her feet shuffled involuntarily.

"You don't stand a chance against me. What kind of idiot would come back here?" She threw back her head, laughing and I could see the fillings in her teeth.

"One with nothing to lose," I said.

In bra and pants I faced her, my body camouflaged by the insects she had placed there, breaking up my silhouette so that I was there and not there at the same time. She stared at her work, a sneer on her top lip.

"How dare you come here!" she said. "How dare you bring your skinny arse back here! I never touched you, bitch. You're deluded! Another street whore with delusions and addictions. Think I'd put my name to those awful... awful things!" She pointed at my body.

"Not your finest work," I said, my body tingling. Keeping my eyes fixed on her, I bent to pick up my clothes, dressing slowly. Alma's eyes burned my body. She didn't move, a mannequin dressed in girl's clothes, the lines visible between her crepey breasts.

"You're old enough to be my mother," I said and she baulked, stepping forwards.

"Don't come any closer," I said, raising my hand. "We're in your studio. There could be a walk-in at any time."

She stopped, momentary confusion on her face. I backed out into reception, sidestepping the reception desk until it was a wall between us.

"I'm your worst nightmare," I said. She tried to laugh but it stuck in her throat.

"You'll never know when I'm coming back or who I'll bring with me." I smiled.

She lunged across the desk, arms flailing as she tried in vain to reach my throat. The wax melt slid underneath her, catching the purple polyester under her arm. A tiny flame sprung from the wax, curling up onto her sleeve. Alma didn't notice, so fixed in her hatred, bent on reaching my throat. The smell of hair burning brought her back; she screamed, patting at the flames which now curled across her body, dropping tiny sparks onto the full skirt with the pile of netting underneath. In a second, the flames had engulfed her skirt. She shrieked again, pointing at the fire extinguisher by the door. I backed towards it, reaching my arm out until it played with the black handle on the top. Her arms flailed, beating at the flames, strangled screams coming from her face, the burning hair extensions orange against the red. The black handle of the extinguisher felt cool.

"Help me!" she called, beating at the flames with frantic hands.

"No." I said.

I stepped backwards out onto the street, waving goodbye as I joined the crowd, walking slowly across the road to a doorway. Here, my heart began to pound, shaking my body. On my haunches, I hugged my knees, watching the closed door, imagining the woman inside, too terrified to reach the phone, slapping herself to put out the flames which licked her skin. My body reacted, retching in the gutter. My mind remained calm. Moments later, the receptionist arrived, pushing the door open as smoke billowed out. I heard her shout through the door, "Call 999. Fire!"

She stumbled back on to the pavement, a crowd gathering around her, mobile phones clasped to ears as flames flickered behind the glass. More people arrived. A construction worker with a drill smashed the glass. Smoke and flames licked the pavement, pushing the crowd back.

"Is there anyone in there?"

"Yes, Alma's in there."

"Someone's screaming,"

"They'll be here in five minutes."

"Five minutes is too late."

The man from the shop next door pointed his fire extinguisher at the window. Foam jetted into the room.

"Get her out! Someone get her out!" Two men kicked at the door. The foam dampened the flames enough for them to step inside.

"Get water."

"Call an ambulance."

"Does anyone have medical training?"

The fire engine arrived, sirens blaring, parting the crowd with a hose. One of them went into the building pushing the two men back on to the street, waving arms to push back the baying crowd. An ambulance drew up, blocking my view. I crossed the road, joining the throng. A woman touched my arm.

"It's awful," she said. "I hope they get them out."

"Me too," I said.

A cordon pushed us back further. Black water dripped from the doorstep. The fireman stepped through, a body draped across his arms.

"She's alive," I heard him say.

"Thank God," I said to the woman next to me.

"It's a miracle," she replied.

The paramedics stepped forward, laying the woman on a stretcher, cloths placed across her face, her body, remnants of purple polyester clinging to her reddened skin.

And she was gone, swept into the ambulance, doors closed against the straining crowd. Police arrived, taping off the area as they had done when Beano died. People talked to each other, to me.

"It's terrible."

"I've never seen anything like it."

"I got it on my mobile."

"The TV will want it; you'll make money off that."

"Poor woman. I hope she makes it."

I listened, unmoved, nodding and frowning in the right places before slipping away, down towards the market and Amy Winehouse, a quiet spot now that Scaramouche was attracting all the attention.

IN THE WASTE GROUND by the railway arch, the buddleia I had planted for Beano had thrust a lonely bloom up towards the sunlight. I drained the bottle of water I had been given by someone in Alma's audience, onto its spindly roots. A butterfly landed on it, bobbing and swaying with the stem, its wings black and orange like the flames. It took off again and I stood to watch it, following it back onto the Holloway Road before it disappeared. I wasn't sure how I had got there, didn't remember the steps. My hoodie was tied round my waist revealing my secret to the world. I left it there, watching the sleeves sway as more pavement disappeared under my feet. Exhaustion flooded my limbs. Safety beckoned, somewhere I could be without explaining, somewhere to be.

In the window of a TV shop, Scaramouche filled every screen. Subtitles rolled along the bottoms, "critical but stable", "lucky to be alive," "fire investigation to take place." The road was cordoned off, the "woman in hospital with life changing injuries". A popular phrase, I thought, life-changing injuries. I kept walking, past the shops and into a tree-lined street, on until I recognised the building where he lived.

Kurt wasn't in. I slumped by his door, staring at the paint peeling on the wall opposite. It would be hours before he came home, time for me to review everything I had seen and not done. Had CCTV caught me entering and leaving the building? It didn't matter. I had left calmly and Alma wouldn't say anything. How could she? I hadn't set light to her; she had done it to herself. As far as anyone else was concerned, I had left before she knocked the wax melt onto herself. The fire investigation would support my claim. Alma was on her own.

Had it been my fault? Of course not. Alma was the architect of her own destruction.

Mother once said that losing her looks would be worse than dying. Had she been beautiful? I wasn't sure. I had never see beauty in her. I wasn't sure it existed out of a mascara bottle and a lipstick. Like Mother, Alma had blinded me with her own sense of entitlement, blocked the receptors for rational thought. She deserved everything that she did to herself.

I hadn't helped her. I waited for shame to redden my cheeks as it had so often before. But none came. Alma had given me life changing injuries, left me to die on a moor, hundreds of miles from home. And she had done it to Beano, Ivy the Terrible, the beautiful child of whom she had been so jealous. No. I had no shame, only the absolute knowledge that karma is a bitch.

I don't know how long I slept for but awoke refreshed, stretching my limbs slowly, filling them with energy from a place deep within my chest. There were pictures on the peeling wall and I stood to look at them; prints of Monet, the ones you find in doctors' waiting rooms. Miniature water lilies merging into each other, a cacophony of colour. From a window on the next floor, light flooded down in stripes. I stood under one, the warmth on the back of my neck soothing and kind. I tried several yoga positions I had seen in books but found them harder than they looked. And I thought of Tutankhamun, his gold face shining in the sun, leading me along a path, holding my hand as I inched along it.

Downstairs, the main door banged shut. Heavy footsteps hurtled up the stairs and stopped at the top.

Kurt stared, slack-jawed, his hand raised to his bald head.

"Oh my God, Jay. It's you."

"I didn't know where else to come."

"You came to the right place," he said, stepping forwards and holding out his hand. I took it, allowing him to pull me into his chest, his arms encircling me completely. We stayed there, silent, for minutes, as I breathed in the smell of his washing powder, the same as Heather's. His grip didn't alter, his arms a haven. Eventually, he gently pushed me away, still holding my arms as he searched my face.

No words came from either mouth, the movements of our jaws mirroring each other until he gave up and dropped my wrists.

"Come in," he said, unlocking the door. The flat was dark, pizza boxes littering the floor. In the corner the television flickered soundlessly. He crossed the room and opened the curtains, unapologetic for the state of it. I stood by the door, remembering every detail of the breakfast I had cooked here, the girl who had eaten and run, the look on his face when he returned from the bedroom with an empty plate.

"What happened?" he said, switching on the kettle.

I pulled at the hoodie, lifting it over my head as his eyes found the creatures I uncovered.

"Alma happened," I said. "Like she happened to Beano too. Ivy, her daughter, a beautiful girl, too beautiful for her mother to love."

"I remember her, a child, I didn't know."

"Why would you?"

"I've just come back from the hospital. Did you…?"

His words hung in the air. I watched them pool on the floor at my feet.

"No," I said. "It was an accident. I just didn't help her."

He nodded. "What do you want to do now?"

"I want my life back," I said and the grin which stretched his face pulled all the geometric designs out of shape.

Joanie cried when Kurt brought me into her sanctuary. "I told him you'd be back," she said. Kurt nodded.

"I've kept a space for you on my beautiful behind," Her laugh filled the room with life.

"I'm out of practice," I said.

"All the better," she said. "Something real and raw. Let me see you."

I moved so that I was in front of her.

"All of you," she said. "I know about your tattoos."

Glancing at Kurt and with Joanie's unabashed nakedness before me, I stripped, slowly and deliberately, until I was as naked as her.

"Wow!" she said.

"With Jay's permission," Kurt said, "I'm going to make them beautiful."

374

"How?" Joanie and I said together.

"I'll paint them a place to live, a tree. Here," he pointed to the blood splatters. "They'll become cherry blossom, female strength. And here," his fingers touched the place where the spider ate its mate, "This thing in its mouth will become Alma, I'll add a petticoat." He laughed, then turned me round slowly, his eyes looking only at the illustrations and not my body underneath. "And I can do a cover-up on this thing." His fingers caressed Baphomet. "It'll become a design representing the elements. I don't know how I'll do it yet, but I will make it all beautiful and colourful, turn you into a walking work of art."

"Like me but with walking!" Joanie laughed and I laughed with her, looking down on myself as I envisaged the extraordinary woman I would become.

"When I've finished," said Kurt, "The tattoo fraternity will think you chose every last creature. You can tell a story of how you tamed the darkness inside you by putting it all on the outside. You can be proud of who you are."

"I'd like that," I said, "Although I'm okay with it now. Nearly."

"Draw something for my little gap," Joanie said and Kurt handed me a pad and pen which I took to the desk by the window, listening as they talked.

"I went to the hospital to see her," Kurt said.

"Why?" Joanie sounded concerned.

"Because I knew she'd seen Jay, I felt it in my water. You know the drill, Joanie, when something sticks inside and you can't shake it off.

Dave told me she'd cancelled the appointment but I didn't believe it. I know her."

"What did she look like?"

"A mess. Covered in bandages. She's out of intensive care and they're sending her to a burns unit somewhere out of town. She'll be there a while."

"Does anyone know what started the fire?" Kurt's eye caught mine.

"Some kind of scented candle or similar, she must have knocked it over and all that froth she wore plus the hair extensions were all flammable. Must've gone up in seconds."

"I'd say poor thing if she hadn't had it coming." Joanie's voice hardened. "After what she did to you and Jay, she's lucky she's not in prison."

I took the design to the bed, laying it on Joanie's lap. "It's a butterfly," I said unnecessarily. "It was the first tattoo I had and they remind me of Beano and how my head used to be. I love the way they find buddleia even in the worst circumstances. They find each other, one feeding and pollinating, the other grateful that its genes live on."

"It's perfect," Joanie said.

"But I don't have the copying thing to get it right on your skin."

"Freehand it," Kurt and Joanie said in unison. I baulked, began to speak and was shushed by them.

"I'm going to go and make some phone calls, get your life back," Kurt winked and left the room.

His mobile tattoo kit was laid out in front of me. "I've never done it on a real person before." I said.

"I know," said Joanie. "Help get me into position. I'll need a pillow between my legs."

Carefully, I moved her, surprised at the effort it needed, gently placing the pillow where she said until she was comfortable. "Go on," she said, "I haven't got all day!"

Plastic containers were lined up in rows as I had seen the other artists do, colours squeezed and mixed until I was certain I had everything I needed. I felt the machine in my hands, the weight of it, attaching an elastic band where Dave had shown me, to steady the needle, to provide cleaner lines and marks in general without damping down too much of the power that drove the needle bar to do its thing. It was large, designed for Kurt's hands, not mine, but it only took a few minutes before it felt comfortable. Drawing a faint line on my own leg, I checked for the pressure I would need, using my illustrations as a rough draft, placing lines on lines that already existed until I was ready for Joanie. I hadn't dressed, hadn't bothered to cover my modesty when Joanie was so comfortable with her own nakedness, preferring to sit with her, skin to skin, illustration to illustration.

"I'm ready," I said. "Tell me if it hurts."
She didn't flinch as the first tentative line scratched her skin. Sweat trickled down my forehead and I wiped it away with a latex-covered hand, cleaning my fingers with antiseptic wipes immediately. The body of the butterfly emerged, long and thin, tiny hairs protruding imperceptibly from its abdomen.

Antennae grew from its head now, long and curled, brushing the trunk of a cherry tree which Kurt had placed there. The first few lines instilling hope in my breast.

Stronger now, my hands pushed the flesh into positions which enabled me to make bold strokes; the curve of a wing, lace-fine on the pale skin. I stopped to breathe, inhaling the peace which surrounded us, exhaling the past. And with each breath, my hand became more confident, looping and curling until the outline was almost finished. I stood back, seeing what I had done, amazed that I was capable, then stooped back over the little area, squinting through concentrated eyes.

The outline done, I washed equipment and stood to stretch, asking if Joanie needed a break. She didn't. Changing my gloves, I wiped her skin, revealing the fine lines I had created there. They were as I had drawn and yet better because they followed the curve of her body, giving the creature a life of its own. Colour loaded, the machine whined again. Orange touched the wings, shading to crimson as though the sun had warmed it. White dots, outlined in yellow, leapt out, the needle producing depth on Joanie that I had not seen on pigskin. Wiping and colouring, I stood back several times to make sure it was developing as I wanted. The colours vibrant, the butterfly was emerging, strong yet delicate. Time passed and my hands worked, eager as Joanie gave life to my art.

The colours complete, I dipped the machine back into black, adding shading underneath, the image becoming three dimensional as the grey appeared. I wiped, shaded, wiped and shaded, checking the angles from which light might come, ensuring that the butterfly wings could take flight.

And as I wiped the last ink from her skin, I heard gentle snoring. Sitting so close to her, the silence punctuated with her breathing, I stared in wonder as the Vaseline brought the colours to life. I stood, covering her sleeping body with a dressing gown, leaving the area on her bottom with my first tattoo, exposed. Turning away for a minute, I pulled on my underwear, jeans and T-shirt, threw the latex gloves in the bin and washed the ink pots and machine as I had done so many times.

In the corridor I could hear Kurt on the phone, the words "Rohypnol" and "doesn't remember a thing" catching in the air. His blue head was bent, supported by a checkerboard hand, a list of phone numbers on his lap. Something new swelled in my heart, filling the void that had been there before. The blue man, asking nothing of me. Leaning against the door frame, I gazed at his visible skin, harsh lines intersecting, the intricate tribal patterns covering his head, the stretched ears reaching almost down to his shoulder. Tears gathered in my eyes; I swiped them away, but like an overfilled water butt, they kept dripping.

Turning away, I entered Joanie's room again, sitting again on the stool next to her noticing the rise and fall of her chest. The butterfly moved in front of me, fluttering its wings as it tried to break free. The body lurched, popping away from her skin, leaving its own image behind as its wings lifted free. Lurching upwards and downwards, it flitted around the room, careering towards walls, never hitting them. At speed, it flew towards me, hovering above my nose, so close that I could feel the beat of its wings on my cheeks. The orange wings fluttered as a head emerged, Beano's beautiful face smiling from the body I had drawn, antennae bobbing on the top of her head. Her blue eyes searched mine, the hint of a smile on her pink lips.

"Thank you," she whispered and flew out into the bountiful garden beyond, settling on the branch of a buddleia, grown giant in fertile soil.

Acknowledgements

I would like to thank Lorelei Press for their faith in me and my work, for taking the time and trouble to support me through the process and for choosing to publish my baby!

Thank you to Will Burgess of the Alban Tattoo Company for his patience, the information and knowledge he shared with me and for his beautiful artwork. I live with his work on my skin and enjoy it every day.

Thanks too to Kate Duffy, who pointed me in the right direction when I couldn't see the wood for the trees and eats cake with me, except when we're not eating cake.

To Claire, a dear friend and supporter who feeds me extremely well!

To memorable tutors at the London Metropolitan University, Sunny Singh, Trevor Norris, Carolyn Hart and Sarah Law, who all gave me the confidence to continue writing. This book started as my dissertation and, although unrecognisable, will always remind me of those days. Thank you all.

To my father, who, although no longer with us, inspired me to write, something he always wanted to do himself. He gave me a first draft of his book to edit as a teenager and I fell in love with the process of writing and editing. Thank you.

Thanks to Callum, Lucy for loving me, being constant and grounding me and for giving me Lyla, a little ray of light and joy to brighten my life. Love you all.

And finally, to Alex, without whose unwavering confidence in me, encouragement and insightful suggestions, this book would not have been written. A great big thank you for always spurring me on. Love you.

Reading group questions

1. What do you think of the book's title? How does it relate to the book's contents? What other title might you choose?
2. Would you read another book by this author? Why or why not?
3. If you got the chance to ask the author of this book one question, what would it be?
4. What do you think the author's purpose was in writing the book? What ideas was she trying to get across?
5. How original and unique was the book?
6. How do you think redemption played out in the book? Was it satisfying?
7. How well do you think the author built the world in the book?
8. What was the purpose of Tutankhamun's presence in the book and what did his presence add?
9. Did the characters seem believable to you? Did they remind you of anyone?
10. There are some larger than life people in the book. Do they seem too far-fetched or believable?
11. **Could you envisage the book being made into a film? If so, which actors/actresses could you imagine playing the parts?**

If you enjoyed Out There, please consider leaving a review on Amazon.

You might also like to read other Lorelei Press books:

In the dead of night, in the height of summer, a house burns. There, covered in ash, unharmed, except for her loss of memory, a child is found. Eva, when no one claims her, is taken into care.

Dan, the firefighter who found Eva, mourns the loss of his own daughter and faces a future estranged from his wife.

Carrie-Anne, near the burnt out house, lives a half life sleeping through the day and drinking away the night.

Ashes brings these three stories together in a beautiful and moving novel about finding hope even in the darkest place.

Hapless Jo Patterson finds life tough. The fact that her best friend, Helen, is uber-confident and formidable only seems to make matters worse. Now Helen has applied for Jo to appear on a pilot dating show called *Date Sensation* and Jo is caught in a panic of mortification and anticipation.

Could appearing on television be the key to romantic happiness? Or will it just cue another series of disasters?

From the London recording studio, Jo finds herself whisked away to paradise. Her bachelor is seemingly eligible, the Greek coast is sunny, and she has a television crew following her every move. Yet, still, nothing goes as planned for Jo. With gorgeous locals, a sympathetic cameraman, and a waiter with a salad obsession, Jo has to keep making choices, even after the cameras stop rolling.

Made in the USA
Columbia, SC
20 March 2018